Let Me Love You Again

ALSO BY ANNA DESTEFANO

ANNA DᴇSTEFANO

Let Me Love You Again

E C H O E S   O F   T H E   H E A R T

Montlake
Romance

This is a work of fiction. Names, characters, organizations, places, events, and incidents are either products of the author's imagination or are used fictitiously.

Published by Montlake Romance, Seattle

www.apub.com

Amazon, the Amazon logo, and Montlake Romance are trademarks of Amazon.com, Inc., or its affiliates.

ISBN-13: 9781477829158
ISBN-10: 1477829156

Cover design by Mumtaz Mustafa

Library of Congress Control Number: 2014958168

Printed in the United States of America

To the warriors of the heart

who never give up on love.

Chapter One

Oliver Bowman surveyed the spectacle beyond the floor-to-ceiling windows of his Midtown Atlanta loft. Disappearing before its setting sun, the dusky sky was a twilight miracle. It made him think of home.

Another high-stakes IT project was behind him, his second since he'd returned to the South. He'd conquered a kick-ass gauntlet of anticipated challenges, more than earning the ridiculous hourly rate he'd quoted his client. Plus a bonus for juggling last-minute crises and beating his deadline.

Two potential deals were in the pipeline awaiting his next pitch: one in Seattle, the other in Toronto. Within the hour he'd pull the trigger on his top prospect. And he would land it, beating out competing contractors—other guns for hire who'd good-naturedly curse him in their congratulatory e-mails. By the first of next week he'd relocate. There'd be no time to focus on anything but work.

But tonight, staring at his sunset view after a nerve-settling run through town, there was nothing to distract him from looking back. From wanting to *go* back—if for no other reason than to silence the question he couldn't stop himself from asking. What did it say that all these months he'd lived and worked only miles away from the foster family he'd crashed out of at eighteen? Yet no one from seven years ago knew he was back except for Travis, the foster brother Oliver had been closest to.

He was focused on the right things, he reminded himself. And working his ass off to make those things possible. Dwelling on the past was a pointless distraction for a man who made his not-inconsiderable living grinding out the day-to-day present. His demanding career fed his drive to compete and achieve. It kept him on track and freed everyone else to focus on what they needed to—including his foster parents. It kept quiet, nostalgic nights like tonight to a minimum.

He'd just ridden the elevator up after jogging through streets heavy with May's suffocating humidity. The temps in Georgia weren't what got to you this time of year. The moisture in the air, rain or shine, made you think you needed a snorkel to breathe. And while he'd been away, he'd missed even that for some godforsaken reason.

He was drenched in sweat, logging five miles in under forty minutes. He'd left himself plenty of time to shower before his conference call to a top-shelf West Coast CIO whose six-month contract would solidify the rest of Oliver's business year. Now he was going to smell like a locker room when he Skyped about cloud computing data solutions. Because he couldn't stop wrestling with the impulse to turn a brief blip of downtime into an excuse to visit Chandlerville—a suburb twenty miles northeast of the A-T-L.

It was natural to want to see how his foster parents were helping a new crop of kids learn they were worthy of love—one hug, one gently set boundary at a time. And if he were being honest, to want to be seen by Marsha and Joe Dixon now that Oliver had "made it."

Grunting, he scanned his sparsely decorated apartment with an objective eye. It was a flashy penthouse unit, its staggering lease covered by the latest corporation needing his expertise. The top-of-the line 4x4 in an underground garage was another high-end perk, freeing up his cash for better uses. But beneath the glossy surface he was still the guy who'd walked away from his last chance at a family with a threadbare backpack over his shoulder and the entire contents of his life inside. Just like he'd have to be wherever and whatever a new client wanted him to be next week.

Joe and Marsha's world was rocking on just fine without him. They didn't need him barging in and mucking with that. They *needed* the money he sent home every month to help them raise a fresh crop of parentless boys and girls. And it was a sweet deal for a man who'd nearly pissed away the second chance he'd been given.

Enough delaying the inevitable. Time to rip off the Band-Aid. One firm pull. A rush of pain, followed by the soothing relief of having done what he'd dreaded. Because living this close to Chandlerville, he'd never stop wondering whether his foster parents were proud of what he'd accomplished. Or if the beautiful girl he'd lost on another late spring night might smile one of her perfect smiles if she could see him now.

He rocked on the heels of the worn running shoes he kept forgetting to replace. The light beyond his windows faded, purple bleeding to gray. Barely realizing what he was doing, he rubbed a hand over the tattoo he'd had inked above his heart after he'd left the Dixon home. The ball-busting teen still lurking inside him sneered.

Why would Selena Rosenthal be thinking of him after all this time?

Since they were eighteen, they'd been as over as two people could be who'd sworn to love each other forever. Travis had said she'd left Chandlerville not long after Oliver. His first love had married, had another man's baby. She'd created a totally new life for herself, light-years from the small-town reality she and Oliver might have made together.

Meanwhile in the last year and a half he'd satisfied two right-place, right-time, big-dog Atlanta clients. He'd regrouped and was working harder and better than ever for his foster family. Work that kept him perpetually on the move. Which made it out of the question—his getting any closer to the people it would gut him to have to walk away from again.

His apartment phone rang, ripping his gaze away from the final streaks of light dusting the horizon. The handset in the kitchen sounded off a second time.

Only one person on the planet knew how to contact him on anything but his cell. Wherever Oliver moved for business, he maintained a landline and the international messaging service it fed into. He'd shared the number with no one but Travis, who knew better than to use it except for emergencies. Their sporadic conversations over the years had been the result of Oliver contacting his foster brother, not the other way around.

Oliver headed across the loft's Berber carpet, his insides twisting. He ripped the phone from its receiver.

"Hello?"

"You need to come home," said the ragged voice on the other end of the line. Travis still lived in Chandlerville, surrounded by the court-appointed family whose love had saved them both. "It's Dad. It's bad, man."

Chapter Two

Oliver was back in Chandlerville.

Through Tuesday morning shadows, Selena Rosenthal locked gazes with the one who'd gotten away. Next door, a ruggedly handsome man stared at her from the front steps of Joe and Marsha Dixon's sprawling house—a yard, a hedge, and another yard away. Dark hair. Dramatic green eyes. Oliver had the face of an angel and a mouth that could tempt a woman into just about any sin on the books. She'd have known him anywhere.

Years had passed. Seven of them, filled with her wanting to go back and fix the mistakes that had led to her and Oliver's last disastrous argument. She'd been too busy to miss him since she'd returned to town. At least she'd refused to dwell on how much she missed him—every time she saw someone from before or stumbled into a familiar place. And instead of reveling in the poignant memories, she'd felt like half a person, because Oliver wasn't there to share the moment with her.

Then he'd stepped out of a shiny red truck in his foster parents' drive just now, dressed in a wrinkled white T-shirt, jeans, and ratty running shoes.

Her mother's screened front door whooshed shut behind her, smacking Selena in the butt. She waited for Oliver to respond, to move, to do anything except stare back. She couldn't stop her smile, or the pathetic half wave that followed it. While his non-response dripped with *you're dead to me*, until she forced herself to look away.

Oh. My. God.

Oliver.

She tried to breathe, to play it cool. And then the head of the precocious bundle of energy and hair bows bobbing in her arms smacked Selena in the chin. She gasped so quickly, she hiccupped.

"We have to water Grammy's flowers, Mommy." Camille struggled to get down. Her first mission each morning was to make certain she and Selena cared for the abundance of buds and bushes her grammy obsessed about. "I left my watering can out back."

"Go find it." Selena set her daughter on her feet. "Hurry, or we'll be late for school."

Two months ago Belinda Rosenthal had welcomed Selena and Camille into her home after a lifetime of estrangement—Camille's lifetime. Selena had reached out to her mother over the phone as soon as she'd had her own child and begun to understand just how complicated mothering could be: on holidays and birthdays and Mother's Day. But for Selena, coming back had never been an option. Until it had become the *only* option.

With a new appreciation for Belinda's hands-off, distant way of caring, Selena was trying to mend fences with her mom despite their differences. Including helping care for Belinda's obsession with all things botanical. Camille's watering pot was a prop. It kept her busy with the flowers that grew in a wild tangle under her bedroom window, while Selena did the heavy lifting of hoisting hoses and sprinklers from beneath the azaleas flanking the front porch.

Most mornings the process resembled a grudge match: her dragging and untangling everything, so the SweeTart-colored blooms of the monstrous hydrangeas that sprawled near the Dixons' front yard could have their morning soaking. Daily watering was a must according to Selena's mother, who'd mastered the art of nurturing delicate buds and blooms to thrive under adversity. While the rest of the country slept off the lingering chill of winter, late spring graced Chandlerville with unseasonable heat. Until September the afternoon sun would revel in its power to wilt even the hardiest of indigenous species.

A rattle from the Dixons' place, the sound of keys jingling, recaptured Selena's attention. She braved another peek. The neighboring yard was empty, almost convincing her she hadn't just ogled a full-grown, ruggedly attractive version of her teenage obsession. But of course she had. Her body knew she had. She was tingling, head to toe, same as always when Oliver was near.

He'd gone inside was all. *Sprinted* was more like it, away from how she'd embarrassed herself.

He'd made her feel safe once upon a time. She'd been special, because he'd wanted her. From the moment they'd met she'd been at the center of someone's world again. He'd tried to protect her. He'd tried to help her, when he hadn't yet known how to help himself.

Her phone blared its *Mission: Impossible* ringtone. She dragged it out of her tote and stabbed the Talk button with her thumb.

"We're already running late, Mom." Selena's little girl returned with her watering can, squeezing through the screen door. "We're taking care of the yard."

"Remember," Belinda said, "we're helping Camille pick out summer shoes after school. We'll have to meet at the store after we're both off work."

If Selena's mother stopped reminding Selena about every single detail of the life she was rebuilding, someone would have to check Belinda for a pulse.

"I'll be there," Selena said, tamping down her frustration. Subtlety might not be her mother's gift. But Belinda was making the best of whatever time Selena remained in Chandlerville while she got back on her feet financially. At the very least, Selena owed her mother the same in return.

"Lock up when you leave." The line went dead, presumably so Belinda could micromanage her Chandlerville post office coworkers into a fugue state.

Selena wouldn't hear from her again until her mother's midday check-in call. During which Belinda would couch her concern for the deplorable state of her daughter's life in even more reminders about nonsense things that couldn't possibly matter.

As a child, Selena had resented her single mom being too busy to offer soft gestures like comforting hugs and encouraging pep talks. Her relationship with her mother would never be the exuberant kind of love Selena had craved since her father walked out when she was five. But Belinda had worked her fingers to the bone for her daughter—the same as Selena was now doing for Camille.

She dropped her cell into the tote bag her mother had lent her. Selena's anemic budget had produced only a secondhand backpack. Before leaving Manhattan, she'd given up her designer purses and most of her Upper East Side wardrobe and jewelry—including her wedding and engagement rings—to a resale shop.

Camille held up her watering can like a prize. "I found it by the begonias," she chirped.

Selena secured the front door and then the screen. She hugged her child, enchanted with the way Camille still embraced each new adventure. She'd fallen in love with her grandmother's blooming world. The outrageous names of flowering plants rolled off her tongue the way other children chattered nursery rhymes.

"Pamper your forget-me-nots." Selena steered Camille toward the perky blue flowers that bloomed beneath her bedroom window. "I'll give Grammy's hedge its morning drink while there's still shade."

And while Selena pulled herself together enough to drive them to Chandler Elementary School.

She peeled off her linen jacket and draped it and her tote over the porch rail. She gave the long skirt of her deep-brown sundress a hike and grabbed both sets of hoses. She dragged the lot across the freshly mown lawn, the ancient sprinkler attachments thumping behind her. As she approached the Dixon property she couldn't help but peek, hoping to catch another glimpse of Oliver.

When word reached Selena yesterday that an ambulance had whisked Joe Dixon to the hospital, she should have realized that some of Marsha and Joe's grown foster children might turn up in town. Even Oliver. Especially Oliver.

After how badly things had ended, most everyone on the other side of Chandlerville from places like winding, affluent Mimosa Lane had assumed Oliver would never come back. But he'd loved his foster parents. He'd lost so much when he'd left. Selena would never forgive herself for her role in hurting him and Marsha and Joe and so many others.

She positioned the sprinklers, focusing on not completely soaking herself with the dribbles of trapped water leaking every which way now that the hoses were fully extended.

"Catch, Mommy," Camille said.

The neon-pink Hello Kitty Frisbee that had been lurking somewhere in the front yard sailed over Selena's head . . .

And landed at Oliver's feet.

Selena was really there.

What the hell was she doing there, so beautiful that she made Oliver ache?

Only a few feet away, she was a paragon of motherhood, while a flood of messed-up and surprisingly sweet memories taunted him. Them as best friends from the moment they'd met. As a teenage couple who'd never let each other go. As a cautionary tale of how much true love could destroy, when you let it slip away.

She'd been the one who'd torched what was left of their relationship. Breaking up with him after high school graduation, telling him he was to blame, and then sleeping with his best friend to rub a little extra salt into the wound. But he'd let her down first. And he'd accepted his share of the blame long ago. Which was why he should have stayed inside his folks' place just now until she was gone. He should go *back* inside and wait for his brother to meet up with him, the way Travis had said he would.

But Oliver couldn't move.

He couldn't take his eyes off of her. Dark hair cascaded halfway to the waist of her gauzy dress. Tall, willowy, fragile, Selena still exuded the vulnerability that had devastated him when they'd first met, first kissed, and eventually became each other's first lover. As if the forever place they thought they'd made in each other's hearts was there for him to claim.

When he was placed with Marsha and Joe at thirteen—after his single mother had been robbed and killed at her night job as a convenience store clerk—he'd discovered Selena living next door. She'd seemed as lost as he'd felt, still dealing with her dad walking out on her and Belinda. One look into her impossibly brown eyes and Oliver had begun to believe that someone else could understand the loneliness sucking him under. She hadn't seemed to belong on quaint, picturesque Bellevue Lane either.

Together, they'd learned how to love and dream and believe again—at least in each other. Then their senior year in high school, they'd let it all slip away, drinking and raging and trying to burn through the kind of loss no one else could possibly fathom. He'd seen the end coming and tried to pull them both out of the spiral. He'd been too late.

More than once over the years, he'd dreamed of stepping around the flowering bushes that separated their front yards and finding a grown Selena waiting for him like this. But whatever she was doing in town after all this time, it had nothing to do with him. Mentally kicking himself, he watched an adorable child— her daughter?—run up to the woman who'd said she never wanted to see Oliver again.

"Hey, mister." The kid's soft lisp was even cuter than her off-centered ponytails. She pointed to the Frisbee at his feet. "Throw it back."

He bent and grabbed the toy. When he stood, an insomnia hangover dug claws into his skull. After hauling ass around the clock for weeks on end, he'd spent the night checking in with Travis hourly about Joe's condition—and wrestling with the pros and cons of driving the half hour between Atlanta and Chandlerville. By sunup Oliver had accepted that he had to get himself home, if only to spend a few hours with his parents before heading back out of town. At this point he was practically seeing double.

He threw the Frisbee over the hedge. It glided in a bright, curving arc. The little girl scampered away, giggling.

Selena made hesitant eye contact, looking a little afraid of him. He knew exactly how she felt. This was pointless. Painful. And avoidable.

Nodding, he walked to his truck, snatched the bag he'd come out for, and headed inside. He was being rude. But it was for the best. He couldn't let their teenage mistakes distract him from the reality that had finally convinced him to return to Chandlerville. Joe Dixon might be dying. It simply wasn't possible.

Oliver stepped into the Dixon house. Its stillness further frayed his calm. Because the small-town simplicity of it was more him than anywhere else he'd lived. He leaned against Marsha and Joe's front door, his head thudding against worn wood.

His father's denim jacket hung from the coat rack beside the entryway, though Joe wouldn't need it for another six months or so. Marsha's flair for throwing color and pattern together still infused the living room with hominess. Handmade slipcovers and throws and pillows softened the edges of furniture sturdy enough to endure the beating it received on a daily basis. Kid flotsam was strewn everywhere, cast-aside books and toys and shoes. Marsha's nightly threats to throw things out if they weren't picked up never entirely cleared the playing field.

Framed images of the Dixon clan stared back at him from the wall across the entryway: his own foster brothers and sisters, plus the newer passel Marsha and Joe were raising. Oliver scanned pictures of himself mixed with all the others, including his senior portrait from Chandler High. He counted at least a half dozen more kids than the ones he'd known.

Footsteps sounded on the wooden front steps. He edged away seconds before the door opened and a tall, muscular man stepped inside. Travis Bryant fully grown would have been intimidating enough dressed in civilian clothes. The sheriff's uniform he wore these days was downright overkill.

"Hey, man," Travis said in a booming voice that he somehow kept at a whisper, in deference to the kids—and their grown foster sister, Dru—he'd warned would still be sleeping upstairs.

"Officer." Oliver smiled for the first time in what seemed like forever.

"That's Deputy to you." Travis took Oliver's measure. "Damn, son, you're looking good. A little Night of the Living Dead at the moment. But if I took you on, it just might be a fair fight."

Oliver jerked his chin. "When I'm done, I guess there'd be something left of you. But I'm not making any promises."

"Before or after I throw your ass in jail for assaulting an officer?"

"Nothing says welcome back," Oliver quipped, "like being fingerprinted and processed."

Everyone who'd lived at Marsha and Joe's when he'd moved in had done their best to make him feel welcome. Travis, too, though he and Oliver had fought like mongrel pups at first. Squaring off, they'd gone at it in a turf war that had evolved into mutual respect and a brotherly bond that still endured.

Oliver reached out his hand to shake. Travis yanked him into a bro-code hug: quick, hard, powerful. They pushed away, leaving unspoken, deeper emotions beneath the surface.

Travis cleared his throat and propped his hands at his waist, shoving aside the gun holstered to his belt at his right hip. "Dru up yet?"

Oliver shook his head—at the question and the changes in his brother. As a teenager Travis as much as Oliver had challenged authority and balked at their parents' well-intentioned structure and limits.

"I just got here," Oliver said.

"That why Selena was standing in the yard next door when I pulled up, looking like she'd seen a ghost?"

Oliver exhaled. "It was just bad timing."

"Not if you want to mend a few fences."

"I need to clean up before we head to the hospital." Oliver hefted his duffel onto his shoulder.

He didn't ask why Travis hadn't mentioned Selena's return to Chandlerville. Just like Travis hadn't pushed over the last year and a half about Oliver taking on two successive client contracts in Atlanta, while still keeping his distance from the family.

"Use Marsha and Joe's bathroom." Travis—using Marsha and Joe interchangeably with Mom and Dad, the way most of their foster siblings had—looked like a man picking his battles. "Dru's bunking on the floor in the baby's room. Teddy's been keeping Mom and Dad up nights. Try not to wake either of them. She'll have to get the brood breakfast and off to school soon enough."

"Sure." As much as Oliver wanted to see his sister, he needed to get to their parents first. "So, she's engaged, huh?"

Travis had said Dru would be at the house with the kids overnight while Travis hung at the hospital with their parents, waiting on updates and keeping everyone else in the loop. Oliver remembered his sister in braces, scrambling after him and the other boys, determined to keep up. Now she had a fiancé?

"Since last Christmas," Travis confirmed.

Oliver narrowed his eyes at the lack of details. His house key bit into his clenched palm. The one his foster parents had presented to him his first day there, the way they did all the kids. Everything that was theirs had been his forever, just like that.

He gazed through the doorway into Marsha's kitchen, where she reigned supreme as the family gathered for meals, making the kind of memories that held on when everything else let go. He and Selena had done homework in there, too, eating cookies or leftovers or something Marsha had whipped up special for them.

"Bite the bullet," Travis said, "and talk with the woman."

"Dru? Yeah, sure. Later, when we get back from the hospital."

"I meant Selena."

Oliver's scattered thoughts refocused on his brother. "Don't go there, man."

"The woman's living right next door. Where else is there to go?"

"I'm going upstairs for that shower so the CICU staff doesn't hose me down on sight."

Travis met Oliver's stare. "Listen, man. I know all of this has to be tough, and you're worried about Dad. Everyone will be thrilled you're home. But are you going to be . . . I mean, after what happened last year, is all of this going to be too much for your—"

"I'm fine." Oliver shoved the house key into his jeans pocket and carried his duffel up the stairs of the sleepy house. He was going to be fine. Over his shoulder, he added, "I just need to stop smelling like the bottom of a rancid gym bag."

He'd yet to clean up from last night's run. He'd botched the conference call with Seattle. He'd prowled his condo like a caged animal for hours before he'd ditched his running gear and thrown on whatever clothes he could find so he could head home. He wasn't certain he'd packed anything but jockey shorts and socks in his bag.

"Ready to head out in twenty?" Travis called after him.

"Down in ten."

Oliver was a mess, and that had to stop. He was going to be where he was needed today—at the hospital with his parents, not wandering around his foster home remembering and wanting it all back. *Not* chasing after Selena and the absurd notion that talking with her could correct things that had been wrong for too long to fix.

He was going to do the best he could for his family with the short time he was back. Then tomorrow he'd refocus on his pitch to a Fortune 100 paper manufacturer that wanted him on the next plane to Canada.

Chapter Three

You need help, Selena, Oliver had said to her forever ago. She'd been drunk. Again. She'd been an alcoholic, though it would be months yet before she'd begin to deal with it. Sober for the first time for much of their senior year, Oliver's gentle encouragement that she dry out, too, had sounded to her still-messed-up self as criticism. Disappointment. Rejection. *This is my fault*, he'd said. *You wouldn't be so out of control if it wasn't for me. Let me help you—let me make this right.*

I don't want your help! Selena had screamed, certain he was dumping her. She'd been certain for weeks. *You want out, just like my dad did. He said he loved me. How long's it gonna take before you leave me, too? Huh? I'll tell you how long. Now! Because I'm the one who's through this time. We're done.*

Anything had seemed better than Oliver finally giving up on her for good.

So she'd raged onward solo, after his parents had insisted he stop drinking or he'd have to leave the foster home he'd already aged out of. Until she'd destroyed the last of her childhood, their love, and Oliver's life in Chandlerville.

"Do we get to stop for doughnuts?" Camille asked, dragging Selena back to the present.

She hadn't moved since Oliver and then Travis disappeared inside the Dixon house. Her heart was still doing pirouettes in her throat. And now her daughter's watering can was empty, and Camille was hopping up and down at Selena's feet.

Ouch! Make that *on* Selena's feet, smearing dirt and Georgia clay all over Selena's soft-soled shoes.

"Mommy, you said we could get—"

"A chocolate doughnut on the way to school." Selena led her daughter back to the house. She banished her memories deep inside, to the emotionless corner of her mind where the past wasn't an old wound forever seeping fresh blood.

The toes of her favorite shoes squished, sinking into the boggy soil beneath Belinda's drippy spigot. Selena mentally crossed off another piece of her once stylish wardrobe that was too delicate for a busy day in Chandlerville. Her silk ballerina flats had been bought to accompany a chic sheath dress embroidered with a matching array of seed pearls and tiny bows. The dress was long gone. The shoes she'd talked herself into keeping, because they were beautiful and made her smile. Now they were another casualty of Selena underestimating just how long her rocky fresh start would be.

"Perfect," she groused at the spigot, twisting the dial on the hose's timer and setting the water to shut off in half an hour.

"What's wrong?" Her six-year-old tugged at Selena's thrift-store dress.

"Nothing, sweetheart," Selena replied to the question no child should ask as often as hers did.

Selena turned the water on. It gushed from the sprinklers. She grabbed her things and knelt in the grass by the porch steps, kissing Camille's temple on the way down. She tightened the ribbons she'd tied around her little girl's wispy pigtails. She always managed to make them slightly off-center.

Had Oliver noticed how beautiful Camille looked, regardless?

"We're snagging your nutritionally barren, dairy-free, nut-free breakfast to go," Selena said, rather than dwelling on questions that would get her nowhere. If she were going to do anything more than stare at the all-grown-up version of Oliver, she'd had her chance twice already. "We want to get to school before Karen Davenport hoards all the best craft supplies."

"I'm going to rule the art table." Camille pumped a tiny fist into the air, celebrating her impending triumph over the reigning mean girl in daycare.

Selena dropped Camille at Chandler Elementary's early child-care center each morning Selena worked as a substitute teacher, without having to pay the fee she couldn't afford until her divorce was finalized. She was fortunate the school's principal, Kristen Hemmings Beaumont, kept her in mind so often for the part-time opportunities that a long list of subs could fill. Practically every day for over a month, Selena had had steady work, custom-made to fill the hours her daughter was in school. Kristen seemed genuinely committed to helping them reclaim their financial footing—at least until school let out for the summer at the tail end of next week.

Until then, Selena had to wake her daughter for school much earlier than when they'd lived in New York, so Selena could get to Chandler and plan for the day ahead. It wasn't what she wanted for Camille, but Belinda headed to the post office each morning at five. So for another week at least, this was the way things had to be.

Selena hugged Camille close. Her earliest memories were of her parents fighting nonstop, and of one or both of them threatening to move out. Then Selena and her mother had had to make their way alone, finally arriving on Bellevue Lane—with Belinda earning barely enough in those early years to keep the lights on and food in the house. Now that was Selena's daughter's reality. And Selena was determined to make all the scary changes and confusion and worry up to Camille. They would get through this—one day, one squishy footstep at a time.

"Let's go, Cricket," she said, using her favorite nickname for her daughter. She led Camille to their car.

Selena had affectionately named the heap Fred. He'd been all she could afford with what remained of the money she'd squirreled away before filing for divorce from her cheating, fabulously wealthy, well-respected yet not-to-be-trusted husband. When Fred slowed as he struggled up a hill, she imagined there was a rusted-out hole beneath the floor mats where she could stick her feet through, like one of the Flintstones pedaling to help the engine along. But he was hers free and clear. She didn't owe anyone anything for him. And he'd come through like a champ on their long journey back to Georgia, charming Selena down to her unpedicured toes.

Slipping behind the wheel after buckling Camille's car seat, she turned the key. The ignition sputtered and then died. Black smoke spewed from the tailpipe.

"Uh-oh," Camille said.

Selena's next attempt to rouse Fred from his funk ended in an emphysemic belch.

"No doughnuts?" Camille asked.

Selena laughed. She dropped her head to the steering wheel. This wasn't happening.

She didn't mean to glance next door at Oliver's shiny red truck and the Dixon home. Her head just rolled to the side on its own. Then she gritted her teeth and turned Fred's key again. Because he *was* going to cooperate. The rumblings beneath his hood warned that he didn't take kindly to being bossed around. But the engine finally caught and roared to life.

"Yay!" Camille cheered. "Chocolate!"

Soaking in her daughter's celebration, Selena cajoled her ancient Chevy into reverse. She steered him out of the driveway and pulled away from their morning's rocky start. Taking the turn onto Maple, she headed for Dan's Doughnuts on Main and settled into the drive. She'd almost cleared her mind of everything but her daughter's morning treat and the workday ahead, when *Mission: Impossible* heckled her from the depths of her tote.

Sighing, one hand on the wheel, she kept her attention fixed on the road in front of her and fumbled the phone from her purse.

"I'm driving," she said after thumbing the call through and putting her mom on speaker.

"Tell me you're going to steer clear of him," Belinda insisted.

"Mom . . ." Selena tried to remember that her mother was trying to help, not obsessed with every new mistake Selena might make.

"I heard he was back. Jonathan Ritter said his mother saw a red truck pull up into the Dixons' drive while you were working in the yard."

"Janet Ritter needs something else to do with her time than peeking out her front windows at what the rest of the neighborhood is doing."

And Jonathan needed to stop being quite so interested in every move Selena made. Her mother's coworker at the post office had graciously offered more than once to let Selena reconsider her hasty decision not to date his fifty-something, single, still-lived-with-his mother self.

"Was it Oliver?" Belinda shuffled things on the other end of the phone.

Selena didn't answer. Thanks to Mrs. Ritter, she didn't have to.

"Did you talk to him?" her mom wanted to know.

"No." A touch of disappointment escaped with the word. A deluge of unwanted questions that made Selena queasy.

Had she missed her last chance to clear the air with Oliver? To make things right with him and his family?

"Tell me," Belinda insisted, "that you're going to steer clear of the Dixon house and the hospital until he's gone again. Don't complicate your life even more."

"I'm not, Mom. I haven't visited the hospital. Neither have you, no matter how good friends you've been with the Dixons, or how serious Joe's heart condition sounds."

"I know, honey." Her mother's work noise stalled. "I feel bad about it, too. But . . ."

"It's better not to rock the boat. I get it, Mom."

Marsha had wanted to have Camille over to play with the Dixon kids. Selena and Belinda and Camille had been invited more than once to join their neighbors for one of the Dixons' Saturday afternoon cookouts. Selena had declined every time.

"It would be asking for trouble," Belinda warned. "You've got more than enough on your plate as it is, right?"

"Right." Except the Dixons were the ones in trouble now. Which made Selena feel shabby for the way she'd rejected their friendly attempts to welcome her and Camille to town.

"Honey?" Belinda asked. "You know he'll be there if you stop by the hospital."

"I'm sure he will."

And that would be even shabbier—Selena insinuating herself into an already tense situation, when the foster son she'd helped oust from Marsha and Joe's home had just made it clear he wanted nothing to do with her.

"It would be a mistake," her mother insisted.

"It absolutely would be."

Except the prospect of losing such a fine, loving man as Joe had hit Selena and a lot of their community hard. And as Selena flipped on Fred's blinker to turn into the lot beside Dan's, she was strategizing how she could carve a few minutes away from school around lunchtime. To offer her long-overdue support to the Dixon family, and to make what would hopefully be her final mistake where Oliver Bowman was concerned.

"I almost didn't recognize him when he first walked in," Marsha Dixon said a few minutes before eleven.

She and Selena were gazing through the large windows of Joe's CICU room. A mother's proud smile bloomed across her weathered features as she watched her husband and Oliver.

"He looks so grown up," she said. "Of course he's grown up. It's been years. But I mean . . . I wasn't prepared for him to look so . . . responsible and, I don't know, corporate or something. Even in those raggedy clothes."

To Selena, Oliver looked all of that and more. He'd changed into different jeans and a plain black T-shirt. There were dark circles under his eyes. His face was shadowed with beard stubble that gave his cheekbones an even sharper edge. From the looks of him he'd been up all night. But there was something coolly sophisticated about him, too.

The rough-and-tumble rebel who'd once mesmerized Selena was long gone. And yet, he was exactly what she'd somehow known he'd become. Successful. Independent. Making his own way in a competitive business where few entrepreneurs thrived. And after Marsha had hugged Selena and thanked her for coming, she'd proceeded to behave as if Selena belonged there beside her, watching the man perched on the edge of his father's bed.

Defying the hospital's frigid artificial climate, a drop of perspiration trickled between Selena's shoulder blades. She felt as if she were staring down a caution sign, flashing for her to turn back before all hope was lost.

"He'll be glad you came," Marsha said, carrying their conversation pretty much on her own.

"Your husband's a wonderful man."

Joe's hand fumbled across the mattress. His fingers curled around Oliver's. Something dangerous rattled Selena's composure.

"I meant," Marsha corrected, "my son will be glad to see you."

Selena kept her focus on the touching scene playing out in Joe's room. "Because of me, you had to boot Oliver from your foster home a week after graduation. He nearly killed his best friend in a bare-knuckles brawl because of me. He was finally sober, and because of me he drowned himself in a bottle of tequila and totaled your minivan. Glad to see me? You and I both know better."

"What I know is that it's been two months since you came back to town. And you haven't brought that beautiful child of yours over once for a proper visit."

"I'd love that, really." It would be heaven. And hell. "But we just can't."

"Can't or won't?"

Selena shook her head.

She wasn't ready for this. She and her daughter were nowhere *near* ready for this. She'd put Camille through enough. She'd promised to make her life and her daughter's as uncomplicated as possible from now on. And this certainly didn't qualify.

But Marsha had kept two generations of foster children in line. The woman could teach an NFL linebacker a thing or two about not backing down from confrontation. And Selena had set this awkwardness into motion when she'd shown up at the hospital. She turned to her neighbor, her hand clenched around the straps of her borrowed tote.

"You deserve your say, Marsha." And then some. "I'm listening."

"It's been a long time since you and my son talked."

"I wouldn't call our last conversation talking." The night Selena had gotten her drunk on and broken up with her soul mate. After which Brad had consoled her, had drank too much with her . . . And, Lord help them, the rest had just happened. "Oliver couldn't get away from me fast enough this morning."

Her neighbor's expression softened with understanding . . . and something more. Selena held her breath, wondering if this was it, if someone had finally guessed. But Marsha went back to watching her husband and foster son. Worry tightened her smile to the breaking point.

Selena placed a palm on Marsha's shoulder. There was frailty today beneath all that strength. "I'm so sorry about Joe."

Marsha shivered. Selena wrapped her arm around the woman whose generosity had smoothed some of the jagged edges of Selena's young life, created by her own mother's bitter fight to survive as a single parent. Selena held on tighter. Marsha and Joe had been a lifeline for her when she and Belinda first moved to Bellevue Lane, years before Oliver arrived. It shouldn't have taken their son's return to get Selena to the hospital to check on them.

Marsha eased away. And like the marvel she was, she squared her shoulders, all five feet one of her.

"We never know how much time we have," she said, short gray hair feathering about her rounded face. "We've got no business wasting a single chance we're given to make things right. Oliver just got back to town. You've been keeping to yourself. But in a matter of hours, you two have somehow managed to see each other long enough for you to think he's avoiding you?" She raised an eyebrow. "Yet here you are, right where you knew he'd head next."

"This morning was a coincidence."

A dangerous one that could cause them all a lot of trouble. Especially given that for Selena, being careful where Oliver was concerned was a Zen state she clearly hadn't mastered.

"The fact that Joe and I got custody of Oliver in the first place was happenstance." Marsha wiped at the corners of her eyes. "Or providence. There's not much difference once you take a closer look. And we're thrilled he's back. Don't throw away your opportunity to at least speak with him, whatever's happened between you two."

"I came to visit Joe to see if there's anything Belinda or I can do to help." Her mother had been more Belinda than Mom for years. "It must not seem like it, but I really do care."

"Of course you do." Marsha hugged her. The wave of peace that washed through Selena should be bottled and sold. "You and your mother have always meant so much to both of us."

Marsha let go. Selena kept her gaze down.

All of Chandlerville admired what the Dixons had accomplished with their group foster home. Belinda's garden club had just last week chosen Joe as Father of the Year. It would be a lovely community ceremony. And Selena knew she'd belonged in the front row, leading the applause. Her marriage was a miserable failure. But the family she still dreamed of giving Camille had always had its origins in watching the magic Marsha and Joe achieved with their eclectic tribe of kids.

Selena had never felt the crush of her reckless secrets more. But how did she face the truth and the people who needed to hear it? How did she create more chaos and confusion for them and her child, when Selena had no intention of becoming a permanent part of anyone's life in Chandlerville again? She'd come home to regroup for a few days, a week tops. She'd never meant to stay this long, get this attached or, God forbid, to be here when Oliver returned. And now . . .

All she knew for certain was that if there was *ever* a right time for her to come clean about her daughter's paternity, this wasn't it.

She took one last look into CICU. Joe smiled at something. Oliver grinned in response, his lips curling higher on the right side. She raised a clenched fist to scrub at her cheek. The needy teenager still inside her longed for Oliver to look up and see her and forgive her and somehow make everything okay the way he'd once promised he would.

"Tell Joe I stopped by. I'll . . ." She forced out the words, the lie. "I'll come back when it's a better time."

"Don't you want to wait until—"

"No . . ." She backed toward the elevator. It dinged, urging her to hurry.

"Selena—"

"I shouldn't have come at all. I don't know what I was thinking." She stopped, appalled at the rudeness of what she'd said. "I didn't mean . . ."

"Stay." Marsha stepped toward her.

"I can't." She was moving again, twisting away. "I have to— Oof!"

She'd barreled into something solid that felt like a wall with arms and legs. She saw a blue shirt and stars. She couldn't make her vision clear.

"Are you okay?" asked a deep voice that was as achingly familiar as Marsha's hug had been.

"Travis . . ." Selena brushed hair out of her eyes.

Oliver's brother wore a deplorably wrinkled version of the starched shirt and dark navy pants that made up his sheriff's department uniform. He looked rumpled and in need of a hug. But he was smiling down at Selena, same as every other time he'd seen her around town.

"I'm fine," she said. "I didn't know you were behind me. Been bouncin' off things all morning. Stuff jumping off practically every table I passed at school. It's been a bit crazed, ever since Camille's and my morning doughnut dash. And I . . ."

Good God. She was babbling. Lines of friendly confusion wrinkled Travis's forehead and ratcheted up his blond, boy-next-door good looks.

"I need to get back to school," she said.

"Not yet you don't." Marsha pushed Selena toward Oliver's brother. "Don't let her out of your sight."

At Selena's scowl, Marsha's eyebrow shot up again.

"Five minutes, my dear." Marsha's voice had shifted into the same *my word is law* tone that kept her kids in line. "You've been running from us long enough. You want to help Joe and me. Then break the ice with Oliver and our family. My boy being back isn't becoming another reason why we never see you and that beautiful child of yours."

Marsha disappeared into her husband's room.

"Make yourself comfortable, darlin'." Travis shot her a wickedly smooth Southern smile. "No one says no to Mom once she makes up her mind."

Selena gave him her best *puh-lease* glare. She'd been immune to his charm since they'd been teenagers and he'd harmlessly flirted with her once or twice, admitting later that he'd done it only to get a rise out of Oliver. But she was also a realist. Marsha wanted Selena and Oliver to talk. Likely as a distraction from the helpless feeling of watching the love of Marsha's life suffer in a hospital bed.

What were the chances of the woman turning the idea loose until she'd had her way?

"Five minutes." Selena rolled her eyes.

Five minutes followed immediately by her avoiding the entire Dixon family again, at least until Oliver was good and gone.

Chapter Four

"Computers?" Oliver's dad was beaming.

Joe also had an intimidating array of tubes and wires coming out of him, hooked up to a roomful of equipment. The hearty, indomitable man Oliver remembered appeared anything *but* indestructible now.

"I make computers do what my clients want them to do," Oliver said, keeping his shock at Joe's weakened state to himself.

His dad hadn't wanted to talk about himself or the past any more than Marsha had. She'd hurried Oliver into Joe's CICU room, and Oliver's dad had instantly insisted on a recap of Oliver's life since he'd been gone. Marsha had slipped away to give them some time alone.

"It takes you all over the world?" Joe asked.

A man could get addicted to hearing the growing wonder in his voice, like a kid opening presents on Christmas morning.

"Wherever they're paying the most," Oliver said.

"Wherever they need the best?"

"Something like that."

"Tell me everything. Not that I'll understand much of any of it." Joe coughed out a soft laugh and winced at the pain in his chest.

Everything . . .

Not the kind of everything, Oliver warned himself, that would unnecessarily worry either of his parents.

"I reengineer systems and software other people can't handle. It's crisis work, usually at the eleventh hour for clients who can't afford for things to stay broken any longer. I untangle whatever mess they've made trying to avoid paying a professional problem-solver who charges what I do. I straighten things out, good as new. Better, usually."

Oliver huffed out his own laugh. He sounded like the kind of PR-pimped-out jerks he avoided at corporate parties. The walking billboard types, touting their brilliance to whoever'd listen. Oliver's work spoke for itself. He was already on the short list of the corporate officers who spent a fortune on damage control. That's all that mattered. Usually. But this was Joe, with pride shining in his eyes . . .

It was a crazy perfect moment.

"Any type of company?" his dad asked.

"I'm wily that way." Oliver winked, when in actuality he'd been called a con man by more than a few of the competitors he regularly finessed contracts away from. Xan Coulter in particular.

She'd made sure to e-mail him that morning during his pre-dawn pilgrimage to Chandlerville. She'd closed the Seattle contract last night, after his less-than-convincing pitch. A rare enough outcome that she'd wanted to know if he was okay.

"But no college?" Joe asked.

Oliver squeezed his dad's hand.

A formal education was what his foster parents hoped all

their kids would try for. Kids who aged out of the system often weren't prepared for or didn't see the point of going to college. Too much of life had landed on them at too young an age, making it harder to believe in things like going for your dreams. Marsha and Joe were having none of that.

"I did tech school for a while," Oliver said. "Scraped my way through, busting it at part-time jobs to make tuition. Then I realized I was pretty much better at what I was doing than my professors."

"Computers were always your thing. They were all you wanted to do, whatever class you were in"—Joe coughed around another soft laugh—"on the rare occasions that you actually found your way to class."

Oliver wanted to hug his dad and hold on to the moment. He wanted to go back and better appreciate every day he'd had his parents' unconditional support in his teenage life.

"I've been lucky," he said. "My first real client paid me crap in return for giving me a shot. The company had contacts everywhere. Now corporations part with a chunk of their bottom line to have me reengineer the communication and data-sharing nightmare that modern cloud computing can make out of business solutions."

"You've worked your ass off making your life happen. That's determination, not luck." Joe pointed with his free hand for emphasis. "Your mother and I always knew you'd figure out how to put being so obstinate to good use."

Oliver grinned, the memories bittersweet. "I was a piece of work, wasn't I?"

"You were finding your way."

"Listen, Dad, I'm sor—"

"Don't you say sorry to me." Joe sounded disappointed for the first time. "You were young and making the mistakes young people have to make. Do you think I regret a single thing that's happened, when I look at the man you've become? What you've done with your life, what you've done for our family, working as hard as you have—it's a miracle. I won't have you apologizing for that."

Oliver shook his head but kept his peace. His dad's praise was everything he'd wanted. And now that he had it, it only made him want more. He got a grip and shrugged. "I solve problems. Wrangle them into submission. Most messes want to be figured out. You just have to dig under the surface, find a place to grab hold, and get to work. The rest falls into place if you keep pushing and don't give up."

It was the mother of oversimplifications. His client schedule on a typical day was loosely organized chaos. Xan Coulter had been hammering at him about partnering up: sharing project loads; *not* working himself into an early grave; maybe even having a shot at a personal life. Which he clearly didn't, if the parade of women he'd torched short-lived relationships with—including Xan—was any indication. And then there was his burnout, spring of last year.

Oliver would have given anything to tell his dad about all of it. Get his advice. But not today. Not ever. *Not* his parents' problem.

"You've done a lot of good with the money you've made," Joe insisted. "There's so much your mother and I couldn't have given the kids without you. Extra school supplies and field trips and computers at the house, vacations for the family, even presents at Christmastime. Tuition for Bethany at the community college after she gave up her scholarship to art school. Specialized therapy the state can't cover because Family Services is forever tightening their budget. My salary's stretched to the breaking point just covering the everyday."

"I'm glad, Dad." So glad, it was downright embarrassing.

"But we'd have been just as proud of you, with or without the money you make." Joe pointed his finger again. "Because you remembered your family. You still wanted to make a difference here—even if being with us is still hard for you. That's worth a hundred times more to your mother and me than the fortune you've sent home."

"It's not that it's hard . . ." Oliver shook his head, wondering how to say what he wanted to say now that he had the chance, without worrying his parents with things that he could deal with on his own. "It's just that—"

Marsha appeared beside the bed. "Travis is back from grabbing a bite downstairs."

Her touch on Oliver's arm felt even better than the hug she'd given him when he'd first gotten there.

"Go spend a little more time with your brother." Her voice was breezy and light. Her smile was the genuine article. But none of it erased the worry from her eyes. "Let me get this trouble-maker to sleep a little."

"Trouble is your favorite thing about me." Joe grinned at his college sweetheart. "And what makes you think I'm going to be able to sleep now that our boy is home?"

Oliver inhaled around the desperate love he felt for these two, dreading already the reality of walking away again. Marsha was at her strongest when life threw its trickiest curveballs. Whatever she had to do, it got done. He'd admired that about her even when he'd been an f'ed-up kid.

You'll be fine, son, she'd said to him his last night in Chandlerville. *You'll make this work. And you'll be back.*

Joe had just brought him home from county lockup—free of charges for wrapping the family van around a tree in a drunken stupor. But the damage had been done. Marsha had packed the few things Oliver owned outright in Joe's old backpack from when he'd gone to college at the University of Georgia. She'd met

Oliver and Joe at the door: Oliver hung over, Joe grimly worried and ominously silent the entire ride home. Marsha had hugged Oliver, and he'd known it was over. For the first time since losing his birth mother he'd been truly terrified.

It was time for him to figure out if he wanted to self-destruct or make a life for himself. And he was going to have to take the next step on his own.

I know this is hard, Marsha had said, her voice strong as she clung to him. *But I have faith in you. And we'll be here. We're your family, Oliver. We'll always be here for you . . .*

Her resilience, her belief that life's hardest struggles could make you stronger, was the constant he'd circled back to most over the years. She'd had confidence in him, even when he'd been at his worst. Now she was just as determined that Joe would get better. Eyes open, arms wide, convincing everyone else to fight a little harder than they thought they could, she was going to will Joe's complete recovery into reality. And Oliver would do his level best to help her.

Joe was studying him with his uncanny ability to see more of people than they often wanted to be seen. "You'll do it?"

Oliver's mom glanced between the two of them. "Do what?"

"The house," Joe explained. "The kids. Teddy."

"No . . ." She shook her head. "I can take care of—"

"You're going to take care of yourself before you end up being admitted, too." Joe held tight to her hand when she would have pulled away. Oliver stood and let his dad tug Marsha down to sit beside him. "You're already exhausted. You haven't left the hospital since we got here. Dru can bring you some things from the house to make you more comfortable. Oliver will take the lead with the kids, at least until I'm on the mend enough for you to divide your time better."

"But Teddy's just a baby," she said. "And Family Services—"

"Oliver helping will show the county that things are still stable. Dru and Travis can shift stuff around at their jobs only so much. Oliver's between contracts, right?"

Oliver nodded, feeling as if a noose were cinching a tad tighter around his neck.

Joe had explained about Teddy, a new baby, a toddler. He was on provisionary placement with the family, to ensure he was thriving in his new environment. Which meant Marsha and Joe needed someone from the family living in the house around the clock, even if that someone was more of a stranger than a big brother. It was the only way to be certain the baby wouldn't be displaced and reabsorbed into the system.

"But you're so busy," Marsha said to Oliver. The rush of worry and relief in her expression would have settled it for Oliver even if he hadn't already made up his mind.

Each minute he was home would cost him when it was time to get back to his own life. He'd lose the Canadian pitch, too, if he didn't get back to Atlanta to work on it before the weekend. He'd become even more attached to his foster family. And as an added bonus, he'd be staying next door to Selena, an off-limits siren he had no business wanting to talk to again as badly as he did. But Marsha and Joe needed him in Chandlerville, so that's where he'd stay.

"I'll take care of it, Dad." He'd find a way through. He always did.

"Thank you," his dad rasped.

Oliver remembered his father's voice booming across a roomful of kids, freezing everyone in mid-mischief.

"I know it's a lot to ask," Marsha said. "But—"

"I got you covered." He knew zilch about riding herd on a battalion of kids who wouldn't trust him, a total stranger, from the get-go. But flying blind had never stopped him before. "Don't worry about a thing."

A fresh wave of pride warmed Joe's pasty complexion. "Your brother and sister will pitch in as much as they can."

"Sure."

"They're good with the younger kids."

"Sure."

Oliver grappled for another word but couldn't find one. Because it was just plain wrong to be feeling this excited. His dad was in cardiac ICU, damn it. But Oliver couldn't help it. He was home for at least a few more days.

"You should make a point of seeing Bethany, too," Marsha said.

Little Bethany Darling . . . Though she wouldn't be so little now.

"She was, what?" he asked. "Fourteen when I left?"

"Fifteen," Joe said.

"Travis said she's mostly steered clear of the family since she graduated from high school and punted on her scholarship to that New York art institute."

"She's confused and hurting," Joe said. "But she's stuck close to home. She keeps up with Dru and—"

"And we haven't seen her at the hospital yet," Marsha said. "Maybe you could find her and—"

"Sure," Oliver said.

He and Bethany had been almost as close as he and Dru and Travis. But he'd kept his distance from her for years the same as from the rest of the family. What's to say him tracking her down now wouldn't *hurt* his parents' chances to reconnect with her while he was around?

"I'll do what I can, Mom. Don't worry about anything."

"Your mother's cranky," Joe teased, "not worried. I've spoiled her plans for tonight . . ." He took a shallow breath. "Belinda

Rosenthal and her garden club ladies-in-waiting were coming over to the house to talk about whatever they've got brewing."

"Father of the Year," Oliver said. "Yeah. Travis mentioned that. You're officially the bomb, Dad."

Joe waved away the suggestion.

"Admit it." Marsha brushed a butterfly kiss across his cheek. She wiped perspiration from his forehead. "You're hiding out in your cushy room here because coffee and dessert with Belinda and her ladies who lunch has you running scared."

"Enough to risk hospital food?" Oliver shuddered. "Tell me you're not that desperate."

He'd eased closer to the door. He wasn't slinking away, he told himself. He *wasn't* desperate to sniff out the caffeine he'd sworn off—a nod to cleaner living, like meaning to get more sleep. He'd handle staying in town just fine, once he had a calm moment to plan an exit strategy that would suit everyone. Once he could see the end of a project, he always found the right path through the chaos.

He reached behind him for the doorknob.

"Get some rest," his mom advised. "You're going to need it once the kids get home this afternoon. Travis and Dru are helping me talk with everyone at the house after school. I could introduce you to younger brothers and sisters then."

"Sounds good."

"Thank you for being here." His father's smile was tighter than before, but just as genuine. "For staying. You don't know what this means to us."

"No worries." Oliver pushed through the door to cover *his* worry about all of it.

At the moment, he'd kill for a quick ride home and a few hours of being unconscious. But he turned down the hallway toward the

CICU waiting area, searching for his brother . . . and put on the brakes so fast his sneakers skidded on the linoleum.

Selena stood with her back to Travis. She stared at Oliver, her bottomless brown eyes rounded like saucers. She was the best part of his messed-up childhood, and she was once more just a touch away.

He'd survived his teenage years by promising himself Selena would be his future. After they'd imploded, too many of his restless nights as an adult had been filled with dreams of what they could have been. And now that they were back in the same place, fate seemed determined to throw them together. Fate, and Oliver's family.

He could hear every hesitant breath she took. He could see what looked almost like regret in her gaze. Only there was something more there—enough to completely lose himself in, if he wasn't careful.

"Hello, Selena." His glance toward Travis promised retribution if his brother had helped set this reunion into motion.

Travis held up his palms, innocence personified. "I just got here."

"I'm sorry about this," Selena added in a rush.

She looked like any second she might hug Oliver or burst into tears or worse. While he wanted to close the distance between them, hold her body against his, and be certain she was really there.

She stayed put.

So did he.

Oliver was officially one surprise over his coping threshold.

"Now isn't a good time," he said.

Dipping his toe into his past with Selena would be like taking that first hit of caffeine. Innocent enough in theory. Just one sip. He'd still be in control. No problem. Until his addiction had him by the gut and there was no shaking it loose.

Selena fussed with the strap of the tote bag she'd slung over her shoulder. She looked ready to crawl out of her skin. But she didn't move. And if she didn't move soon, one of them was going to scream. Most likely Oliver.

Then the elevator at the end of the hall dinged, its doors rolling open, and Brad Douglas stepped onto the ICU floor.

Having Oliver close was better than Selena remembered. Every part of her wanted him even closer—when reason said she should be getting the hell out of there, while Oliver stared at her, and then Brad, and then her again.

Brad had stopped just outside the elevator. Even taller than Oliver and Travis, he managed to look both easygoing and badass in a sheriff's deputy uniform identical to Travis's. Except Brad's was neatly pressed, and Travis looked like he'd slept in his.

Brad had steered clear of Selena since she'd come home, to spare her the mortification of having to face him. Or maybe to spare himself—since he was engaged to yet another person in Chandlerville who had reason to despise Selena. He seemed as shocked as Oliver to find her in CICU. Meanwhile Travis was gazing at them as if all the oxygen hadn't just been sucked out of the hallway.

And it felt so . . . right, somehow.

"The Three Musketeers," Selena couldn't stop herself from saying. "Together again."

Travis chuckled and popped his chewing gum. "I'd forgotten about that."

Brad flicked an answering grin toward Oliver, looking as self-conscious as Selena had felt back at the house.

"I'm sorry about Joe," she said to Oliver. She really was. And she *really* had to get out of there.

Because, God, she wanted to hug him instead—all of them—and catch up. Empty seconds ticked by, filled with everything she and Oliver couldn't say to each other. Not now, in front of Brad and Travis. Maybe not ever.

"Thank you for coming to check on Dad." Travis's hand gently closed around Selena's elbow. "It's great to see you again, even if—"

Selena tugged free. If he said one more nice thing while his brother stared daggers at her . . . Why was she still there, letting herself hope for the good things that might still be possible for her and Camille—*if* Selena and Oliver could find a way to at least be civil to each other?

"I have to go." Her legs finally cooperated, moving her toward the elevator.

Halfway there, with Brad aiming his hesitant smile at her, she sensed someone closing in from behind. Her control finally snapped.

"Travis, I—"

She turned and Oliver was there instead. Right there. Belinda's tote slipped off Selena's shoulder and whacked him in the chest.

"Shit," she said.

Selena swallowed another of the curses that had come far too easily since her marriage imploded. Then she lost herself in Oliver's emerald gaze. It was as pure and clean as spring rain. Her desperation to leave shimmered into instant need. This close to him, all she'd ever be able to do was want.

I'll love you forever, Selena, he'd said the night she'd thrown him away, *no matter what. I'm not like your dad. I'll never leave you.*

"I'll walk you to your car," he said now.

Marsha poked her head out of Joe's room. She smiled as Oliver reached for Selena's arm, touching her for the first time since that long-ago night.

"We should talk," he said.

No.

No, no, no no.

"No," she said emphatically. "We shouldn't talk. Not like this."

She felt her resolve to do the responsible thing evaporate.

If he stayed in town and Marsha kept meddling the way she was, some kind of showdown was inevitable. There'd be no escaping it unless Selena bolted again for parts unknown. And having things finally in the open would probably be for the best. She'd put it off long enough. But the heat rolling off Oliver's powerful frame made her want far more from him. And she had to get that nonsense under control.

He seemed so . . . distant. So completely different suddenly. It was possible her heart was going to melt into nothing.

"Watch out," Travis said as Marsha headed their way. "Matchmaking mom, incoming."

"I hope Joe's okay," Selena muttered to both brothers. "I'm so sorry, Oliver . . . for everything."

She raced for the elevator, sidestepping Brad.

"I'm sorry about this," she said to him, too, as she stabbed the call button.

The elevator opened with a cheery ding. Inside the car, she turned back. Brad and Oliver and Travis were side by side, their hands braced on their hips, identical perplexed expressions on her musketeers' faces.

Her cell phone played its "Danger Zone" ringtone, saving her from walking back onto the CICU floor. Marsha joined her sons. Selena turned her back as the elevator closed and answered the call from her, *if there was a God*, soon-to-be ex-husband.

"What is it now, Parker?"

Chapter Five

"Go after her." Marsha stood close to Oliver without touching him, the way she had the first day he'd come to live with the family.

He'd felt unbearably raw then, after losing his birth mom. A similar flood of violent emotion clawed at him now.

"I'll go," Brad said.

He hesitated. He blinked at the killing stare Oliver cut him and headed for the elevators, shaking his head.

Marsha followed at his heels. "This is all my fault. Poor girl."

"You're just going to stand there like a chump," Travis asked, "and leave Mom to deal with this on her own?"

Oliver wanted to snarl and rip into something, preferably his brother. But Travis was right. Marsha looked almost as rough as Joe had. She needed to be caring for her husband, not consoling Selena. And Oliver could have prevented all of this if he'd had the balls to deal reasonably with Selena from the start.

His mother and Brad had already disappeared, their elevator heading down. Oliver punched the button to follow. He could still feel the softness of Selena's skin beneath his fingers. Travis joined him, stepped with Oliver into the car, and punched the button for the ground floor.

"Butt out," Oliver said. "I can handle this on my own."

"You bet. You're one smooth devil."

"Do yourself a favor and back off."

"Hey." Travis cuffed Oliver's shoulder with an open palm. "Don't hate your wingman."

"Is wingman slang for 'dead man walking'?"

Travis chewed his gum, unfazed.

The elevator dinged. The doors opened in time for them to catch Selena hurrying across the lobby toward the front entrance. Brad and Marsha watched her leave. By the time Oliver and Travis reached them, Selena had disappeared outside.

"I feel horrible," Marsha said.

She wasn't the only one. It had gutted Oliver upstairs—the stricken look on Selena's face.

"I'm sorry if I made things worse." Brad's remorse was as genuine as his earlier *welcome home* smile. "But it's good to see you, man." He offered Oliver his hand. "It's been a hell of a long time. Too long."

Oliver shook out of habit, while watching Marsha stare after Selena.

"I stopped by on an early lunch break." Brad's uniform, identical to Travis's, explained the rest.

Travis had conveniently forgotten to mention that he worked with the guy.

"Dru's tied up at the restaurant," Brad continued. "She dropped Teddy at the church daycare after getting the kids off to school. She'll pick him up on her way back for this afternoon's meeting at the house. She wanted me to see if there'd been any updates from Joe's doctors."

"Dru?" Oliver pictured his baby sister, forever tagging along after him, Travis, and Brad—the Three Musketeers, Selena had dubbed them.

"My . . ." Brad turned to Travis. "You didn't tell him?"

"Tell me what?"

A fresh batch of memories attacked, images of Oliver's kid sister and his then best friend. Dru and Brad were dancing together when Dru had been a high school sophomore and Oliver, Travis, and Brad were seniors. She and Brad were slow dancing *way* too close while the spring formal's band played "Endless Love."

Oliver's head was going to explode.

"Brad and Dru were engaged last Christmas," Marsha explained. "After he came home to help his grandmother."

Brad.

And Dru.

Whose crush on Oliver's best friend had been so big, she'd been the first to guess that the boy she'd fallen for had hooked up with Selena. She'd been the one to break the news to Oliver and had been just as devastated as he was. She'd sworn to never forgive Brad.

"When Vivian died," Marsha added, "she left Dru the Dream Whip to run. Your sister and Brad have been doing a fine job with it. They're living in the Douglas house now, exactly the way Vi thought they always should have."

"Seriously?" was all Oliver could manage.

Brad's good-natured vibe dimmed at Oliver's underwhelming response. What? Was Oliver supposed to congratulate the guy who'd helped Selena kick him to the curb, because Brad had moved on to Oliver's sister?

Marsha laid a comforting hand on Brad's arm. "Joe's resting better this morning. We're still waiting to hear from someone about what's next. They ran more tests and scans early this morning. Another EKG about an hour ago. Tell Dru to head over to the house whenever she can this afternoon, and thank her for running Teddy around. We should know more by then about what the next few days will be like. But at least Oliver's agreed to stay for a while."

Travis grinned. "Well, hell, man, that's great."

Brad looked like he wanted to agree. Oliver saw the precise moment the other man decided that keeping quiet was a wiser course of action. Marsha crossed her arms at the lot of them.

"Seriously?" she mimicked. She looked ready to knock their heads together, the way she'd frequently threatened to when they'd been kids. She never had back then, but there was a first time for everything. "Tell me you boys aren't planning on keeping this up the entire time Oliver's back."

"Why don't I stop by later?" Brad suggested. "I'll have some time when my shift is done, unless Dru needs me to cover the restaurant. Unless . . ." His attention shifted to Travis. "I don't want to make more trouble for anyone."

"Come by anytime you can," Travis said.

"Thank you," Marsha added, "for taking such good care of Dru and the Whip through all this, so Dru can be wherever she needs to be."

"Anything I can do." Brad included Oliver in the offer.

"I'll walk you out." Travis steered Brad away.

"Brad and Dru?" Oliver asked his mother.

"You need to talk with Selena," Marsha insisted.

After the stunt she'd just pulled, her gentle reprimand finished pissing him off. "I need to focus on helping you and Joe. Other than that, I should probably steer clear of conversations that tempt me to take my sister's fiancé apart again with my bare hands."

He rubbed the side of his nose. A delay tactic when he was close to doing or saying something he'd regret. He was supposed to breathe deeply and regroup. He sneezed instead.

"Bless you." Marsha rooted in the pocket of her cardigan. He'd never known her not to have a spare tissue whenever someone needed one.

He stopped her, keeping his hand on her arm until she looked up. The worry in her gray eyes damn near broke his heart.

"Let me take care of you and Dad right now. Please, let the rest go."

"Dealing with Selena—and Brad, too—is one of the best things you can do for your father and me."

"Not if you want me to stay."

He would handle diving headfirst into his family. Somehow he'd still find a way to walk once his job here was done. But how did he do that if he opened the door any wider to reconnecting with Selena? He'd treated her like shit twice already because he didn't trust himself to get closer and be able to find his way out. Some part of him was still so stuck on her, he'd come close to punching Brad—just for breathing near her.

"If you're going to give us a hand with everything else," Marsha insisted, "you're going to have to at least talk with Selena. She lives next door. Brad and Dru are engaged. He's over at the house all the time, pitching in as much as your sister does. And—"

"Hold on." Oliver's vision narrowed to one suddenly obvious detail. "Before you sent me out of Dad's room to talk to Travis, when you knew Selena was there . . . You were stalling. Brad was already on his way. Dru called ahead, right? Damn it, Mom. What were you thinking? Throwing the three of us back together without at least warning me, while Dad's in the next room fighting for his life?"

"Take it easy, man." Travis stepped beside their mother. His gaze was the kind of intense that must put the fear of God into people he confronted on the job. "Mom's trying to help."

And maybe she *was* helping. Oliver's first confrontation with Selena and Brad was done. The surprise of it was behind them. But that's where this ended. Selena's sweet face and sad, hurting eyes while she'd apologized for their disastrous end that had been as much Oliver's fault as hers . . . What was the point of repeating that, just so they could all hurt some more?

"I'm sorry," he said to his mother. "But, please. Lay off whatever the two of you were angling for upstairs."

Oliver's fist clenched at the memory of Brad's *friends again* handshake. The man was going to be his brother-in-law, which meant at the very least Oliver had an uncomfortable conversation ahead of him with Dru. He had no bandwidth left for additional drama.

"If you won't go find that girl for your own sake," Marsha said, sounding dug in, "do it for our family."

The wanting place inside Oliver ripped wider open. He rubbed a hand across his face.

"I need some air," he said. Except Marsha's complexion had turned deathly white. He grabbed her elbow. "Mom? Are you okay—"

"Dr. Kask," she said over Oliver's shoulder.

He and Travis turned to see a middle-aged man in a lab coat heading their way from the elevator bank.

"You've met Travis," she said to the fifty-something doctor with a fifty-something comb-over. "This is Oliver, another of our boys."

Comb-over looked up from his clipboard to acknowledge Oliver and Travis. His attention tracked to Marsha and held. The clipboard dropped until it was in front of his waist.

"The charge nurse thought perhaps you'd headed to the cafeteria. I wanted to speak with you and Mr. Dixon together before I went off shift."

"Okay." Marsha's voice was hushed, as if whispering might soften the blow of whatever the doctor had to say.

"We have your husband's test results back. Unfortunately, they're not what we'd hoped. He's not responding to the medication well enough for that to remain our only course of action. This morning's electrocardiogram isn't showing enough increased blood flow. Given the significance of the blockage to his left coronary artery . . ."

The doctor glanced at Oliver and his brother as if they should find somewhere else to be. Neither of them budged.

"I need to discuss a few options with you and Joe," Comb-over said.

"Options?" Travis and Oliver asked in unison.

"More invasive alternatives, to get blood flowing properly to the patient's left ventricle. Interventions that will increase his oxygen levels and reduce the degree of permanent damage done to the heart muscle."

"The patient?" Oliver bit out. The man sounded like a walking, talking textbook.

"I'm sorry to be so technical," the doctor said to Marsha. "Occupational hazard when I spend most of my days with other doctors, poring over lab tests and research. We're wasting muscle, Mrs. Dixon, the longer we wait to try something else. I'm afraid there's no clear recommendation for me to make. There are two procedures that offer you similar potential results, with different sets of risks and probability for complications. It will take me some time to explain them. But I'd like Joe scheduled for surgery later tonight, first thing tomorrow at the latest."

Marsha turned to Oliver and Travis.

"I'll let you know what your dad and I decide as soon as I can," she said, ready to battle onward. "Travis, could you give your sister a call? Let Dru know I might not make it to the house this afternoon. You kids talk to the younger ones on your own if I can't."

"Sure," Travis said.

She left for the elevators with Comb-over. A flash of panic shook Oliver—a premonition that he might never see his father again. His next calming breath did little to loosen the dread clogging his windpipe. He shook it off.

Marsha would have made damn sure Joe had the best doctor for the job, even if the guy had the bedside manner of a chunk of computer code. She and Joe would make the right decision. And, surgery or not, Joe would be fine. He had to be. Then he and Marsha would pick up the pieces the way they had after every other setback they'd faced. Oliver's whole family would.

A firm grip closed around his shoulder and yanked him from his thoughts, spinning him to face his equally worried brother.

"You're coming with me," Travis said.

"Mom and Dad will be awhile." Travis shoved Oliver toward a hallway to the right of visitor reception. "Let's go."

Oliver rounded on him. "Hands off, man. I'm not going anywhere but back upstairs."

"I'll text Mom. She'll join us if she's finished with the doc before we're back."

"Back from where?"

"Hell freezing over."

Travis kept a firm grip on Oliver's shoulder as they walked. Oliver's options narrowed to cooperating or starting a brawl.

"That ass kicking we've been talking about?" he said. "Considered yours kicked."

"Looking forward to it."

Something was slipping inside Oliver, more out of his control by the second. Listening to that doctor talk medical options reminded Oliver of how he laid out system specs to a waffling client who had a mother of a design mess on their hands. By that point it usually didn't matter what decision was made. Oliver was already focused on the inevitable fallout. Either option was just as likely to blow up in their faces.

Only this time it was his dad's life on the line. Not some faceless IT application he felt no attachment to beyond getting paid.

"Let me go, Travis. Seriously."

"Not until I'm done ruining both our mornings. We're settling a few things."

Travis, biceps bulging beneath the short sleeves of his uniform, hustled Oliver down a hallway a sign said led to the cafeteria. People were staring.

"I asked Brad to wait for us," Travis continued. "You two are going to have it out before you spend another moment with Mom. *Before* you see Dru. I'll contain the carnage, enough to keep your ass out of jail this time. But you're giving him the benefit of the doubt, or I'm throwing you in a cell myself."

"There's nothing to have out." Oliver yanked his arm free, but he kept walking.

"That's right. You both got on with your lives. You *both* learned everything the hard way. And what does any of it matter now? We've all made peace with the crap we pulled when we were kids. The rest is holding a grudge, Oliver, and nobody needs that from you."

"So?"

"So talk to the guy, without looking like you wanna have his spleen for dinner."

Oliver treated his brother to an under-his-breath, anatomically impossible suggestion. "I'm just as sick over Dad as you are."

"I know that. Brad's worried, too. So let's get this out of the way, so everyone can focus on what Joe and Marsha need."

Oliver marched down beige corridors washed with the kind of fluorescent lighting that seemed manufactured to effect maximum gloom. They cornered into the cafeteria and were assaulted with skylights. People. Ambient noise. Oliver squinted through his growing migraine.

Brad was at a just-this-side-of-shabby table, in a corner where he sat with his back to the wall. The rest of the room was packed with a fast-eating lunch crowd. Doctors, nurses, visitors of patients. Groups talking with hushed intensity.

Brad watched Travis and Oliver settle across from him. His resigned expression had taken a definite tilt toward pissed. He was expecting a fight. Maybe he was looking for one.

"I don't give a shit," Oliver said straight off. "About you and Selena and seven years ago. I did." His hand clenched into a fist on top of the wobbly table. "I still do, I guess. And let's be clear, I'll knock you from here to next Tuesday if you do anything to hurt Dru again. But I figure she's a grown woman. She knows what she's getting into. If you weren't one hundred percent into her this time, she'd have stomped you into the dirt when you came sniffing at her again."

Travis's chuckle loosened some of the tightness between Oliver's shoulder blades.

Brad scratched behind his ear and stretched his legs under the table. "Your sister did a fine job stomping on me herself when I first got back to town."

Oliver was cheered by the image. "Go, Dru."

"But I couldn't let her slip away again."

"Obviously."

"She still gives me hell on a regular basis if that sweetens the deal for you."

It did. Not that Oliver cared to admit it. "You and my sister fighting like a married couple already doesn't square things between us. But I haven't been part of this family in a long time. If they want you here, at the house, wherever, then be there. Be there for Dru. Don't hurt her again, and you won't have a problem with me."

"I care about your mom and dad." Brad braced his forearms on the table. "I care about your whole family. And I couldn't live without your sister in my life."

"He makes Dru happy," Travis said. "Brad's grandmother was the first to guess how much Dru was still stuck on him. Vi made sure Dru had one last chance to realize it herself. Stick around long enough and you'll see it, too."

Oliver stood. He got it. Dru and Brad were tight. No harm, no foul. All better. Except while Brad and Travis talked about second chances, images of Selena's face kept flashing through Oliver's mind.

"I'm sorry to hear about Vivian." He had genuinely liked Brad's cantankerous grandmother. She'd been a nice old lady, if you liked them brutally honest and loyal to the bone. "She was a real dame."

"Thank you." Brad stared at Oliver.

Meanwhile, Oliver couldn't seem to get moving. He caught his brother checking his phone. Travis shook his head. No update yet from Marsha. Oliver dug into his pocket for his truck keys, then remembered his brother had driven them over. Travis's raised eyebrow confirmed that Oliver wasn't going anywhere just yet. Oliver threw himself back into his chair.

Brad had grabbed coffee. He took a long sip from a foam cup. Oliver's mouth watered. Brad had always drunk the stuff black as sin, wicked strong. Exactly the way Oliver liked it. Except he'd cut all stimulants out of his life and made a commitment to keep it that way.

"You need a line on a local meeting?" Brad asked.

Oliver strummed his fingers on the table, letting the subtext of the question sink in. "Excuse me?"

Brad shrugged. "Sisters talk, man. You're back. Dru's worried about you sticking with your program. I'm saving her the angst of asking you herself later."

Oliver's threats to pound on Travis held new appeal.

He owed his brother big time. He'd called Travis eighteen months ago for help, and Travis hadn't blinked before using his local contacts to muscle Oliver last-minute into a top Atlanta rehab facility. But they'd agreed to keep that and the outpatient counseling Oliver had completed afterward between themselves. Oliver was taking care of himself again. He was following the guidelines of his program—eat better, no stimulants, try to sleep more and work less, let go of the past and focus on what he could accomplish today and why it was important to stay clean.

There'd been no sense in worrying their folks or anyone else over Oliver landing in rehab after nearly blowing a project for a top client. There was definitely no reason for it to be a topic of conversation now with Brad or Dru or anyone else.

"Evidently," Oliver said to his brother, "sisters aren't the only ones who talk."

"It's barely been a year and a half, man." Travis plunked his smartphone down, display up. "I thought maybe Dru would see you more. I asked her to let me know if she noticed anything we should be worried about, assuming you stayed in town for a while. Now that you are, there's a solid local meeting I can hook you up with if you need one. I know a couple of guys who go, good men. Friends who'd keep an eye out for you."

Brad and Travis calmly waited for Oliver to respond, as if they were talking about where he should gas up his truck.

The Three Musketeers.

Together again.

"Who else knows?" Oliver asked.

"No one." His brother shook his head. "But I don't see the point in keeping it a secret. No one's going to judge you. But if keeping quiet about the fact that you've finally laid your demons to rest is what you want, I've got no problem with it. As long as being back doesn't mess with your sobriety."

Oliver thought of his dad upstairs, Marsha's reaction to Kask just now, Selena running from facing all of them, his reaction to seeing her . . . There seemed to be demons everywhere he looked. He shifted gears, glaring at Brad.

"Hey," Brad said, "I'm not talking."

"Except to my sister."

"She told me."

"Because," Travis said to Oliver, "she's worried about your ass."

"We all are," Brad added. "This would be a lot for me to take in all at once."

"This?" Oliver asked. "What the hell do either of you know about it?"

"We know family hasn't been an easy thing for you to be close to for a long time," his brother said. "So go to a meeting, man, if that's what you need to do."

"I need . . ." Oliver wished to hell he knew. He pushed out of his chair. "I need to get back upstairs and hear what the doctor's saying to Joe."

"So you can barge in on our parents looking half-crazed?" Travis asked.

Brad eased deeper in his chair. "You're not going to dump your problems on your parents. Sit back down and get yourself together."

Oliver sat, his brother and former friend's support an unwanted comfort. And as unsettling as watching Selena bolt as if loving Oliver was the worst mistake of her life.

"Thanks." He exhaled a razor-sharp breath.

Brad nodded. "The doctor's talking with your parents?"

"Surgery." Travis grabbed Brad's coffee. He shot it back and grimaced like it was two fingers of bourbon. "We don't know what type or when. All Kask said was soon."

Chapter Six

"How can I help you today?" Ginger Reid Jenkins asked Selena. Her attention dropped to Camille, whom she flashed an indulgent smile. "Aren't you just the cutest thing? And the spitting image of your mama when she wasn't much older."

"Except my eyes are lighter." Camille preened. "I get new shoes, 'cause my feet are getting too big for my old ones, and Grammy says I need good ones, and I should get them here, 'cause yours won't wear out as fast as the ones from Walmart."

"Sometimes it's better," Ginger agreed, "to spend just a little more for something you want to last."

She gave Selena a wink. The more than causal interest lighting Ginger's eyes hinted that the rumors about Selena's current financial straits had made the rounds to her old classmate.

"We've got some real nice things on sale," Ginger said to Camille, "that I think your mommy and grammy will love. We're making room for the summer trends. A pretty good selection of sizes, too." She pointed to the back corner of the Neat Feet boutique that occupied the same Main Street address as it always had. "Go check them out while I catch up with your mom."

With a nod from Selena, Camille took off toward the colorful display. The sale wall was in the same place as always, decorated today like a spring garden. Each flower sported a shoe atop its cheery green stem. As a child, Neat Feet displays had been Selena's favorite part of each visit to the store. That and the fact that buying good shoes, even for growing feet, was one of the few things Belinda never scrimped on when she'd made her quarterly budget. And every time she'd brought Selena to the boutique, Ginger's father had treated Selena like a princess—no matter that sale wall shoes were the only ones Belinda would let Selena choose from.

"It's crazy," Selena mused while Camille inspected each blossom. "It feels like just yesterday that I wanted one of everything in this place. Your parents had a knack for making you believe that pretty shoes you can't afford can magically make your life better."

Ginger's attention snapped up from eyeing Selena's tragically muddied silk flats. Her smile didn't waver, but some of its soft-sell sparkle dimmed.

"What are you in the market for?" she asked, tactful if curt. "So we can be sure to get your little one exactly what she needs."

"I'm sorry." Selena cringed at her rudeness for the second time that day.

It was a sore spot, that she'd let herself dream that everything really would be okay, just because she'd met a successful businessman in New York who could buy her and her daughter all the pretty things that Selena and Belinda had never been able to afford. But comparing the master salesman Ginger's dad had been to the soulless man Selena married was horribly unfair.

"I swear," she said, "I don't know what's wrong with me. It was a long day before I even left the house this morning, and things went downhill from there. Belinda's supposed to meet us here, but she's late. And I'm afraid I'm too distracted to be good company. I've always loved being here—your parents made coming to Neat Feet feel better than going to a candy store. I couldn't believe it was still around when Belinda first mentioned it. It looks the same, smells the same, feels the same. How are your mom and dad doing?"

Ginger ducked her chin. A lock of hair fell to half cover her face the way Selena remembered happening a lot when they'd first met in third grade. Mrs. Shultz would always ask Ginger questions in front of the class, and Ginger would get so shy and tongue-tied she'd look down at her desk, hiding behind her hair, until their teacher moved on to someone else.

Suddenly—too late—Selena remembered a snippet of gossip her mother had shared about Lizzy Reid, who was a member of Belinda's garden club. Lizzy had missed most of this year's meetings because her husband had advancing ALS.

"Dad's not doing too well," Ginger confirmed. "He's in a rehab place just outside of town. It's the only way insurance will cover his care. Mom goes to be with him every day. It's weighing on her, not keeping him at home. I'm mostly holding down the fort by myself now."

She'd answered in a casual way, seeming to expect Selena not to really care, or to be looking for a reason to change the subject. Instead, Selena gave Ginger a hug. They'd been friends once, both of them with pigtails like Camille's, long before the world had gotten so complicated they'd forgotten the simpler things that had once made them giggle and smile and twirl around each other's backyards.

"I'm sorry about George." Selena stepped back. "Your dad's the best. He always made us laugh. And he loved this store. I'm sure

he'd be proud to bursting if he could see what you're doing with it."
She took a moment to watch Camille pick up a pair of black-and-white oxford shoes, her smile ear-to-ear. "You're carrying on your family's legacy. I'm glad my daughter got to see this place. I really didn't mean to be so rude."

Ginger turned from watching Camille, too. She fiddled with the pearls she wore at the neck of a silk sweater twinset. A multi-karat diamond twinkled atop the thick platinum band on her wedding finger.

"I can understand the long day part," she mused. "The whole town is talking about it. Honey, I'd have sprinted for the hills, too. Both times."

Selena's mind blanked, not following at first. She was so tired, she was practically dead on her feet. And it was only four o'clock.

"Oliver being back," Ginger explained. The bell atop the door jingled, announcing another customer's arrival. "It's going to stir up a lot more people than just you. The town's buzzing about you two meeting up at the hospital this morning, after he drove right up his parents' driveway earlier and just stood there, staring at you."

"Which is why"—Belinda breezed to their side, joining the conversation without missing a beat—"I thought we'd discussed you steering clear of the hospital while he's in town. Why would you go and open yourself and Camille up to even more gossip?"

The bell over the door chimed again.

"Let me go see if I can help Camille make her selection." Before she slipped away, Ginger exchanged smiles with the new mother and daughter who'd come in, the little girl skipping along instead of walking.

"Tennis shoes," Selena called after her. "Something that will last through a summer of playing outside in my mother's yard."

"So," Belinda said, "you've definitely decided to stay awhile longer?"

The other mother glanced over from the table of dress shoes, the patent leather kind that little girls in the South wore to church on Sundays. The woman looked away when she realized she'd been caught eavesdropping.

A growing part of Selena would have liked nothing better than to pack her and her daughter's things and leave Chandlerville by nightfall.

"We don't seem to have a choice but to stay," she said to Belinda, keeping her voice down and praying her mother followed suit. "Parker's got his lawyer delaying the divorce again, asking for new briefs about joint assets. Something about categorizing them differently. The school year is almost over, taking my anemic income stream with it until I can find something else. Parker's and my joint accounts are still frozen. And I haven't saved nearly enough yet to get me and Camille set up with a place of our own."

"He called again?" Belinda turned her back to their still-avid audience. When Selena nodded, Belinda sighed. "Why do you encourage him? Stop answering when you know it's him."

"I was leaving the hospital." Selena stared the other mother down until the woman finally moved herself and her child across the store. "I was distracted. Besides, I can't risk agitating him more than he already is. He's swearing he'll hold things up until I agree to fly myself and Camille back to New York to meet with him in person."

"The more your lawyer has to do to get you out of this marriage, the less money you'll ever see from whatever settlement you're awarded."

Selena shrugged, despising the no-win limbo her husband and his financial resources had exiled her to.

It had all been explained to her. Why a judge's ruling would be better than a protracted trial. How a mediator might be an option. But that would require either Parker's agreement or a judge's order, and so far Parker's attorneys had prevented the latter. And while she didn't owe her own legal team a dime until a settlement was awarded, they'd take their fee out of whatever she received. And that bill was growing at an alarming rate, given that Selena had filed to end her marriage six months ago.

"I hate this, Mom. Owning nothing of my own, having nothing to offer Camille that Parker doesn't control, and owing you more every day we stay here."

"All you owe me," Belinda said, her tone brooking no argument, "is your promise to do what's best this time for yourself and your daughter. Be smart about this, Selena."

Belinda was trying so hard to be supportive. Selena knew that. But her mother's concern, her disappointment at the state of things, dripped from every word.

"Be smart about Parker," Belinda insisted. "About Oliver. About Camille. Stay as long as you need to. I've told you that. Get your life straight and figure out what you really want. I'll take care of what I can in the meantime. You save your money for you and Camille. We'll make it work."

Liquid sprang to Selena's eyes, emotion she wouldn't let fall.

We'll make it work.

How many times had her mother said that when Selena had been a little girl and wanted something they couldn't afford? Something that her friends like Ginger had gotten so effortlessly from their parents. Belinda would inevitably have to say no, but that they'd *make it work* somehow. Selena would see, her mother had promised. And now Selena did.

She'd blamed both her parents for how hard life had been after their divorce. But Belinda had borne the brunt of everything Selena had thought she'd gone without. Material things Selena had been obsessed with, like pretty new shoes, shiny churchgoing shoes, while her mom insisted on buying sturdier ones that would do just as well for nice as for everyday. Now Selena was relying on Belinda to help her navigate the same limited-income choices for Camille.

"Thank you, Mom." She hadn't said it enough as a child. She'd never again forget to say it as an adult. "I am going to make this work."

"I know you will. Just steer clear of Oliver Bowman, honey. Don't go down that road again, unless you're one hundred percent sure of what you want."

"What I want?"

Sometimes Selena wondered exactly what her mother knew, or what Belinda thought she knew, where Oliver, Selena, and Camille were concerned. And after the mess Selena had made of things at the hospital, today of all days, she found herself wishing she and Belinda were close enough to talk about everything. The way other mothers and daughters seemed to so effortlessly share life's ups and downs.

"Mom," she said, "do you—"

"Let's go make sure your daughter's not buying out the store." Belinda left to chat with Ginger and Camille about shoe options.

Selena stared after her. She didn't have the energy to follow. The rest of her day and the decisions she still had to make about Oliver and the Dixons and Camille—while the entire town watched on—were for once making her issues with Parker seem like the least of her problems. Except that if Parker hadn't been yanking her around financially all this time in an attempt to manipulate her into taking him back, she and her daughter would be long gone from Chandlerville. Then there'd be no Oliver for Selena to have to deal with. At least not until she'd settled down somewhere with Camille and begun building the happy life she was determined to give her child.

Maybe then Selena would have been able to see her way clear to reach out to Oliver on her own terms. Instead of it feeling like the worst possible timing for her to tell the man she'd loved the deepest secrets of her heart—and hope he didn't crush both her and her daughter with more of the cool indifference he'd shown Selena that morning.

"Leave the boy be for a while," Joe cautioned Marsha. "Let him settle in before you throw more at him."

Marsha shook her head, her thoughts more scattered than she ever remembered them being. Her Joe was getting worse, not better. And Oliver was back—still struggling with seeing himself as part of their family, no matter how honest and responsible he'd become in the rest of his life. But there was one thing she was certain of.

"We don't have time for him to settle in," she said.

The doctor was gone. The decision between the available surgical options was made: angioplasty, scheduled for ten o'clock that night. There was only the waiting now. The wondering if they'd made the right choice. And the worrying over their kids. Joe's mind was preoccupied by family, same as hers, even now. The kids had always been their priority since the day they'd begun fostering.

"Besides"—she smoothed salt-and-pepper hair back from her husband's forehead—"when has Oliver ever settled in anywhere? From what he told you earlier, I'd be surprised if he's stayed in one place all these years more than a few months at a time."

And now they had him home—their brilliant boy, all grown up, with his heart in his eyes each time he looked at Marsha or his father . . . or Selena. That fine mind was no doubt already fixated on getting away from them again. Which was unacceptable. She was done enabling his believing that being responsible to the family was all he had to offer. That sending home money was all the contact with life in Chandlerville he needed.

Joe shook his head. "He's not going to put up with much more meddling from you, love. Not if he doesn't understand why."

"Then I'll have some fast explaining to do at the house, won't I?"

After which she'd talk with the younger kids and get herself back here, to make certain Joe had whatever he needed.

They'd scraped by without opting for bypass. But angioplasty was invasive enough. Kask and his team would attempt to widen the main artery leading to Joe's heart without cracking his chest open to do it. And if they couldn't . . .

She brushed the backs of her fingers over the stubble of her husband's beard. "I want our son back."

"I do, too. For longer than a few days. But he's seen staying away as the answer for himself—and us—for a long time. He's never been ready to—"

"Give his whole heart away again? Have we waited too long?"

"He reached out first," Joe reminded her, "when he contacted Travis about sending money home. And we didn't give him a reason *not* to keep that door open. He felt comfortable coming home again because of that. If we'd pushed for more, he might not have."

"He'd have been here for you."

"He needs to stay for more."

"And if he's not ready to? I won't be at the house after today, to make sure he sees what's right in front of him, waiting for him to want it, too."

Joe eyed her. "So you're going to cut to the chase this afternoon?"

"He needs to know, before it's too late and he makes a mistake he'll regret."

"He's a fine man. He'll do the right thing."

"He doesn't know what the right thing is yet."

"Neither do you."

"He still believes he's let us down." Marsha stared at the clock across from Joe's bed until her vision cleared. "It's breaking my heart to see how much being back means to him, and to know he's already decided that being elsewhere as soon as possible is what's best for everyone."

He *was* a fine young man with a bottomless heart that had refused to let him cut ties completely with the people who wanted to love him. He needed to give folks in Chandlerville a chance to see that—especially Selena. He needed to give himself the chance to finally belong to all of them.

"The years away have taught him good things about himself," Joe reasoned. "The next few days will teach him more."

"If he stays."

"He won't turn his back on the promise he's made."

Marsha wanted to believe that. "If anything can show him what's still inside him, diving headfirst into helping with the kids should."

Her Joe's eyes sparkled. He drew her palm to his heart, his hand trembling as it covered hers.

"The kids get what they need," he said.

It had been their pact from the beginning of this crazy dream of theirs—to still have a huge family, despite learning that they couldn't have babies of their own. They'd from the start put doing what was right for the kids first. The rest had worked itself out every time.

"Brad and Oliver and Selena and Camille," Marsha said. "It's not a coincidence that they're all back now."

"Not if you have anything to say about it," Joe teased.

"I don't know what has Oliver more spooked. Agreeing to stay in town for longer than he'd planned." She could still see her son's shock in the hallway. His anger downstairs. "Or the prospect of still being so tangled up over Selena."

"They weren't ready for what they had when they were younger. Or how hard it was going to be to keep it. Not everyone gets it right from the start."

The way she and Joe had. "Brad and Dru worked past their issues."

Their Dru had learned how to believe in someone, something, as her very own. Oliver needed the same confidence in himself—in his heart. A lot of their kids struggled to trust the best of what life had in store for them.

"What if he's still not ready?" Joe looking worried—for her and their son.

"What if Selena isn't?"

The young woman was so deliberate now, so careful. Like Oliver always had been, even when he'd been drinking and self-destructing in high school. He and Selena had worked hard for their new lives. And both were determined to believe those lives should be far away from Chandlerville.

"This may be their last chance." Marsha rested her head on her husband's shoulder. "*Our* last chance to help them. We have to do something."

She and Joe had guessed for a while now that there was more going on than Selena admitted to. They hadn't said anything to anyone else. There was no way to ask questions about Camille without making the situation worse. But after what had just happened in the hallway, Marsha was even more convinced that Selena was hiding something, and isolating herself because of it.

Her husband sighed. "You're determined this is the right time?"

"Is there ever a *right* time to dig into the past and hope the truth doesn't make things worse?" Marsha was thinking of Dru now, and everything she and Brad had already been through. "The last thing I want is to cause more hurt."

"A lot of good can come from believing that people will support each other, even if it hurts a little."

"Camille," Marsha whispered. "She's a very good thing."

"She's the most important thing. Oliver will see that. Dru and Brad, too. Selena already does, the way she dotes on the child. We'll have to convince her that she belongs with us, too. Or no matter what Oliver does next, Selena might bolt."

"Oliver will make sure everyone's taken care of." Protecting his own was a soul-deep part of the man he'd become, the same as with Travis. And Joe. "But . . ."

"He needs to want Camille for himself—not see her as another responsibility to throw money at while he keeps himself from getting too attached. *If* she turns out to be his."

"She's so beautiful. And she's *so* Oliver's." Marsha had hoped so at least, since the first time Camille had flashed her crooked, heart-catching smile.

"Our first grandchild."

Joe sounded exhausted—and positively bewitched. Then his breath caught on his next chest pain. He insisted they weren't nearly as bad now as when he'd collapsed in the heat of the late afternoon sun, mowing their lawn. Fin Robinson, one of their newest kids, had found his father and run screaming inside to get Marsha. Her own heart clenched at the terrifying memory.

Straightening, she made her smile wider, softer, wanting Joe to know. Did he know? He was her everything—their family's everything. He had to pull through this.

"I can't wait to see Camille wrap her grandpa around her little finger," she said. "You'll be toast. You're always such a push-over with the girls."

He smiled through whatever discomfort remained, reassuring, determined, and then somber. A tear trickled from his eye.

"I . . . I don't want to miss any of it. But I know it's going to be okay. All of it. And I believe in you, love, whatever you think you need to do for Oliver."

Marsha wiped his cheek, wiped her own. Her Joe's belief was a powerful thing. It had gotten them through so much. It wouldn't fail them tonight.

"After your angio's a smashing success," she said, "you'll get to see plenty of Camille and Oliver and everyone else. All the kids can come for a visit once you're on the mend and out of CICU."

Her husband's eyes slid shut, the weakness that struck without warning stealing him away.

"My first grandchild," he whispered.

Marsha kissed him. "You better believe it, Gramps."

She slid into the chair beside his bed. Useless tears welled behind her closed lids. But there was no time for that kind of nonsense.

Time, she'd learned years ago, slipped by too quickly to waste wishing things were different. Whatever was coming next always arrived, regardless. Steering into the current was the only way. Making life work the best you knew how, instead of fighting what needed to be done or giving up and going under.

Maybe Joe was right. It might be safer to let things follow their own course. But everyone needed to be navigating the same troubled waters sooner rather than later. It was the only way to tackle the hard work that had gone undone for too long.

"Leave it to me, love." Her hand still covered her husband's heart, desperate for the feel of its steady beat. "I won't let our boy leave again without him knowing how much we all need him."

Chapter Seven

"No, Parker," Camille's mommy said on her cell phone, while Camille played out back of her grammy's house. She was in the shade by the tall bushes next to the Dixons' yard.

It was one of her favorite places to play, near all the pretty white flowers—camellias—that were like her name. 'Sides, it was too hot to play anywhere else, even in the front yard where she wouldn't have to hear Mommy argue with Parker.

And she'd already spread out one of Grammy's quilts where she was. It was Camille's favorite—the one with the big flowers all over. And she had her bubble wand and the big bottle of bubble stuff Mommy had let her buy at the dollar store. And bubbles kinda made it not so bad that Parker had ruined the drive home from the shoe store by calling and making Mommy sad again. *And* since Camille was sitting next to Grammy's camellias, she could watch all the people next door. And that was even more fun than bubbles.

There were lots of people to watch today—extra cars in the driveway, plus all the kids were home from school. The man from that morning and his truck were back, and Dru and Travis and Mrs. Dixon now. Plus, Camille was close enough to still hear what her mommy was saying if she wanted to. And she kinda wanted to, even though she wished they really had left Parker behind for real, the way Mommy kept saying they had. Only Parker kept calling and calling. And Camille worried about her mommy when he did that.

"No," Mommy said. "We're not coming up there. I told you this morning, last week, last month, *two* months ago. My answer hasn't changed. It's not going to change. You don't want a family. You want to look like you have a family, while you live your life however you want to. We don't need to see each other again to agree on that. And Camille doesn't need to be any more confused by what you think being a father and a husband looks like. We both know what we want and what we don't. *You* need to tell your lawyers to release enough money so I can get Camille settled somewhere else. I've said yes to mediation. I'll say yes to whatever's fair, including not asking for child support. But that's not enough for you. We agreed . . . "

Mommy kept saying that to Parker—the man they'd lived with all of Camille's life. The man who'd married her mommy so they could be a family forever, and had kept asking Camille to call him Daddy when Mommy said she didn't have to, 'cause he wasn't really. The man who made her mommy cry at night sometimes still, when Mommy thought Camille was asleep and wouldn't hear her talking to Parker on the phone.

We agreed . . .

Her mommy saw Camille watching and turned away and started whispering. Like she didn't want Camille to worry. Like she didn't want Camille to miss the things they used to have when they lived with Parker in his fancy apartment in New York. But it was okay with Camille, all of it, 'specially leaving. Because now they got to live with Grammy. Whatever *we agreed* meant, New York had never felt as good as living here, and living next door to Grammy's neighbors.

Watching the Dixon house around the shady bushes in the hedge, Camille sat in the middle of the old quilt on one of the tulips—the flower that had a little tear she didn't mind on one of its purple petals. She dipped her daisy bubble wand and waved it and thought about all the times in New York when Mommy had taken her to play in the park next to Parker's building. And Mommy had kept telling Camille how great it was to live where they lived, and all Camille had ever wanted was a house of her own, with other houses all around them and kids her age to play with, like the ones she saw on TV.

She watched her bubbles fly and sparkle and sink, the sun making rainbows in them, and wondered what living at the Dixons' house would be like. There were always tons of kids there. She'd even snuck over a couple of times to play, when Grammy wasn't watching and Mommy was out, even though Camille wasn't s'posed to.

The Dixon family was so cool. All those kids. All of them looked different. They weren't a real family, someone at school had said. But they were bigger than any family Camille had ever seen, and they looked so happy, and she kinda sometimes wished . . .

She looked behind her.

She wished her mommy wasn't upset so much still. She wished Parker would stop calling. She wished she could believe her mommy and grammy when they acted like nothing was wrong, no matter how many times Camille asked 'cause she knew something still was. In New York Mommy had smiled and said things were okay, too, only they hadn't been.

Camille wished that whatever the fresh start was that Mommy kept saying would happen would go ahead and happen now.

"No, Parker," her mommy said. "Camille and I can't live that way anymore. We've moved on."

Mommy said *moved on* a lot, too.

Moved, Camille understood. They'd moved from their apartment with Parker to a friend's place in New York. Camille had slept on the couch and Mommy on the floor, and they hadn't been able to bring most of their things. Then they'd moved from New York with Mommy's new, funny car, Fred. And that time, they'd only brought the stuff they could pack inside him. They'd been at Grammy's longer than Mommy had said they would, and Camille loved all of her new things here—mostly Mommy's old things, because Camille was staying in her mommy's old room, and the other cool stuff Grammy didn't mind Camille playing with, like her quilts. But Mommy said they'd be moving again soon.

Once Parker did whatever Mommy said he'd *agreed* to.

Camille dragged her floppy blue bunny, Bear, into her lap. She'd brought him outside with her quilt. She liked to pretend he was the pet she'd never been able to have in Parker's apartment. She blew fresh bubbles while she stared next door. She bet no one over there wanted to move. Why would they, in a family like that?

She noticed the man from that morning standing at the kitchen window, the same place Mrs. Dixon stood sometimes on the weekend, when Camille stayed home with Grammy, and Mommy did errands or jogged the way she did every day she didn't work. Camille stood, leaving Bear on the quilt. She bounded up and down on her new pink tennis shoes and twirled her bubble wand the way she sometimes did with Mrs. Dixon, wanting the man to see how many great bubbles she could make.

Mrs. Dixon always clapped. She liked bubbles a lot. The man didn't clap, but he kept staring. So Camille waved her hand, the way Mommy had waved at him that morning. He waved back this time, and it looked like maybe he was smiling. Then Mrs. Dixon was there, waving, too.

Chapter Eight

"She's adorable," Marsha said to Oliver.

"Hey, Mom." He pulled her into a hug, both of them looking out the window. He hadn't realized she was home yet.

Marsha rested her head on his shoulder. "Selena was about that age when she and Belinda first moved next door. That was, what, eight years or so before you came along?"

Oliver grunted.

He blinked the sleepless grit out of his eyes.

After Travis dropped him at the house, Oliver had jogged a quick couple of miles to clear his head, nearly having a heat stroke under the midday sun. He'd showered. Hanging until Dru got home with Teddy, he'd downed what must have been a gallon of water and tried to nap. Epic fail. Then he'd heard Selena's dilapidated Chevy pull into the driveway next door. He'd dragged his ass off the couch so he could peer through the blinds, and he'd been borderline or not-so-borderline spying on the Rosenthal place ever since. When he'd heard her out back, how was he supposed to have looked away from the sight of her and her daughter on the other side of his parents' hedge?

"She seems happy." He glanced again at Selena's *adorable* little girl, who'd gone back to playing. He hadn't had the heart not to wave back just now.

"They dote on her." Marsha leaned against the kitchen counter and crossed her arms. An ominous sign. She had something to get off her chest—resistance was futile. "It's a side of Belinda most people don't remember. The way she'd loved so freely and showered so much attention on Selena—back before Ben left them, and Belinda and Selena moved out of their big house across town and into that tiny thing next door. Belinda never completely recovered from it. But Camille's been good for her grandmother. She's a special little girl. People fall in love with her on sight."

"What's not to love?"

He watched Selena talk on the phone, her daughter nearby on a colorful blanket. Sweet, domestic, a picturesque scene. Selena seemed to finally have what she'd always wanted, whatever had happened with her marriage. A family of her own to care for and be loved by, including reconciling with her mother.

"There's evidently some kind of delay with her divorce," Marsha said. "Selena's helping Belinda make ends meet while she's here, working a part-time job at the elementary school."

Selena was divorced. Oliver couldn't wrap his head around it. He tuned back in to the growing chaos that had rocked the house once Dru returned with Teddy—the kid screaming from being awoken from his car-seat-induced snooze. She and Oliver hadn't exchanged more than a few words before Travis turned up again. Then the school busses pulled to the curb, one every half hour, spitting out the rest of the kids. The noise factor in the house had quickly escalated to eardrum-bursting decibels, distracting Oliver from imagining Selena with another man, raising their child, living their life. *Leaving* their life to move back here.

Two older kids, a teenage boy and girl, raced through the kitchen. Ignoring Oliver and Belinda, they tramped up the back stairs, bickering.

"You played first yesterday," said the girl who'd been introduced as Shandra. She wore a jeans skirt and graphic T-shirt and had turned a bright blue bandana into a headband. "It's my turn."

"No one's playing nothin'." Gabe's cargoes were wrinkled almost as badly as his short-sleeved, plaid button-down. "Not if we don't find the controller."

"In your pit of a room?" Shandra raced past him.

"Stay out of my room! I didn't take it upstairs last night."

Marsha watched them go and chuckled.

"Video games." She shook her head. "They take turns after school. Sounds like Shandra has first dibs today."

"*If* she can make Gabe produce the controller. And she's infiltrating enemy territory to hunt for it, so he'll think twice before he hides something from her again. Smart girl."

Oliver's running grudge match with his own siblings over anything and everything had been legend back in the day. Marsha and Joe had mostly let them work things out for themselves, the way Travis and Dru seemed to be this afternoon. And before the full-tilt after-school mayhem could torch the last of Oliver's rapidly declining sanity, he'd excused himself to the kitchen to make coffee—for Marsha. He'd wanted to have something comforting waiting for her when she got home. Instead, he'd let himself get sidetracked.

He sneaked another glance out the window. Selena and her daughter were gone.

"Honey," Marsha said, "have you—"

"Can we get this started, Mom?" Travis came in from the living room, still in uniform. He'd been grousing since he'd arrived about the mound of paperwork still waiting for him at the station.

"Sure," Marsha said. "Let me grab that cup of coffee."

She scanned the unused stovetop. Her gaze tracked back to Oliver. So did Travis's.

"Take all the time you need, bro," Travis said with a WTF stare. "I think Dru's teaching the older kids how to play craps. The younger ones are finger-painting the walls. And I'm showing Teddy the finer points of Hatha yoga. We've got all day."

He left Oliver and Marsha alone again, in the room where she'd cooked for Oliver, where he'd learned to clean up after himself and others. He'd helped her sort and fold laundry on the counter. He'd tutored the younger kids with math homework. He'd helped bandage skinned knees and elbows when there'd been no one else around to see to someone smaller than he was.

All the family he'd known since he'd lost his birth mother had happened in this kitchen, the living room, upstairs where he'd bunked with Travis in what was likely Gabe and Fin's room now. And being part of it again as an adult felt . . . so much better than he should be letting it. He chugged from a bottle of water he'd snagged from the refrigerator.

Leaning his hip against the counter, he faced the music.

"What's on your mind, Mom?"

"You're sure you're ready to be point for dealing with six kids who've never met you?" Marsha's smile said she'd guessed he'd been hiding out in the kitchen. "A baby, three in elementary school, and another two in high school who come fully equipped with the attitude that anyone older than nineteen loses ten IQ points just getting out of bed in the morning?"

"If Dru and Travis can handle them, I can. My work's portable," he assured his mother, when the reality was that he was in danger of losing Canada to Xan, too. "I'm here for as long as you need me."

A burst of angry shouting in the other room—sounded like

Fin—set off gales of girl laughter. From Lisa Burns, most likely. She was the one closest to Fin in age, the both of them in upper elementary school.

"And what about the rest?" His mother smoothed a hand down Oliver's arm.

"The rest?"

"You, Selena, and Brad. And Dru. And Travis, now that I think about it. He's kept up with the lot of you. He and Brad are close still, the way you and your brother have stayed in touch."

"Yeah," Oliver admitted. "We have."

"There are other people here besides Travis who'd like the chance to know you again." Another whoop of laughter sounded off from the living room. Kid curses, adult chastisement, more laughter. "Some of us will continue to inflict ourselves on you as long as you're around. Others, you're going to have to take the initiative with."

"I've already talked with Brad."

"And Selena?"

"Mom . . ." Oliver stretched his neck from side to side until it finally cracked.

"Now that you're home, make the most of it. Don't let your past deprive the rest of us of the good things we could all still have."

Deprive the rest of them of what?

"What's really going on?" he asked.

Marsha didn't answer right away.

Oliver glanced toward the living room, hoping for someone to misbehave and require her intervention. When that didn't happen, he braced his hands on his hips and bit the bullet.

"I'm listening," he said. "As long as it doesn't involve concocting another way to maneuver Selena and me together. I'd do anything else for you and Joe, I swear I would. I'll deal with Brad and

Dru and whatever else I have to around here. But Selena and I are off-limits. You didn't see how hard it was for her both times we were together today. I'm not putting either one of us through that again, not even for you."

"Both times?"

"This morning when I first got here. She and her little girl—"

"Camille"

"—were out front of Belinda's. And it was just so . . ."

"What?"

Painful. "I don't want to hurt her again."

"Of course you don't."

"After all these years, it's just . . ."

"What?"

"Over." And *over* was a whole lot easier to process from a distance. Through the kitchen window. Or from Atlanta or another state or even another continent.

"Okay." Marsha gave a firm nod. "If over's what you want, what you need, that's fine. Just hear me out before you make up your mind. Then if that's still your decision, I'll consider the subject closed until you bring it up again."

Oliver hung his head, because his mother was being reasonable. How was a man supposed to outmaneuver reasonable?

"Let me have it," he said.

Marsha's smile should have taken some of the sting out of his surrender. But there was something in her expression that had the hair rising on the back of his neck.

"Selena turned up a few months ago," she said. "She and Belinda have shared very little with anyone in town about Selena's life since she left. Except that she's divorced and starting over. And that she has a little girl she keeps pretty close tabs on. It's almost like Selena's afraid to let anyone get too close."

"Travis said they weren't planning on staying."

"Her divorce is holding her up. But, no. No one sees her putting down roots here again."

"So she doesn't want her daughter getting too attached." Reasonable enough for a kid that young who'd been uprooted from one home already. Selena certainly knew how that felt. "They seem happy together."

His mind replayed an image from that morning: Selena holding her daughter, smiling at her, sweet, perfect, content. It was like a living cameo burned into his brain. And it was none of his business.

"Did you talk with Camille?" his mother asked.

"Not really. Look, I'm glad Belinda's helping them. If she and Selena have patched things up, good for them. Good for Selena's daughter. What does any of this have to do with me?"

Marsha looked uncomfortable. She'd never been big on gossip. This was so out of character for her, it was downright spooky.

"I think there's more going on next door than meets the eye," she said. "Your father does, too."

"Like what?"

His mother linked her hands in front of her. "Selena and Belinda have been telling everyone that Camille's four, going on five years old. My guess is she's older. Just tiny for her age. She's snuck over to the house a few times when she plays out back on the weekends and her grandmother's watching her. You know Belinda. She can get so caught up in her yard, I swear if a bomb went off she'd never know the difference."

"You've been spending time with Selena's daughter, when Selena doesn't want her over here?"

"Camille wanted to play with the kids," Marsha said. "At first, I didn't have the heart to turn her away. She's always scampered back home before they notice she's gone." Marsha was wringing her hands, for God's sake. What the hell? "We've had some lovely chats. She's just . . . wonderful."

"I'm sure she is, but you need to stop. Do you want me to talk to Selena for you? Is that what this is all about?"

"I'd already have told her myself if I didn't think I'd get Camille in trouble, and . . ."

"And *what*?"

"Camille's already finished kindergarten in New York. She talked to me about her teachers there, when I asked her about her class here. Her mother's reenrolled her in the program at Chandler. Now that's not all that unusual for kids who are in between age groups, whose parents or teachers don't think they're ready to move up yet. But my guess is Camille's closer to six than five. Maybe a little older."

"And . . . ?" Oliver stared at his mother while she waited. And waited. He'd reached his limit.

To keep from storming up the kitchen stairs himself, he turned to deal with Marsha's beaten-up kettle and the coffee he'd promise to make but had no business drinking once he did. The shiny brass kettle had been dented all to hell and back, covered in tiny pit marks it had collected over years of dedicated service. It sat where it always had, on the stove's left back burner, forever ready to feed the endless pots of herbal tea Marsha made for young souls in need of soothing. For the older and more sleep-deprived, there was the best damn coffee on the planet, made by pouring boiling kettle water into his mom's stovetop slow-drip pot.

Walking to the fridge, needing some distance, he found his mother's favorite blend of ground beans in the door, same as always. Dru had said to make sure he made decaf, since it was already late afternoon.

He headed to the sink with the right container and the kettle.

Maybe he could bash himself over the head with the thing. That would stop everything Marsha had said, and not said, from rattling around in his already aching brain. Then something froze inside him. Bits and pieces of conversation, seemingly disconnected details, finally aligning.

"What did you say the little girl's name was?" He set the kettle on the stove, his ears ringing. His hand shook as he turned the burner on high.

"Camille. Just like—"

"Selena's favorite flowers."

Oliver covered his heart with his palm. His tattoo felt like it was burning through the material of his T-shirt.

He hadn't smelled camellias in years until that morning. A row of them grew between his parents' backyard and Mrs. Rosenthal's, and Selena had loved their blooms. Once they'd started dating, Oliver had given her a camellia every morning there was one to give.

She'd named her child after the fragile blossom that would always remind him of her. Of them. Of the perfect year they'd spent loving each other.

"I'm so sorry, Oliver . . ." she'd said that morning. *"For everything."*

For running from him again? For ending things so destructively seven years ago—because she was incapable of loving and trusting anyone, even him? Or was she sorry for something more? Something impossible for him to believe.

Except more pieces were snapping into place while his mother stayed silent, letting him work things out for himself.

"Wait just a damn minute." He redid the simple math Marsha evidently already had.

Jesus.

The kettle whistled, slicing through his shock and punching his headache to DEFCON 1. How long had he been standing there, staring blind, his world narrowing to one crucial detail?

"How old do you think Selena's daughter is?"

Marsha stepped in front of him and took care of the coffee. "A lot closer to six, maybe a little older." She put a hand on his shoulder. "Which means Camille would have been conceived—"

"Seven years ago . . ." Oliver glanced toward the living room, where good-natured bedlam continued. "Is anyone else wondering the same thing?"

"Joe and me. Maybe Travis, but he wouldn't cause trouble for anyone unless he was sure."

Anyone . . . "You mean for Brad and—"

Dru burst through the doorway.

"What's the holdup?" she asked.

Blonde and tall, she was as beautiful as ever, even with worry dragging at the gorgeous smile she flashed their mother. She had a sniffling Teddy perched on her hip, his red hair spiking in the back from his nap.

"Oh my God," she gushed. "Is the coffee ready? Is it decaf? Count me in. But we've got to get this party started. The kitchen crew needs me at the Whip. And Travis wants to check in on Dad before he heads to the station for his night shift."

"Let's do it, then." Marsha poured a mug of coffee, black, and walked it over to Dru, exchanging it for Teddy. "Hey there, big boy," she cooed.

The toddler beamed at her, besotted, and then over her shoulder at Oliver, as Marsha walked him away from the bomb she'd just detonated in Oliver's life.

"You okay?" Dru asked.

Oliver realized his mouth was hanging open.

"Sure," he managed.

I just might be a father.

Or an uncle.

Which would make you a stepmother, if your fiancé knocked up the girl of my dreams when we were teenagers.

He pulled his sister into his arms for the first time since rolling into town.

"God." The rightness of home washed through him again, crowding out the rest. It was the first chance they'd had to be alone. "You're a sight for sore eyes."

Dru hugged him back.

She made a happy, watery sound, half laugh, half cry. "I can't believe you're back. We've missed you. *I've* missed you."

"Me too." He made himself set her away.

"Yes." She punched his shoulder. "I could tell how often you thought of us, with all the letters and phone calls and attempts to stay in touch."

Oliver tousled her bangs like he used to, when she'd been five inches shorter but just as sassy. He rewarded her next punch with a satisfying grunt. He deserved it. He didn't have a clue how to explain the distance, his need for it.

"I just wanted . . ." He'd wanted *here* to be right for all of them. He still did. He looked out the kitchen window at the Rosenthals' empty backyard. "I'm really sorry, Dru."

Dru hugged him again. "No apologies. Not between us. I understand. Really. Brad does, too. He told me a little about the hospital. Sounds like it was brutal. No one blames you for wanting to be somewhere else all these years. What happened, it was horrible. I felt responsible for it for years."

Shocked, Oliver sputtered, "Why the hell would you think any of this was your fault?"

"I'm the one who got Brad to admit he'd slept with Selena. I was so mad. I had such a crush on him. I wasn't thinking about what it would do to you if the rumors were true. I refused to believe Brad when he said it just happened. That it meant nothing. I needed company in my pity party. So I found you and tattled."

"It was a long time ago, and you were hurting, Dru."

"I was the reason you two fought and you got yourself in trouble again. If I'd just stayed out of it . . ."

"You couldn't have." And he couldn't take the tears in her eyes. "You cared too much about everyone to just let it go. I'm the one who made Selena feel like she had no one on her side. I might as well have driven her into Brad's arms."

Dru winced at the image.

"None of this is your fault," he insisted. "You got hurt because of me." And it might not be over yet. "*I'm* sorry."

Dru cocked her head to the side. She'd always been sneaky good at reading him.

"You were in love with Selena," she said, "even after she broke up with you."

He nodded.

"And now . . . ?" She blew on her coffee, took a sip.

"And now . . ." If Camille turned out to be Brad's, how would Dru and her fiancé weather the shock? "You're engaged. I'm happy for you, kiddo."

Dru's smile was just shy of believing him. "Brad said Travis had to drag you into the cafeteria this morning. Don't be an asshat, Oliver. You're going to have to do better than that."

"I shook your guy's hand. We cleared the air. It's all good." Or so Oliver had thought.

Dru took another sip of the coffee he wanted to drown himself in. But even decaf had enough stimulant in it to affect him. Then she smacked the back of his head with her palm, like when they'd bickered as kids.

"Hey! Careful, brat." He lifted his half-empty water bottle to douse her. "Payback's a bit—"

"Knock it off, you two." A scowling Travis reappeared in the kitchen doorway. "Kill each other on your own time. Mom's talking with the kids."

The quiet in the other room registered. Blessed peace reigned for the first time since the kids had commandeered the house. Oliver's gut clenched.

"Right," he said.

Joe. Angioplasty. Keeping things at home on an even keel for his parents and for kids who'd already survived more insecurity and loss than anyone should have to.

He'd help his family through this. He'd deal with Selena, if there was anything to deal with. He'd deal with any fallout for Dru and Brad. His *take care of things at home* project list was growing by leaps and bounds. But the kids came first. It was Marsha and Joe's mantra. And for as long as Oliver was back, it was his now, too.

Travis ducked into the living room. Dru held back.

"I can understand your work being a priority," she said. "But don't let being messed up about Selena or Brad or anything else take you away from us again. Not until you absolutely have to go. Promise?"

Oliver smiled down at her, not used to it yet. "You grew up while I was gone."

"I got my dream come true." She kissed his cheek. "Gives a girl clarity. I got cuter, too. I'll give you a pass for not noticing. But that's one you owe me. I'll collect, if I'm ever in the mood to be particularly bratty."

"*If?*"

He hooked an arm around her, the old and the new and the somewhere in between feeling right in that moment. They followed Travis into the circle of Marsha's soft, steady voice.

"Joe's going to be laid up for a while longer," she was saying, holding Teddy in her lap and surrounded by the younger kids, Lisa and Fin and Boris, who'd piled on the sofa next to her. "He needs a procedure tonight the doctors are saying will take time for him to recover from. Which means I'll need you older kids"—she looked at Shandra and Gabe, who each had taken over one of the chairs beside the couch—"to help pick up some of the slack around here. And you've all met Oliver by now, right?"

Marsha smiled at him, like he was the best part of her day. Then she smiled down at Teddy the same way and bounced him in her lap. The blue slipcover on the oversized couch used to be red. She'd sewn the new one, no doubt, like all the others.

"Oliver's going to be staying here at night, in Joe's and my room, while I'm at the hospital with Dad." She sounded exhausted, no matter how upbeat she kept things. "I'll have my phone with me. If you need something important leave a message and I'll try to check regularly. I can't keep it on when I'm in CICU. But for now, for everyday stuff, Oliver's taking the lead. Travis and Dru will be around as much as possible. I know you're just meeting Oliver for the first time, but he's family. He's been where you are. And Joe and I are so grateful that he's home. The family's lucky to have him, just like we're lucky we have the rest of you kids."

Like they'd be lucky to have Camille, too, her lingering glance toward Oliver seemed to say.

Or was it his conscience working overtime? Because the part of him itching to escape back to the all-consuming job he'd built his life around was already looking for ways to justify *not* forcing the issue of Camille's paternity. Except he wasn't alone in this decision. This was Bellevue Lane, not his cutthroat, transient business world.

He took in the somber faces of the kids circled quietly around Marsha, almost like she was about to read them a story. To someone else they might look like a mismatched litter of cast-off lives. Instead, Oliver saw a thriving family. Because of Marsha and Joe's determination to love and heal as many children as they possibly could.

Travis stepped to his other side, completing a united front for their younger brothers and sisters to see.

"You're all worried," Marsha said. Love filled her voice and fisted in Oliver's throat. "I know. I'm worried, too. I don't like the sound of things like surgery and more tests and Dad having to stay away from the family. I don't like my Joe being sick, and how worried he is about all of us. But I'm grateful. Because I'm not going through this alone. Neither is your dad, even though we can't get you younger ones in to see him yet. We're a family. No one's going through this alone."

Just like Oliver steering clear of Selena the rest of the time he was in town was no longer his choice alone to make. He hugged his sister closer. He would do what was best for his family.

Marsha smiled at him, as if she'd read his mind.

"Whatever we have to face," she promised, "everything's going to be just fine, as long as we face it together."

Chapter Nine

"Thanks for coming in again today," Kristen Hemmings Beaumont said, bright and early the next morning. "We've really put you through your paces the last couple of months. Can you believe it's almost summer?"

"It's really heating up outside." Selena smiled at the six-foot-plus former college basketball star.

Chandler Elementary's much-loved principal was newly married, as of March, and still glowing from the whirlwind romance that had matched her with Chandler High's soccer coach and in-demand local musician, Law Beaumont.

Kristen dabbed at her forehead with a Kleenex. "It's steamy enough inside. I don't know who's more ready to be sprung from school—the kids or the faculty."

Same as any other school day, Kristen was wearing a suit this morning—a jacket and skirt in a beautiful aquamarine color. Plus low-heeled pumps that screamed classic sophistication without adding to her height.

"Thank you for keeping me working all this time," Selena

said. "I know there are a lot of other moms on the sub list. It's made a world of difference for Camille and me."

Selena and her boss had never talked about it, and Kristen had never asked for details. No one in town had had the nerve to come out and pump Selena for information about her divorce. How when she'd come home at the end of March, it had been for only a few weeks' visit.

"Math as flowers?" Kristen motioned to the project Selena had been prepping.

Selena smiled and kept working. She needed everything ready before her class arrived. She and Camille had had another late start—this morning because Selena had been up most of the night, obsessing about yesterday's scene with Oliver and Brad. And the news about Joe's overnight angioplasty. And now Oliver would be staying in town indefinitely, while his father recovered—which explained him and Marsha waving at Camille yesterday afternoon from the kitchen window, as if Oliver had settled in for a nice long visit.

Selena surveyed the colorful pile of cut construction paper on the desk and thought of her mother and daughter's shared love for growing things.

"I seem to be working on a running theme." She pasted together a second example of today's exercise in simple fractions—left by the third-grade teacher she was subbing for.

Each child would create three different types of construction-paper flowers. Selena was then to divide the kids into teams of two, to take turns making gardens with one or more of each other's flowers, and then talk with the class about how many halves, thirds, and fourths of each type of blossom were in their beds. The result would be a magnificent garden they'd staple to the bulletin board next to their storage cubbies.

"You know . . ." Kristen leaned a hip on the teacher's desk at the front of the classroom. "If this ever turns into somewhere you'd like to stay, Chandler Elementary would be lucky to have you for more than part-time hours."

"I . . ." Selena gaped at her boss.

Part of her plan for the funds she kept asking Parker to release had been to take college classes at night—to finally earn the degree she'd never gotten. To begin building toward a career that would enable her to take care of her daughter on her own. Becoming a teacher had definitely been at the top of her list of possible occupations to pursue. But even if Parker stopped dragging his feet, and she had enough money to start getting serious about school again . . .

"Working on staff at Chandler Elementary?" she asked Kristen.

"We just had a full-time sub position open up."

"For next year? I . . . I hadn't really considered that an option."

Staying with Belinda. Living next door to the Dixons—with Oliver possibly popping in and out now, after Joe came home from the hospital. Committing to being in Chandlerville for an entire year, so Selena could be sure she had a job lined up. It should sound like a lifeline.

"You're becoming our go-to mom," Kristen said. "The teachers love your work with their kids. You keep the students happy and focused and on task. The most overactive of our students don't seem to faze you, and neither do the shyer ones. You come early and stay late. I've even caught you tutoring a time or two after everyone else has gone home. Have you considered making teaching a career?"

Selena nodded. "Wherever we end up. But any kind of degree would be too expensive right now, and impossible to schedule around Camille's day."

"Not necessarily. Not if you stay here."

Selena began cutting and pasting again, needing the soothing rhythm of the work to cover the panic. What Kristen was suggesting sounded amazing. What Selena would have to face with her daughter, her mother, the Dixons . . . with Oliver, if she were really to contemplate staying in town for good, was terrifying.

"I'm sorry," she said. "I appreciate the offer. But . . ."

"There's an excellent community college just down the road. My husband's there nights working on a joint music and education BA."

"There'd be no money for classes," Selena reminded herself, "even if I subbed full time next year. And I need to get my daughter settled in a home of our own first before I commit funds we don't even have yet to something else."

"That's what scholarships and grants are for."

Kristen reached into her skirt pocket and pulled out a slip of paper covered in the loops and curves of her stylish handwriting. She laid the list on the desk.

"Look into them. I'm happy to be a reference, and I know half a dozen teachers you've subbed for who would, too. I'm sure you have your reasons for moving on. No one's trying to pry or even change your mind. But if you decide you'd like to give Chandlerville a chance, call me and we'll set things in motion."

"I . . ." The scissors clattered from Selena's fingers.

"My cell number's at the bottom." Kristen took in Mimi Stone's bright, colorful classroom and smiled. "I can see you in a room like this."

"I hope I'm not interrupting anything." Travis stepped into the room, wearing civilian clothes and looking even more ragged than yesterday. "The front office said Selena was working today."

"Of course not," Kristen answered while Selena composed

herself enough to deal with her second interruption that morning. "I'm sorry to hear Joe isn't doing well."

"Thanks," Travis said. "Dad's awake and out of recovery, back in CICU. More tests are happening today. More doctors. We're hoping for better news than yesterday. Mom's pretty much insisting on it."

Kristen smiled fondly. "You let your parents know we're keeping an eye on their kids here. We can send work home if it's easier to keep them closer for a few days. Whatever the family needs."

"We appreciate it. So far it's business as usual at the house. My brother's back—" Travis glanced at Selena. "We're getting him up to speed on everyone's schedules. I just stopped and signed Oliver up to be able to drop off and pick up the kids if he needs to."

"Great," Kristen said. "I better get. Bus call in fifteen," she said to Selena. "Could you help take care of the car riders getting dropped out back at the cafeteria?"

"Um . . . sure."

Kristen stopped next to Travis on her way out, just as tall as he was, delicately feminine in comparison. She patted his shoulder. "I hope your dad's home soon, good as new. The whole school is rooting for him."

The way she'd just said people were rooting for Selena and Camille to stay in Chandlerville while Selena competed for scholarships, worked full time, and took classes to become a teacher. While she made her own money no matter how long it took Parker to finalize their divorce.

And all Selena would have to do was face down the worst of the mistakes she'd made in her young life, come clean with the Dixons, and hope the fallout didn't make things worse for her daughter.

"I'm sorry about Joe, too," she said once it was just her and Travis.

"Yeah. It's been a long night. But so far the doctors are saying encouraging things, whatever the hell that means. Until they tell us for sure they don't have to crack Joe's chest open, no one's going to sleep easy."

"I hope they clear him soon."

Travis stared. Because of course he hadn't searched her out just to talk about his dad.

"You're wasting your time," she told him, "if you're here on another mission for Marsha." Selena moved around the classroom, putting things away, bustling, not trusting herself to sit still and let Oliver's brother look closely enough to see her own sleepless night. "And I have a lot of work to do."

He dropped onto the edge of Mimi's desk. "Will you just talk with me for a second?"

She circled back and sank into the teacher's chair, resigned. "I don't have much more than that. Once I help unload a couple hundred kids and herd them toward their classrooms, I'll have twenty-five of my own, bright-eyed and expecting me to not to bore them senseless."

"It's about Oliver."

Of course it was.

Travis stopped her from stacking the multicolored flower pieces. "It's about giving him another chance."

"I hope your family does." Selena really did. "I'm sorry it took Joe getting sick, but I'm glad Oliver's found his reason to come home."

"He's staying for at least the rest of the week."

"That must mean a lot to your mom." And it *couldn't* mean anything to Selena.

Excitement shot through her, though, from the possibility of seeing him again on a daily basis, even if it was only from across their parents' yards. Followed by the dread of knowing she wouldn't be able to keep her distance any better than she had yesterday, the next time they stumbled across each other. And she had no idea how she was going to tell him what she needed to.

She stood and stepped around the desk, needing to move again, and tripped. The stack of math project instructions she'd intended to place on each desk flew out of her hands, sliding across the floor. Travis caught her before she took a header into one of the filled-to-brimming bookcases. He set her back on her feet and bent to gather up her materials, handing them over.

"Thanks," Selena said. *Get a grip, Selena!* "Sorry."

When she tried to edge away again, he caught her elbow. "Oliver's a good man."

"I know that." She'd always known it, even when she'd broken up with him.

He'd been determined to make her life better, his way. On *his* timetable. A trait she'd run from, and then homed in on all over again with Parker.

"Then why not stay at the hospital yesterday and work things out with my brother?"

"I don't know, Travis. Why do you think?"

"Brad . . . and other things."

"Yeah. And other things. Oliver could barely look me in the eye."

"I don't think he's holding a grudge. Brad either. Or Dru. We'd all like to put what's happened behind us. Maybe that's possible now. You talking to Oliver, the two of you getting everything out in the open. It might make it easier for my brother to stay a little longer. You know, for my parents' sake."

Selena pulled her arm away. "That's hitting below the belt, using Marsha and Joe to manipulate me."

"I said Oliver was a good man." Travis grinned. "I'm a totally different story."

"Has he really not spoken to anyone in your family in seven years?"

The town gossip mill was desperate for details. But the Dixons never talked about family.

"He's kept up with me, once he got himself situated in business. The family doesn't know, except my parents, but he's been financing a lot of the extra stuff Marsha and Joe need for the kids, pretty much from the moment he made his first dollar. Money for additional tests and tutors for the kids that the state couldn't justify. Extras for school and family activities. A whole lot more. Even Bethany's tuition now. Joe makes good money, but—"

"A family as large as yours, it must be a constant financial drain on a single income." And of course Oliver would have done whatever he could for his parents. His ratty sneakers and worn clothes made more sense, even if they didn't jibe with the flashy truck he'd prowled into town driving.

"My brother's sent every dime he's made home, best I can tell, as long as he didn't have to be in Chandlerville to put it to good use."

Selena blinked. "And I'm the reason he left in the first place. If you want him not to disappear again, doesn't nudging me in his direction seem a tad counterproductive?"

Travis scratched the side of his head. "I think he's dealing with a lot of stuff. And if I don't miss my guess, you both have secrets you think won't hurt anyone else as long as they stay secret."

The intensity of Travis's gaze had Selena looking closer, then looking away.

"Give talking to Oliver another try," he finally said.

"Sure." Why hadn't Selena thought of that? "I'll just pop over later today and chat him up."

Travis smiled at her sarcasm, then grew serious. "Find a way to clear the air. If my brother cuts and runs before the rest of us get to know him again, don't let any of it be about you this time."

She glanced down at the list Kristen had given her. What an amazing gesture. The opportunity of a lifetime. A fresh start that wouldn't be possible if she could never completely let her guard down with anyone in town, not even her mother.

"You don't understand," she said. "Things are so much more complicated than you can possibly imag—"

"Mrs. Rosenthal?" asked a female voice laced with static, piping into the classroom over the intercom.

"Yes?"

"Your daughter's in the infirmary. I think the nurse has already used Camille's EpiPen."

Selena rushed past Travis and out of the classroom, desperate to get to her child.

"Is everything okay?" he called after her.

"No." Not since Camille was a baby.

"'Bout done with that plan?" another deputy asked Brad as Oliver approached Brad's desk. "After you sell Willis on it, I want first dibs on some of the action."

The working end of the Chandlerville Sheriff's Department looked pretty much like it had the last time Oliver had been there. The night he'd been hauled in for DUI by an officer who'd known Joe for years. Oliver had been sober enough by that point, after the single-car wreck that had somehow managed to leave him with only a busted lip, to nearly wet his pants in fear when the guy had dumped him into a cell out back. Since no one else had been hurt, the officer had sprung Oliver the next morning, into Joe's custody, without filing formal charges—saying if he ever saw Oliver in the precinct again, he'd throw the book at him.

The deputies' work area was small. Utilitarian. Dated in an outgrowing-itself way that begged for someone to put it out of its misery. Five desks dominated a space barely big enough for four. A couple of them were two-sided, with chairs and computer monitors facing off across the two halves. Brad was working at a keyboard on a half desk covered in printouts and books and what looked like enough research to feed a college-level term paper. He had a spreadsheet open on his monitor.

"Oliver?" He set aside the notebook he'd been balancing in his lap while he typed. He stood and reached out his hand, making Oliver the asshole if he didn't reciprocate. "It's good to see you again. I wasn't sure, after yesterday . . ." He glanced at the officer beside him. "After Joe's procedure last night, I wasn't sure when we'd get another chance to talk."

Oliver shook Brad's hand, marginally less inclined to deck the guy this morning.

"You remember Lee Bennett?" Brad asked.

The other officer offered his hand next. "Oliver Bowman?"

"Lee." Oliver shook. Football. Cornerback. That explained the man's size. "Sure. You were a year behind us at Chandler."

The hulk of a man smiled good-naturedly. "Close enough to know exactly who you were when I saw a strange truck in the Dixons' drive at the butt crack of dawn yesterday and ran the plates."

Brad slanted Lee a quizzical look. "You're casing the Dixon house?"

"Keeping an eye on the place. Sheriff's orders." Lee hooked his thumbs into the belt loops of his uniform pants. "Now that we know you've got someone there round the clock, we'll leave off.

Unless you two are still plannin' to slug it out like some folks thought you might at the hospital. The guys are taking bets already. You know . . . who'll be left standin' when the dust settles." Lee laughed. "My money's on Travis and Marsha Dixon, after the two of them wade in to settle you down."

"I think Oliver and I can handle things on our own."

Lee glanced a not-so-subtle warning toward Oliver.

"We'll keep the bloodshed to a minimum." Oliver checked his watch.

Dru had Teddy at her place—she'd begged off at the Whip for the entire day, leaving an assistant manager in charge after spending the night at the hospital with Travis and Marsha, waiting for news on Joe's angio. Then waiting for him to wake up from the anesthesia. She'd shown up at the house several hours ago, dragging ass but ready to show Oliver the basics of getting the kids off to school, so tomorrow he could take over on his own.

His sister needed a break this afternoon, not more trouble. And there Oliver was, about to pretty much make that impossible.

"I come in peace," he assured Lee. "I need to speak to my future brother-in-law."

After a nod from Brad, Lee gestured toward the hallway leading to the holding cells. "Gonna grab a soda. Want anything?"

Oliver and Brad shook their heads.

Oliver watched Lee's retreat, reconciling the guy, one of their high school drinking buddies, with the responsible keeper of the peace he'd become. Finally alone with Brad in the empty squad room, he grappled to meld another night of no sleep with his determination not to *F* this up.

"Where's everyone else?" he asked.

He'd seen only the female officer at the front desk who'd waved him back. The squad room was too quiet. Creepy. It smelled the same. God, it *felt* the same. Like it was still seven years ago.

Brad leaned back in his chair. "Folks filter through before or after patrol. We have a couple of warrants being served today. There's an in-school field trip at Chandler Middle School. A *policemen are your friends* community outreach thing. The sheriff is there. I'm covering Travis's shift, so he's free to hang with your parents this morning and be at their place later if you need help with the afternoon stuff. Dru's pretty wiped."

"She's been a trouper. I'll let everyone get back to their lives tomorrow. My brother and sister seem to think the kids are going to scare me away."

"Hell." Brad laughed. "They scare me every day I go over there."

"It's a little . . . much. But I'll rally."

Actually, Oliver hadn't made a dent in the inbox full of e-mails he needed to deal with. He'd been up and down with Teddy most of the night. The baby was teething, Dru had explained—which evidently meant the kid was suffering 24-7, so everyone around him should be, too. And while Oliver had been trying to console an inconsolable toddler, his mind had refused to latch on to anything but getting his ass over here this morning—and then to the Rosenthal house, once Selena was home from work.

"You got a few minutes to talk?" he asked.

"I have a proposal to finish for Chris," Brad said, "but it'll keep."

"Chris?"

"Chris Willis. The new sheriff. Took over for Ben Higgins five years ago or so. He's a good guy. You'd like him."

"Yeah." Oliver had never been a law-enforcement-liking kind of guy. "Listen, I'm really sorry to be doing this, but . . ."

He crossed his arms, more pissed again than sorry suddenly.

Brad stood and mirrored his stance. "Sorry about me and Dru?"

"Jury's still out. But I got to talk with her some yesterday. She seems happy. You must be doing something right."

"Not everything yet, but we'll work the rest out. It's only been a few months. It was pretty rough at first."

"Still, you're already engaged."

"Extreme circumstances. But you have to know, man. It's what I've wanted for years. Pretty much since things went to hell and I left and my grandmother took Dru in."

"After you blew it with Selena, me, and Dru, all in one night?"

Brad inhaled. "Your sister and family are over it. It'll make things a hell of a lot easier for everyone if you could be, too. Maybe it would be gratifying to lose control and blow off steam like the old days. If that's what you're here to do, I'm happy to oblige. By my recollection, I owe you a beat down. But pounding on each other'll just hurt people we both care about. And it's not the same thing as dealing with the problem."

"The problem being Selena?"

"We're all in one place again. It's a small town."

"And she's living next door to the family you're signing up to be a part of whenever you and Dru make it legal."

"This fall. We were thinking later this fall, when the leaves turn. We met again just before Thanksgiving last year. But we might move things up now. Dru wants to be sure . . ."

"That Joe's there."

Brad stared at the toes of his polished work shoes. The guy actually polished his shoes. Which meant Travis must, too. And Oliver had a personal tailor for the suits he wore for top-shelf clients.

The Three Musketeers had gone legit.

Brad's expression oozed regret. "Damn, we were a mess back then. The three of us."

"Four. Don't forget my brother. And while we're on the subject, how exactly did you and Travis end up as cops, working for the Chandlerville sheriff together?"

Brad snorted. "Another long story. But to sum up . . . I was on the force in Savannah. Now I'm trying to re-create a killer job I walked away from in the Low Country. Chandlerville could use a community safety officer." He motioned to the paper and notebooks strewn across his desk. "And if it happens, it'll be because of Dru and your brother. Travis kept up with me, same as Dru says he has you. Probably the rest of your siblings. He's like your folks. He doesn't have it in him to give up on people."

"Neither does Dru."

"She gave me a second chance to love her," Brad said. "We've both moved on."

"From this business with Selena, too?"

"There is no *business* with Selena."

"Yeah, about that."

Jesus, how did Oliver say it?

"My family needs to know the truth," he said, "and so do I. So do you, Brad. You and Dru. And I need to know you're on board before I go after Selena, trying to get this done."

"The truth about what?"

"Camille."

"The kid?"

"Marsha was already pushing me toward Selena yesterday morning when you walked off the elevator."

"Like my grandmother did with me and Dru."

"Not exactly."

"Then what?"

"She wants to know whether or not she and Joe have been grandparents all this time."

Panic did a slow, greasy glide across Brad's features. He held up a hand. "Are you telling me Marsha thinks . . ."

Oliver nodded.

He still couldn't get the words out himself.

"Joe, too," he added. "Travis might have the beginnings of a clue. Who knows? He keeps everyone's secrets. Most of them," Oliver qualified. "Mom doesn't think Dru's there yet, but . . ."

"Dru . . . ?" Brad sputtered.

"If I can talk Selena into it, I want to sit her down with you and my sister and get to the bottom of things."

"Her daughter could be yours?"

"Or yours, buddy, if your hookup was as unplanned as you've said."

"Selena and Camille could have belonged in one of our lives all this time?"

"And if she knew she was pregnant and ran anyway, stayed away all this time, that means she doesn't want Camille to be part of our lives. Which would explain the way Marsha's said she's been avoiding everyone since she came back."

"God . . ." Brad slumped into his chair. "She must have really hated us, or thought we hated her, if she figured she had to have a baby all on her own."

"I don't know anything for sure. And the hell of it is, if we handle this wrong we may never know, unless we force the issue legally. The person we need answers from ran from both of us yesterday."

"Damn it, man, it never occurred to me . . . It was just once. But yeah, we were stupid drunk and not thinking about protection. Of course she could have gotten pregnant. And then I was too busy dealing with the fallout of you leaving and then Selena, and my grandmother telling me to get out on my own and learn how to stop being such a selfish ass. My life was a mess after that."

"Mine, too."

But Oliver wasn't a mess now. He was a responsible, respected businessman. He could fix anything. Even this. Somehow he'd get Selena to see that *not* dealing with him wasn't an option.

They'd once promised each other forever. She shouldn't have had to face raising her daughter on her own. *If* that's what had happened.

Oliver and Brad sized each other up.

"We both dropped her," Brad said. "But shit, man. She had family here. Belinda, your parents, Vivian. She'd have been taken care of if she'd just told someone."

"She found someone else to take care of her." Maybe marrying another man to give Oliver's baby a home.

"We've got to talk with her." Brad sounded ready to hunt Selena down now to talk it out. "We've got to know for sure, before we . . . Jesus, how am I going to break this to Dru?"

"Don't. Not yet." It was the main reason Oliver had come here. "She's holding it together for Mom, but she's as wrecked as the rest of us about Dad's surgery. My gut says not to drop this on her until we know more. But you . . . You know my sister better than I do now. I wanted your take before I did anything else."

Brad winced. "She can't sleep. She's running herself into the ground. Visiting the hospital, taking care of things at the Whip, spelling you and Travis whenever she's needed at the house."

"Then let me try talking with Selena first. Yesterday at the hospital I wasn't . . ."

Ready?

To what—forgive *her*?

He'd hurt her so much more than he'd known, if she could have kept Camille from him. Or from Brad. Oliver should be pissed, but all he could think about was going back to that horrible night everything had begun to unravel and holding Selena until she'd let herself truly trust him.

He'd finally worked it through in rehab. How he'd pushed Selena too hard to clean herself up, to be like him, to move on from how lost they'd both felt. She hadn't been ready. She'd needed someone she trusted to stay lost like her. He hadn't been able to anymore, not and stay with his family. So at least to her mind, he'd abandoned her. While she'd still been hurting and self-medicating, and convincing herself that he no longer cared.

Now you're going to leave me, just like my father!

"I'll try to get her to open up about Camille." And not to push her even farther away. "I'll let you know what she says."

"Then we'll all do what's best," Brad agreed, "for Selena and her little girl and Dru and the rest of your family."

"*Our* family." Oliver reached out his hand to his soon-to-be brother-in-law. His friend. And possibly the father of his first niece. "Instead of taking care of ourselves this time, we'll protect the people we care about."

Brad shook. "One for all?"

"And all for one."

Chapter Ten

Selena would have given her last dollar for a cab and the disposable income to pay someone else to drive her and Camille home from their very long day—capped off by a lengthy visit to Camille's pediatrician.

"I'm sorry, Mommy," said the bedraggled moppet huddled in Fred's backseat.

"You couldn't help throwing up, Cricket. Mommy's not mad at you." What Mommy *was*, was certifiably freaked. It was terrifying each time her daughter's allergies attacked—even when an episode turned out to be relatively minor like this one.

Camille's doctor had said she'd be fine, just to keep an eye on her for the next twenty-four hours to make sure her symptoms improved.

"You told me not to eat other people's snacks," Camille said, "and I did. Karen called me a baby because I wouldn't. I did it just to show her. I'm sorry."

"It's okay, honey. You had your EpiPen, and Nurse Mallory took care of you until I could get there. But you never know what foods might have peanuts in them." Nuts had been the culprit this time, the pediatrician suspected. "The doctor said we can't be too careful, okay? Next time, talk to Mrs. Preston if Karen won't leave you alone. Promise me?"

"I promise."

Even Camille's ponytails were drooping when Selena checked her daughter's reflection in the rearview mirror. Her cheeks were flushed and sweaty, and her pretty pink dress was stained from her stomach's attempt to expel the candy she'd let herself be bullied into eating. Selena pushed Fred's air conditioner to Max, patting his dashboard when, without the slightest hesitation, he blasted colder air toward her daughter.

Chill bumps scatter-bombed Selena's body at the thought of how much worse things could have been. She shivered and pressed the brake too hard at the corner of Maple and Branch. Fred jerked to a stop. He backfired, a gentleman's warning not to push her luck. Selena took a more leisurely turn onto Bellevue.

She was losing it. Even her car could sense it. And Kristen's and Travis's visits that morning hadn't helped. Even while she'd been dealing with Camille and the rush to her pediatrician, Selena hadn't been able to get her future in Chandlerville, and Oliver and his family, out of her mind.

At least it was the middle of the day and Belinda wouldn't be home from work until later. Selena hadn't let her mom know about Camille's emergency. Everything was fine. Selena was holding herself together. Adding Belinda to the equation might tip her over the edge to completely coming undone. She refocused on the angel sliding lower on Fred's cracked vinyl seat.

"We're almost home, honey."

Her daughter's miserable gaze met hers in the mirror. Then she caught sight of the red pickup once more parked in the Dixons' driveway.

"None of my concern," she reminded herself—even though she'd spent a large chunk of last night on her mother's front porch swing, staring through the shadows at the yard and the house next door.

"What's wrong?" Camille wanted to know, looking out the window, too.

"Nothing."

Except someone was walking through the hedge between the two yards. A very tall, determined-looking someone heading toward Belinda's porch, then standing there, watching Selena drive closer, looking ready to wait all day if that's how long it took her to face him. She slowed at the curb, drowning in the déjà vu sense that Oliver belonged there, had been there all these years no matter how long she'd stayed away, waiting for this moment of reckoning.

She pulled into the drive, almost taking out the mailbox when she couldn't look away from him. He waited, hands clasped behind him. Angry? Calm? Lethally patient? She couldn't tell.

Leaving Camille in the car on a day this hot while Selena talked with Oliver was out of the question. So was running the engine and air conditioning for her daughter while Selena took care of things alone. Their weekly gas budget barely covered their drive back and forth to school. Selena turned off the engine. Fred rumbaed into his shutdown routine, various parts of the car shimmying in conflicting tempos until the racket settled to a random series of pings.

Oliver loomed on the porch steps, like a storm cloud rolling in on itself—more threatening the longer it held back its fury. It could have been Selena's imagination. It could have been more of the guilt riding her for months that had become intolerable as she'd tried to sleep last night. But somehow she was certain . . . her secret was out.

"Mommy?" Camille asked.

"Let's get you inside." Selena opened her door with a grinding screech that resembled the mating call of the bobwhite quails nesting each fall in the countryside near Chandlerville.

Camille's door didn't make quite as much racket. She kept insisting hers sounded like a parakeet. Selena lifted her daughter from the car and held her close. Oliver waited for them to come up the walkway, more than anger in his shifting expression. Selena saw longing. And fear. As if something he'd wanted badly his entire life was within his grasp, and he had no idea how to hang on to it.

Selena bit her lip. She'd promised herself never to dream about what this moment could mean. But she felt her heart stumbling all over itself in excitement as she walked toward Oliver. She couldn't stop herself from hoping.

Her child in her arms, Camille's head nestled against her neck, Selena stopped at the bottom of the steps and waited.

"I could hear your car coming down the street from a block away," he finally said.

The man who'd wanted to be anywhere else yesterday but near Selena had been listening for her. And now he had eyes only for Camille.

"Please," Selena asked, "let me put my daughter down for a nap." *Let me catch my breath before we do this.*

Not once in the nearly seven years she'd lived with Parker—a lot of them truly bad years—had Selena been tempted to have another drink. But in less than twenty-four hours of living in the same town again as Oliver . . .

This should be the most precious moment of her life, having Camille meet the man who could very well be her father. Instead, Oliver's jaw was clenched, terrifying Selena that he'd say too much and scare her child. He inhaled. His attention slipped to Selena's ringless left hand where she was gently rubbing Camille's back.

Then her daughter straightened and turned enough to see who was there.

"Hello," Camille said. "You're the man who threw the Frisbee."

Oliver's breath came out in a rush. The two of them studied each other, connecting silently with an ease made sweeter by the look of wonder Oliver flicked toward Selena.

"Who's the father?" he said cryptically.

He didn't sound angry. But Selena sensed something surging through him, silent thunder rolling closer. Then the rebel of her misspent youth smoothed a palm across Camille's cheek. Selena's little girl smiled back, thankfully not catching on to the tension escalating between the adults.

"I don't know for sure," Selena said, giving her awful truth its voice, even though she'd always thought of her daughter as Oliver's.

She thought of Brad and Dru and Marsha and Joe, herself and Oliver, and even Belinda, and the confusion and chaos that were about to descend, ratcheting up what the Dixons were already dealing with. And, God help her, she thought of Parker, a part of her wishing she were weaker. More practical and able to go back to him and not care how many other women he slept with, as long as he came home, made the pretense of their marriage believable, and provided the financial security that to some other woman—to a younger Selena—might have been enough.

"I didn't want to know at first," she explained, needing Oliver to understand her long-ago decision. "I was alone, which meant I was going to handle it alone. And I did." Except the happy, secure family she'd wanted for her baby had never materialized. "Please, let me settle Camille in her room. Then give me a chance to explain the rest."

Chapter Eleven

A father was a good thing, so whoever's father the man from next door was looking for, Camille hoped he found him.

As much as Camille had always wanted a big family with tons of kids like the Dixons, she'd settle for just a daddy to go with the mommy she already had. A real daddy was one of the best things she'd never had. She figured a daddy would be even more fun than living with Grammy the last few months, and all Grammy's flowers and quilts and bubbles, and Mommy's old toys from when she was little.

A daddy would be better than anything Camille could think of.

One who'd be there when the other kids' daddies were. And he wouldn't do things to make Mommy decide to leave. He'd love Camille more than his job. He'd make Mommy laugh and smile, and he'd want to go to the playground and play games. And he would never make Mommy cry, not like Parker had, or the way Mommy looked like she might cry now, while Camille looked between her and the man from next door. The one who'd smiled and waved at Camille from the Dixons' kitchen window.

"Just tell me the truth." He sounded like someone was in trouble or something, the way Parker did a lot of the times.

"I . . ." Mommy was shaking, the trouble kind of shaking Camille felt when she'd done something wrong, like eating Karen's M&M's when Camille had known they were bad for her. "I am, Oliver. I don't know. I couldn't . . ." Mommy made that sound with her throat, like when she and Parker had fought and she'd been crying—only she didn't want Camille to know. "I don't know how things got this far, but I promise. I never meant for anyone to get hurt."

The man looked at Camille again, smiling now, at least at her. Camille remembered Grammy saying he was part of the Dixon family, too. Even though Camille had never seen him before yesterday.

Camille's stomach rumbled, like it wanted to be sick again. She swallowed, not wanting to make Mommy worry again. Her mommy looked so sad.

"Don't cry." Camille patted her mommy's cheek and smiled at the man. "You're not mad anymore, are you, Oliver?" Mommy had said his name was Oliver. "Say sorry, and Mommy will get you lemonade like she's going to get me because I'm sick. Grammy makes the best, Mrs. Dixon says. And Mrs. Dixon makes the best chocolate chip cookies, and she brought some over awhile ago, and we saved them in the 'frigerator so they would last. So, say sorry, and we can have cookies and lemonade."

Oliver smiled at her again. He had green eyes, almost as dark as hers.

"She's been sick?" he asked Mommy.

Camille's mommy headed up the steps, hugging her again. "Come on, Cricket. Let me get you out of this heat."

"I'd like to come in." The man stopped Mommy from opening Grammy's screen door so she could get to the wood one behind it, the one Camille couldn't get open on her own.

"Please, Oliver," Mommy whispered.

"It's okay," Camille said. "I don't feel so bad now. He can come in. He'll be nice. Won't you?"

Oliver agreed, and Mommy sighed the way she did when she agreed to do something for Grammy that Camille knew her mommy really didn't want to do. She nodded her head, and Oliver held the screen door open while Mommy unlocked the wooden one.

Grammy's shady porch felt so good after being in the hot sun. Camille wished she could just take her nap on the old metal swing in the corner. It had Grammy's pretty pillows all over it. It was where Camille's mommy snuck off to late at night when she couldn't sleep.

"I'll be nice," Oliver said to her mommy. He smiled at Camille again. "And I'd love some lemonade and one of my mother's cookies."

"Mrs. Dixon's your mommy?"

"Since I was thirteen."

"That's so cool."

Mommy put Camille on her feet and got down in front of her.

"It's rest time, honey. You can barely keep your eyes open since Nurse Mallory used your EpiPen. And your doctor said it was important that you take things slow if you don't want to end up right back in his office. So let's get you cleaned up. You can lie down for a while. And then we'll try a snack."

"Cookies?" Camille wrapped her arms around her mommy's neck, really tired, and not really sure if she ever wanted another snack ever again.

"Toast." Mommy held Camille's hand as she stood and opened the door to the house.

"And lemonade?" Camille checked behind them while she and Mommy walked inside. Oliver didn't follow them. But he kept holding the screen door, and Mommy didn't close the wooden one. "I'm really, *really* thirsty."

"Once you're tucked in for your nap," Mommy said, "we'll give lemonade a try."

"I'll take some, too," Oliver said.

Mommy hugged Camille to her side. She looked at him, not saying anything for a long time.

"One glass." Mommy stepped back a little. When Oliver followed, she looked at Camille. "To bed with you, my little friend."

But then Oliver was down in front of her the way Mommy had been on the porch. And he seemed to really like her. And Mrs. Dixon was his mother. And Camille wished more than ever she hadn't snuck a piece of Karen's candy at school, so she could stay and listen to him and Mommy talk about whoever's daddy Oliver had come to talk about.

"It was nice to meet you, Camille," he said. "And I promise not to eat all the cookies the way I used to when I was your age, so you have some left when you're feeling better. Deal?"

Parker used to promise things, too. He'd promised a lot of things that never happened. Camille was pretty sure that's why they'd left, her and Mommy. Because Parker mostly never meant anything he promised. But Camille would bet Mrs. Dixon's son never did that. There'd be lots of cookies left when she woke up.

"Deal," she said. "How do you know my mommy?"

"This is an old friend of mine," Mommy said. "He and I . . ."

"Knew each other when we were kids." Oliver stood. "When I lived next door for a few years."

"If Mrs. Dixon is your mommy, then you and Travis are brothers, right?" Camille liked Deputy Bryant.

Oliver didn't answer right away.

"Travis visited Camille's school," Mommy said. "She's seen him and Dru going in and out next door, and she loves the Dream Whip. Dru's always there. Travis, too, sometimes."

"Yes," Oliver said, "Travis and Dru are my brother and sister."

"That's so cool. And the other kids, too?"

Like Teddy, who Camille wasn't supposed to have played with, but he'd been so much fun the couple of times she'd snuck over to see Mrs. Dixon.

"They're newer, but I'll get to know them now that I'm back for a while."

"That's so—"

"That's your last *so cool* for a while," Mommy said. "Bed. Lemonade. Nap. No more eating other kids' snacks. And I don't care how much theirs look better than yours."

Camille let her mommy lead her away, even though she wanted to stay and talk to Oliver. She didn't understand why her mommy and grammy didn't want her to play next door. Mrs. Dixon was nice. And Oliver seemed nice, too, just like Travis and Dru.

"See you later," she said, thinking that Oliver didn't look anything like Deputy Bryant. Or anyone else next door. Because they were a foster family, Grammy had tried to explained. They'd come from different homes that hadn't been so good, before they moved in with the Dixons.

Lucky, Camille thought to herself as she and her mommy finally got to her room, and Camille crawled into her bed and closed her eyes.

The Dixon kids were so lucky now, she thought sleepily. No matter how bad the other families had been before they'd come to Chandlerville.

Chapter Twelve

"Snack?" Oliver asked when Selena returned from settling Camille down for a nap.

Selena grabbed two glasses from the cabinet beside the sink and the pitcher of lemonade from the fridge. She hadn't taken any to Camille yet. Her daughter had fallen asleep as soon as her head hit the pillow.

"She's allergic," Selena explained.

Oliver waited patiently. He was giving her plenty of space, hanging across the kitchen while she poured their drinks and refused to look at him. But she could feel his mind working, analyzing. The emotions that had been riding so high outside, when she was terrified of what he might say . . . he had them firmly in check now.

And it was bugging her.

She crossed the kitchen, handed over his drink, and sipped hers. He stood unmoving in the doorway to her mother's tiny living room, evidently content to wait until she said something more. She'd bet every penny she'd socked away in her savings account—in her name alone so Parker couldn't touch it—that Oliver could wait her out all afternoon.

"Camille's allergic to peanuts." Selena's throat felt raw, like she'd been shrieking.

Her whole body was silently screaming from being too close to a man she hadn't been alone with since she was eighteen. She took another drink, flooding her taste buds with summery tartness.

"A lot of things can make her ill," she explained. "Luckily, today it was peanuts. Camille ate another child's candy. She wants to be like other kids so badly, between episodes she forgets how quickly her body wants to get rid of what it can't process."

"Luckily?" Oliver sipped from his glass, his eyes widening.

Belinda didn't believe in indulging in too much of anything, especially sweeteners. Fresh-squeezed lemonade was supposed to taste like lemons, not sugar.

Selena swallowed her smile. "Peanuts aren't the worst potential offenders on Camille's list."

"What's the worst?"

"Milk, so far. But nuts are bad enough. And a lot of the prepackaged convenience foods kids like have them, or they're made in facilities that process them. Other parents send things to school for lunches and snacks that could make Camille react. Even freshly baked things like doughnuts. Except for Dan's on Main."

Selena heard herself babbling. She tried to knock it off. But it was so surreal, Oliver being in this house again. And from the moment he'd stepped inside, Belinda's had felt right to Selena— for the first time since she'd come back.

So she rambled onward. "DJ has nut allergies in his family. Three of his kids. He has five now. Can you believe it? Five kids in seven years? When he took over the business from his father, Dan Junior made Dan's Doughnuts and Bakery completely nut-free.

And he has a shelf just for dairy-free items. We go there every now and then as a reward, to help Camille not feel so bad that she has to be careful the rest of the time. DJ's chocolate doughnuts are her favorite treat, just like . . ."

Selena blinked.

Just like Dan Senior's pastries had been Selena's. And Oliver had spoiled her rotten, buying them with his summer job money.

They'd been merely friends still when he'd caught on to the insatiable craving that was her sweet tooth, while Belinda was adamant about keeping unhealthy food out of the house. He'd teased Selena unmercifully about it for years, but never in front of anyone else. And once they started dating, he'd surprised her with her favorite treats when she least expected it. Just because. He'd said he loved the way her smile tasted after she'd eaten one. She'd let herself forget that when DJ took it upon himself to pamper Camille.

She motioned to the drink Oliver had hardly touched. "It's getting warm."

He drained the glass.

Good.

"Now, if you don't mind . . ." She tried and failed to sound nonchalant. "I'm going to ask you to go, so I can get on with our afternoon here."

She couldn't do this yet—have the potentially life-changing conversation they needed to have. Not with Oliver once more acting as if they'd barely known each other.

"And if I do mind?" he asked

"I've had enough. You asked the question you came here to ask. I've answered it as best I can. And I have to get back to my daughter. I might need to run her to her pediatrician again if she starts to feel worse. Leave the glass on the counter when you're done."

He grabbed her arm before she could brush by.

"*Your* daughter?" he bit out, anything but in control now.

Then his head lowered, his breath catching Selena's as his kiss erased everything but her memories of wanting to love him forever.

She'd had enough?

How could anyone get enough of something that felt as good as holding Selena?

Her lips trembled beneath his for a second, as if she were afraid. Then she was kissing him back, ripping free of his hold. But only so she could throw her arms around his neck as if she'd been dying to from the start.

God, Selena.

No other woman had ever felt like her, tasted like her, tempted him to crawl inside her and never find his way out. Since yesterday, he'd been dreaming of having her body plastered against his again. And she'd clearly been wanting him with the same desperation, while he'd agonized all this time over not letting his need for her show.

Her nails bit into his biceps, causing his hands to clench at her waist. He hauled her onto her toes and fisted a hand in her hair. Their mouths opened with identical groans. Their kiss deepened, rocketing from exploring to carnal. Their tongues mated, their teeth nipped, their lips crushed, both of them remembering and needing and demanding where this was taking them. Sprinting toward it, agreeing without speaking that—

"No." Selena shook her head, her hair hopelessly tangled around his fingers. She was panting, the same as him, but she was pulling back. "Please, Oliver. No more . . ."

Scraping together his sanity, he licked her lower lip a final time. A tender rasp of his tongue, while the rest of him throbbed in tempo with his thundering heartbeat. Then he let Selena slip away.

She stumbled backward, catching herself against the kitchen counter, bracing both hands behind her on its edge. She was breathing so heavily she could have been running wind sprints. And he couldn't watch anymore. He picked up his empty glass from where he'd set it on the tiny Formica dinette table—he needed something to do with his hands besides grabbing her again. He headed into Belinda's cramped living room, thinking, *Not smart.*

Nothing about what had just happened had been smart. It was the least smart thing he'd done yet. But Selena had been brushing him off, and before he walked away again . . . He'd needed her there, right there, next to his heart.

Damn it, focus.

Focus on something besides yourself this time.

He looked around the living room. To him, the Rosenthal place had always seemed like a dollhouse, with its grand total of five rooms and a single bath down Belinda's short hallway. He'd always worried about bumping into something or accidentally knocking things over. He'd never known what to do with himself here. He still didn't.

He flexed his shoulders. He went to take another sip of lemonade and curled his fist around the empty glass. *Stay cool, man.* Like Selena, who was ice-cold now, staring at him from the kitchen as if their meltdown hadn't happened. But he'd felt her shock, felt her shaking. She'd gasped. And the soft sound of her wanting him had pulled him deeper into the kiss she'd been returning with abandon.

He'd envisioned several potential outcomes to him showing up on Belinda's doorstep. He'd considered each one while he'd waited for Selena to come home. But his grabbing her like he still had a right to, and her grabbing back, had been nowhere on his list. Instead of getting her to see reason, her barriers were even more firmly in place.

And damn if he wasn't spoiling for another chance to rattle her cage.

But he needed to make some kind of amends. There had to be a speck of common ground left for him and Selena to build on, so they could discuss Camille sensibly.

"It still feels like I'm going to catch hell," he said, "if your mom comes home and finds me alone with you."

"We're not alone." Selena glanced down the hallway, finally joining him in the living room.

She paced back and forth. Then back again. She sat on the love seat Belinda used as a couch. The thing sported the same plaid tweed fabric as years ago. The same drooping cushions. The recliner beside it looked different, but it was just as faded. Both faced what looked like the same TV, rabbit ears perched on top. It was an almost self-righteously primitive setup compared with the state-of-the-art entertainment center Oliver had covered the cost of next door.

"If my mother could see us," Selena muttered, "Belinda would definitely have something to say about this one."

"This one?"

Selena looked like a queen amid the midcentury ranch's fraying décor, with her silky length of mink hair and pale skin. She was wearing a sundress like yesterday. This one was made of a filmy lemon-yellow material that had him thinking of sherbet—and sipping every inch of Selena's smooth skin while she melted all over him.

"You know my mother," she said, yanking his attention back to their conversation. "She means well these days, but she can't help but obsess over my running list of poor life choices. No degree. No husband for much longer. No savings. No baby daddy. No success keeping any of it from dumping back into Belinda's lap, no matter how welcoming she's been. She'd say I deserve better than to be hitting rock bottom with you again."

"Camille deserves better, too." At least they could all agree on that.

Selena winced. "Better than me?"

"Better than not knowing my family, even if your mom's not going to be wild about you associating with me again. I'm assuming you haven't told her about any of this."

"I haven't told anyone. Not even Parker—not the details, at least. That was the deal breaker for me when we got married. He wanted to know more about my past and who Camille's father was. I wanted everything that had happened before New York to be over and done with. He either took us as we were, or not. My child deserved a fresh start. A clean slate where my mistakes couldn't hurt her the way . . . the way they will now."

Oliver sat in Belinda's recliner. "You're a good mom, Selena. And I can understand why you felt you had to do what you did seven years ago. But a part of you must realize the positive influence my parents could have on Camille's life."

"You don't know anything about me." Selena smiled, as if that sad fact comforted her. "And I know your parents are good people, Oliver. I just don't know how my daughter would react to finding out about them, only to have us move away again. And not upsetting her life any more than I already have is *all* I can let matter to me now."

This Selena was stronger, he realized, than the girl who'd been so terrified of losing him. Stronger and potentially even more self-destructive than she'd been as a teenager, when she'd been trying to protect only herself from him.

"What's happened to you?" he let slip out.

Selena shrugged, when she should be telling him to go to hell for judging her. "I've grown up, the hard way."

"You're giving up on my family without letting us prove we could be good for Camille."

"I've learned a lot about second chances. The number one thing? That this is my life, my chance, my mistakes to make and make up for. It's my responsibility to do the best I can for my daughter. She deserves that from me. And she'll have it."

"I don't doubt she will. But why the hell does it have to be just you?"

"Because I'm all she's ever had," Selena continued, reasonable and calm while he could feel his blood begin to simmer again. "Because she's not yours or your family's to worry about. Not yet. Not until I'm sure it's the right time. I wish I had a different answer that would make things easier. But I don't. And don't think I haven't lain awake nights since coming back, wanting to talk it all through with someone. Get it out in the open. Make this right."

"Then make it right."

Selena shook her head. "Once we open that Pandora's box, there's no backing things up, regardless of what we discover. And springing a father Camille's never met on her at this point in her life, when we're *not* staying in town for any longer than it takes me to come up with the money to move again, would only con-fuse her more."

Confuse Camille, Oliver wondered, or Selena?

It was a believable speech, fiercely delivered. Selena hadn't so much as blinked while she'd spoken. She'd barely taken in air. But he'd just had her in his arms, felt her needing him the same bottomless way as when they'd been lovers. And she was wound so tightly now she seemed to be holding herself together by sheer grit.

"I'm not asking you to do anything you and Camille aren't ready for."

"Sure you are."

"I want to do what's best for everyone involved."

"By forcing your way into my daughter's life?"

"By talking with you about our mutual problem."

"Camille's no one's problem."

"Someone's her father, Selena. Assuming you're sure she's not your ex's."

"Parker came along after I already knew I was pregnant."

Oliver stared into his empty glass. "Does Camille know that?"

Selena nodded. "She's always called him Parker. I've been honest from the start that he wasn't her birth father. That her only blood family was a grandmother she'd never met before we moved in here."

Oliver swallowed the reflex to argue the point on his parents' behalf.

"I . . ." He tried to think of a gentler way to say it and couldn't, when he'd smooth-talked countless skeptical CIOs into giving him their business. "I take my responsibilities seriously these days, Selena."

"Me too. And Camille's *my* responsibility."

Which in her mind meant that the both of them were completely beyond his reach. "Your daughter's my family, too."

"You don't know that."

"If she's not your ex's, she's either mine or Brad's." Another possibility struck him. "Could she be someone else's?"

Selena choked as she sipped her lemonade. "Could you be more of a jackass?"

He let out the breath he'd been holding, relieved, grateful. "Then she's either my daughter or my niece." He slipped to the edge of the recliner. "Is it so hard to believe that that could matter to me?"

She went to put down her glass and missed the edge of Belinda's scarred coffee table. She cursed and caught it before it could crash to the hardwood. But liquid drenched her arm, her dress, and the floor.

Oliver leaped forward and took the glass from her. He handed her the fresh handkerchief he'd slipped into his pocket that morning. She looked at the pressed white square, at his wrinkled jeans. Then she was gazing straight into his eyes, connecting again, crushing him with the mixture of home and loneliness he saw there. And her determination not to feel this . . . whatever this was between them.

She mopped up the table and then herself.

"You carry a handkerchief?" she sputtered, like she was accusing him of something. "Of course you do."

He let her clean up, let her settle. He took in all of her, as if it were the last time. Smooth features, solemn eyes, and a guarded soul that he still felt tangled up in, whether either of them liked it or not.

"You really were hoping," he said, "that no one would catch on."

She handed him the soaked handkerchief. "I told Belinda we'd be in town for only a few weeks. There have been some complications."

"Like what?"

When she clammed up again, she finally succeeded in pissing him off. He gave himself credit for not exploding and scaring her or the sick little girl sleeping in a bedroom down the hall. But, *complications*?

"We're going to deal with this," he said. "If you'd just listen—"

"I have listened. I listened when your brother came by school this morning, to try to get me to see reason. But—"

"Travis?" Damn it.

"Don't tell me you didn't know. And don't think it helps your cause for your family to be coming at me, too. Travis. Your mother. What's next—Joe begging me from his hospital bed? I don't want anyone to get hurt by this. But—"

"This is no one else's business right now but ours." And Oliver would make certain Travis and the entire Dixon crew understood that. "Once we break the news, I'll get my family under control."

She shook her head, a sad kind of envy overtaking her features. "They love you, Oliver. There's no controlling that. And I wouldn't want you to try. You need them too badly still."

He stared at her, his heart feeling like it was teetering on the edge of a cliff, destined to fall and take him with it, no matter what he did next. His family did love him. They couldn't have made that more clear, or the fact that they wanted him in town for as long as he could stay. So why did it feel as if none of that could make things right, not without Selena in his life, figuring this mess out with him?

"I'm not sure what Travis thinks he knows," Selena said. "But he seems pretty certain I'm a threat to you settling in Chandlerville. Reassure him that I'm not, and he'll back off. The best way you can keep everyone else out of my business is to drop your questions about Camille."

"Drop them?" Drop the fact that he could be a father—to a little girl who thought he was cool. To Selena's little girl.

"Give me some time. I can't make a split-second decision about verifying her paternity. Don't ask me to do that. We have to do this carefully, if we do it at all. Be reasonable, and—"

"I've been reasonable. But I've already talked with Brad. Do you understand what I'm saying? You need to tell your mother as soon as possible, because mine's the one who started this. And I don't see Marsha letting this drop. I'm sticking in town for as long as I have to—to deal with whatever my parents need me to. And my mother's asked me to deal with this."

"So now you're *dealing* with my daughter . . ." Selena spat the words at him. "Is that what that display was outside? You cupping her cheek and smiling at her and crouching down in front of her to talk about cookies and lemonade? Maybe even kissing me just now. It was all for your parents' sake, right? But now you want me to believe that Camille's paternity means something to you personally."

Oliver gritted his teeth. He felt just as incapable of helping Selena see reason now as when they'd been kids.

"Camille matters to me," he insisted. "Even if the last thing you want is for anything about her to be about me. Let me help you see a different way through this. You're ignoring the reality that there's nothing I take more seriously than my responsibility to my family."

"I see reality just fine." Selena collected both their glasses. "And the reality is that I get to decide what's best for Camille. And you get to leave. Don't think you can bully me into agreeing to what you want. I'll deal with telling Belinda. Then everyone's just going to have to accept that I'm doing the best I can, the same as I have since Camille was born. I'm handling *my* responsibilities. I'm going to make sure my daughter has a happy life, whatever it takes. And the last thing she needs is another man wanting to call himself her father, while he's only thinking about himself and what he wants. Now get out."

"Funny," an older, more lived-in version of Selena's voice said, from the doorway to the porch. Neither Oliver nor Selena had heard it open. Belinda stepped all the way inside. "That's pretty much what I said the day I told your daddy to leave and never come back."

Selena watched Oliver leave without responding to Belinda's bombshell.

"Mom . . ."

She had no idea what had just happened or what her mother had meant. Not for certain. And she didn't dare ask. Not right now. Not when she'd just been kissing Oliver and wanting to keep kissing him—a man who was smiling at her daughter one minute, grabbing for Selena the next, then making not so thinly veiled threats about doing whatever he had to on his family's behalf about getting to the bottom of Camille's paternity. Now, evidently her mother might have booted Selena's dad out twenty years ago, instead of the man abandoning them the way Selena had always believed.

"I got a call from Gladys in the school office," Belinda said. "That Camille had gone home after having an allergy attack. I had to call the pediatrician myself to find out that you two were on your way home. I took off early to make sure everything was okay. I tried calling your cell."

"I turned the ringer off in the doctor's office." Selena ran her hands through her hair. "Sorry. It's been a long day. I was rushing to get set up for my class this morning when Kristen stopped by to talk . . ."

She took her glass and Oliver's through to the kitchen. Kristen's offer was a topic for another day.

"Then Travis interrupted us," she added, arriving at even more details to skip over. "Before we could talk long I got a page about Camille. We just got home. I know I should have called. But—"

"Yes." Her mother pulled down the hem of the post-office blue shirt she wore to work every day. "I obviously interrupted something important with Oliver. And I should have kept my opinions to myself. I'm sorry about that, honey, really."

Selena returned to the doorway between the living room and kitchen. She realized she was smiling—completely inappropriately. And so was her mother.

"You should have kept your opinions to yourself?" Selena repeated.

Belinda set her purse on the entryway table. "You thought you'd never hear that from me, didn't you?"

"With or without checking the sky for flying swine?"

Belinda actually chuckled. She passed Selena, heading for the automatic coffee maker. It could be 110 in the shade, high summer, a Southern heat wave with no end in sight, and she would put on a pot of coffee the second she walked in the door. An entire pot, even if she was preparing it only for herself.

No single-cup fancy maker for Belinda. Selena had wanted to buy her mother one a few Mother's Days back—the swankiest must-have model available in New York. It had had a feature for practically everything except giving you a mani-pedi while you waited. But coffee was coffee to Belinda. Ground beans. Boiling water. The rest was just trappings to get you hooked on buying things you didn't know you needed until some marketing team said so.

Selena leaned against the arched doorway, watching her mother go through the soothing ritual of setting things up.

"I've been all over you since you came home." Belinda measured out grounds. "And I know I could have handled things better when you were growing up."

"You don't have to apologize, Mom." More than anything, Selena couldn't take that right now.

"For how I raised you? I'm not. I did what I thought was best, the best I could. The same as you are with Camille." Belinda finished up and faced Selena, the kitchen's small table and three chairs between them. "But you've got enough people forcing their opinions on you. You don't need more pressure from me about the choices you're facing."

"About?"

"About Oliver, dear. I should have butted out just now. I shouldn't have called you about him yesterday morning. I had no business at Neat Feet trying to talk you out of doing whatever you need to do. I'm not very good at keeping my worries and thoughts to myself. But this is one time I'm going to do just that. It's your decision to make, not mine. Just know that I'm here to talk if you ever want to. That's all I'm going to say. About Parker and Oliver . . . about your father. When you're ready, if you're ever ready, I want to be here for you."

Selena sat in one of the chairs, her legs as wobbly as the unsteady flutter of her heart. "Like you waited for me to tell you about Parker?"

Belinda frowned. "That man never loved you or your daughter. Not enough. He wasn't going to give you and Camille the family you deserved. I could hear it in your voice, the way you described your lives together. I knew you hoped he'd change. I knew from personal experience that men like him never do. But . . ."

"You let me come to my senses on my own and ask you for help."

Belinda joined her at the kitchen table. The legs of her chair creaked as she sat. "Me telling you that you deserved better than a man you thought was your savior wasn't going to get either of us what we wanted. You'd never have trusted me if I'd been the one to say it first."

Selena inhaled the comforting aroma of her mother's coffee. She cherished the care and patience Belinda had shown her all this time, no matter the bumps in their relationship they were still working through. But she couldn't talk about Oliver yet. Or whatever had really happened when her dad left.

She just wanted to sit there with her mother, she realized, and enjoy the simplicity of the birds chirping in the backyard—the way they had when Selena was a little girl, doing her homework at this same table and dreaming of growing up and moving away and making a bigger, better life for herself. She didn't want bigger and better these days. She wanted simple. She wanted honesty and hope and a belief in tomorrow she hadn't felt in a long time.

"Thank you, Mom." She didn't know what else to say. "For waiting, and for not asking too many questions yet."

Belinda smiled and left, only as long as it took to pour coffee and stir sugar into her cup before she sat back down. "There's time to work up to the rest, as long as you keep letting me be part of your life." Her steady gaze said she knew how much even that was asking. "I realize I'm set in my ways. I'm not easy to live with."

"That's not it."

Even if the last thing you want is for anything about her to be about me, Oliver had said. And Selena had no idea if *that* was it. She couldn't see anything clearly now. She had no idea what to do next.

"I know how hard you're trying," she said to her mother, grateful that she wasn't doing this alone.

"We both are." Belinda smiled. "You're trying not to run again before you're able to make ends meet on your own. And I'm trying to talk less. Listen more. I know I'm not good enough at it. But I'm getting better. *We're* getting better. We can get through this together this time. I know we can."

Selena blinked.

If you decide you'd like to give Chandlerville a chance, call me . . .

Let me help you see a different way through this . . .

You both have secrets you think won't hurt anyone else . . .

We can get through this together this time . . .

Selena had left New York, determined to make it on her own. Only to surround herself with people determined to help her find her way.

"You have a meeting tonight?" Belinda asked.

Selena shook her head. "Tomorrow. I'll probably take the day off to stay home with Camille. If she's still not feeling well by tomorrow evening, I don't need to make a meeting."

"Oh yes you do. I saw your face when I walked in on you and Oliver. You've had quite a day—Travis, Camille's allergic reaction, then whatever was happening just now. On top of yesterday. You don't have to talk about any of it with me. But you're going to be where you need to be tomorrow night to feel supported."

Selena's sobriety and how hard she'd worked at it since before Camille was born had so far been one of the few conversations Selena and Belinda had muscled all the way through—two adults talking, instead of falling back on the dysfunctional parent-child dynamic that wouldn't have gotten them anywhere. Since then, Belinda had made it a point to be home anytime Selena had an

AA meeting. In fact, Belinda had regularly insisted on it, just as she was now. Supporting. Pushing. Loving Selena in her own way.

"I'll be there," Selena promised.

Belinda sipped her coffee, her eyes full of questions that she didn't ask. Selena rose and headed for Camille's room. But her daughter was sound asleep still—curled up with the stuffed blue bunny she'd always called Bear, in her window seat now. Selena covered her little girl with Belinda's tulip quilt and slipped quietly away, lingering in the doorway.

She hadn't realized until she'd returned home that the décor she'd chosen for her daughter's room in Manhattan had mirrored her own childhood haven. Pink and white, fussy and little-girly, cluttered enough to be cozy without feeling messy. Only here, Belinda had meticulously sewn every stitch of it herself, slaving away for entire weekends after they'd first moved in, wanting Selena to have a taste still of the bigger, grander home they'd been forced to sell across town. Now Camille had that same fanciful world to dream in. And maybe it was helping Selena's baby believe, just a little, that everything really was going to be okay.

Selena stepped across the hall to her mother's sewing room. Belinda's old Singer sat atop its cabinet in front of the window, where it had always been. Selena had taken over the tiny couch in the corner and crammed her diminished wardrobe into the closet where Belinda stored old coats and outerwear that were rarely needed in Georgia.

Looking back, looking around her mother's tidy sewing retreat, thinking about how much time Belinda had spent creating things over the years they couldn't afford to buy outright—clothes for Selena, gifts for her friends, even band uniforms for her and her classmates . . . Selena no longer saw want or the lack of things they hadn't had, or the coldness that had once grown between her and Belinda. She saw her mother's need—Belinda's bone-deep desire to make things better for her child under extraordinarily difficult circumstances. Selena saw the love she'd always had within her grasp, even when she'd believed there was something better for her somewhere else. All while Belinda had given her enough space to make her way back home.

Her mother seemed content to wait again. And to support whatever Selena decided to do next. Only for once Selena wished Belinda *would* weigh in. Selena had put a lot of people she cared about in an impossible situation—Camille most of all. And for the life of her, she couldn't decide what to do about it.

Oliver had stomped through the front door to find his brother instead of Dru sitting on the couch, supervising the kids as they did their homework. Which was code, evidently, for driving each other and any grown-up within hearing range bat-shit crazy. Oliver had ignored everyone and hauled himself into the kitchen to root in the fridge for beer. Of course there hadn't been any. He'd been counting on it.

He'd chugged a glass of milk instead, rinsed it out, and dumped the glass in the dishwasher. He'd just finished doing the rest of the plates and bowls and things in the sink, left over from the tribe's after-school snack.

Teddy sounded off in the other room, waking from his afternoon snooze, prompting Oliver to wade back in. He snatched the toddler from his playpen. One look at Oliver's face had Travis closing whatever book he'd been quietly reading.

"Homework upstairs," he said. "Oliver will make sure it's done, so don't even think about ditching."

Kids grumbled and pried themselves off the couch, the floor, the surrounding chairs, dragging their feet and marching up to their respective rooms the way convicts would to the gallows.

"Where's Dru?" Oliver bounced a sniffling and nuzzling and soon-to-be-starving eighteen-month-old in his arms. He took a wary sniff, gratified to discover that the inevitable post-nap poopy diaper was so far a no-show.

"I cut her loose," his brother said. "She's exhausted after last night. I'm not on shift for another hour, and she's got to be at the Whip early tomorrow. She doesn't need to be hanging around here—"

"Because I keep bailing on you guys. I get it. I'll be where I'm supposed to be from now on."

"Do you get it? Do you even know where you need to be?"

"I know I'm here now. Which means you're sprung. Don't let me keep you, bro."

"So we've got nothing to talk about," Travis said mildly, his expression hotter than the hell they used to raise together. "Is that it? I haven't seen you since before Dad's surgery. I hear from Brad and Dru you've had an eventful twenty-four hours. And that was before your little jaunt next door. But I should just get the hell out of your way, with you looking like you want to wreck something, because we've got nothing to say to each other? What the hell, man?"

"Okay . . ." At the moment, hell sounded like a cakewalk to Oliver. "Let's talk about you backing off."

His brother set his book aside. *The Count of Monte Cristo.* The jerk who'd tried to pay Oliver to do his lit papers in high school had been sitting there calmly reading the classics while Oliver's heart rate hadn't settled since Selena and Camille walked up to him next door. And now the kid in his arms was crying loud enough for ten babies.

"How about first," his brother said, tossing Oliver the pacifier that had been sitting on the coffee table, "you tell me what's got you so cranked up. Dru said you were on edge when she got here with Teddy, but you wouldn't tell her what's going on before you headed next door. Neither would Brad, when he let her know you two talked this morning."

Oliver plugged Teddy's mouth with the pacifier and glared silently at his brother.

"So things went well with Selena?" Travis asked.

"Did you know?" If Travis had, and he hadn't said anything, Oliver was going to do bodily harm. "Is that where all of this is coming from? You knew about Camille, and instead of calling me months ago when she and Selena showed up in Chandlerville or at the very least telling me once I hit town, you've been playing games like helping Mom throw Selena and me together yesterday. And stopping by the school to have a friendly chat with Selena this morning. You're my brother, damn it. This is about our family."

Travis's expression evened out into the kind of calm that only a dimwit would believe meant he was about to reasonable.

"I don't know what you're talking about," he said, "but I've got my own reasons for thinking that you and Selena dealing with your issues is the best thing for everyone. And as far as me not calling you the last few years about anything going on here, while you've been gallivanting all over the country and half the globe . . . you've got a lot of nerve throwing us being brothers in my face after everything I've put up with."

"From me?"

"*You* call *me*, remember? I don't get to call you up and chat about current events. Emergencies only, right? Because being close to any of us again isn't what you wanted. At least that's what you've been telling yourself. So us being brothers or family or whatever else you're feeling indignant about right now seems to be a convenience that only you get to indulge in, and only when it suits you."

The bitterness curling at the edges of Travis's Southern drawl doused Oliver temper like a bucket of ice water. "That's not true. I—"

"Called me out of the blue five years ago. I get a call from you from God knows where saying you just want to be sure things are okay with the family. Did Mom and Dad need any help? Because you were finally in a position to start paying them back. Was there anything anyone needed money for? So, sure, I came up with something—I can't even remember what now—and the folks were happy enough when the dough started pouring in like clockwork. And they've been real sports, haven't they? About keeping their distance, just like you wanted. Of course you don't have to see how worried they are, or how much it hurts when nothing ever comes their way except your next deposit. No note. No pictures. No way for them to know that you give a damn whether you ever make a personal appearance here again. All anyone in Chandlerville needs from you is money, evidently, satisfying whatever responsibility you feel minus the hassle of you actually letting yourself care about what it's being spent on."

"You think I didn't want to come home? You think it wasn't driving me crazy, needing to be here and knowing that—"

"If you came back, it wouldn't be so easy to ignore how people here have always wanted more of you than you've been comfortable giving them?"

Oliver swallowed, feeling like slime. Except for loving Selena, he'd never known how to be close, to dig in, to belong—not since losing his birth mother. Not even to his foster family. Especially not to them.

He dropped into one of the chairs beside the couch, his anger fizzling. Teddy's head and soft, fuzzy baby hair nuzzled in. It was like having a sweet-smelling, living blanket soothing away the confusion and frustration and excuses.

"I've been doing what I thought everyone needed," Oliver said.

"How's that working out for you?" Travis propped his ankle on his knee.

"Lousy." Oliver checked Teddy. He couldn't contain his grin at how cute the toddler looked, back asleep and drooling on one of Oliver's last clean shirts. "I'm making a mess of everything except being a human baby cushion. But you're not helping, stirring things up with Selena."

"I talked to Selena this morning," his brother said, "for the same reason I've always taken your calls, and Mom and Dad would have taken your money even if they hadn't needed it. The same reason Mom tried to get you to deal with Brad and Selena yesterday. We're trying to keep you close the only way we know how, you jerk. And not because it feels so spectacular to be an afterthought you've been plotting to get away from again, from the moment you rocked into town. I want my brother back—pain in the ass that you are. I want you home for good. So do Mom and Dad, even if they'd never pressure you about it. Not the way I'm going to. Because, damn it, when are you going to get it?"

"What?"

"Having family in your life is a good thing, even when bad things happen. Even when we screw up. We care about each other and take care of each other through it all, the way no one else will. That's what Mom and Dad taught us. That's why I called you when Dad got sick, because I knew you'd want to be here. And now even though it's driving you nuts, and you're driving *me* nuts, you're staying. And what about you asking me to help you find a place to rehab when you needed it? Or you squatting in Atlanta since then? Or going next door today to face Selena?"

"What about it?"

"Are you telling me you haven't had a serious case of wanting to be in Chandlerville, and back with *her*, for a good long while?"

Before Oliver could formulate an answer that consisted of more than a string of four-letter words, Travis stood and lifted Teddy away, laying the baby in his playpen with practiced ease. He turned back. Oliver had gotten to his feet, too.

A large thud overhead made the ceiling shake to the accompaniment of gales of muted laughter. The rhythmic sound of Teddy sucking on his pacifier paused for a second or two before the baby got back to soothing himself and dreaming in slobbery bliss. Whatever had happened upstairs settled down, leaving Oliver and his brother squared off across the living room, their hands jammed in the pockets of their respective jeans.

Oliver didn't want to get into how much sense Travis was making. Or how Oliver would be lying awake tonight stewing over every word, once the rest of the house was asleep and he couldn't close his eyes or drive to the hospital to check on Joe or slip next door to beg Selena for another chance to come to some kind of compromise. Or even work. He hadn't gotten a damn bit of work done since he'd come home.

What the hell did Oliver really know about family? And now he was supposed to be a hands-on son, a brother, maybe even a father himself. Maybe more—if Selena could let herself want more with him again.

He stared at Travis, who had been there every step of the way, since Oliver's first phone call five years ago, since he'd walked in the door at thirteen. He had to talk to someone. Someone neutral who could help him chart a course through the minefield of options facing him. All of them threatening to blow up in his family's face.

"Do you need to get to work?" he finally asked.

Travis checked his watch. "I've got a few more minutes. Why?"

Oliver sank back into his chair. "There's something I need to tell you."

Chapter Thirteen

Oliver dragged himself into the Dream Whip at nine the next morning. He pulled up short.

"Bethany?" Shocked, thrilled to find her there—he hadn't had a chance yet to hunt her down—he pulled her close, feeling clumsy. Feeling her surprise and confusion.

He'd come to see Dru. Brad had called the house late last night, saying he'd broken the news to his fiancée about Selena and Camille, after Oliver flubbed things so badly at Belinda's place. Travis was pitching in at the house again this morning. He'd been one hundred percent behind Oliver making sure their sister was okay.

Oliver had promised to cut his brother loose within the hour. But he couldn't just brush past Bethany. Not like this. Only a year younger than Dru, she'd always seemed so much more fragile.

"I didn't know . . ." he said.

"That I still existed?" Bethany finished.

She had no clue how much he'd kept up with her since she'd aged out of Marsha and Joe's house. Because, as Travis had pointed out, that's exactly the way Oliver had wanted things. He cleared his throat, hating how much he'd hurt her. Refusing to make lame excuses.

"I didn't know you worked for Dru and Brad," he said.

Petite, bordering on sprite-like, she'd streaked her shoulder-length auburn hair with waves of deep purple. A diamond chip winked on the left side of her nose. She'd thrown on cowboy boots with her denim shorts and a Whip It Good T-shirt that from the looks of it she'd cropped and shredded herself. Possibly with a pair of gardening shears.

"The Whip's something to do." She finished wiping down the red leather booth by the door. "Somewhere to be, whenever Dru needs me. When I'm not doing my thing. And since Dru and Brad are giving me a place to stay at Old Lady Douglas's house, it works. For now. You know about *for now*, right. The way you told Dru and me you'd be back that night Mom and Dad moved you out. You said leaving was just for now. No worries. You wouldn't forget about us."

He nodded, promising himself he'd make it up to her somehow. Then he noticed the stains under the nails of one of her hands, a smudge on the back of the other.

"You're painting?" He smiled, surprised after the choice she'd made about her scholarship.

She shrugged. "When I'm not working or taking classes at the community college."

She'd enrolled in general business courses mostly. It was nowhere near what she should be doing with her talents. But at least she'd stayed close to home while she tried to figure out what all foster kids had to at too young an age—what their life would become after the system said they were grown.

Last he'd heard, Bethany hadn't painted in years. It looked like her passion to create had finally trumped her fear of never being good enough. She glanced to the framed painting on the wall beside them. He needed only a second to understand why.

"It's beautiful," he praised.

The landscape was of a field just outside of town. He remembered the place vividly. The scenery and the tree at the center of the painting—he was guessing it was a watercolor, but what did he know?—was an old oak with sprawling, ancient limbs that he and Selena used to sneak away to. Their senior year, they'd hung out under it for hours at a time after ditching Brad and Travis and Dru. Selena would bring an ancient quilt to lie on, and they'd stare up at puffy white clouds and bright sunlight, or at stars and a soft, winking moon. They'd talk and make love and drink . . . and then make love some more, keeping the rest of the world out for as long as they could.

He turned back to his sister. "You've gotten really good."

She stared at the floor.

"Bethie?"

"Don't call me that." She slung the rag she'd been using over her shoulder. "My big brother called me that. The guy who would have e-mailed or written or sent up smoke signals, so we'd know he was still alive.

"I'm sorry."

He'd let his work keep him from his family. He'd told himself that was okay. Like he'd believed letting Selena go free and clear was the right thing to do. He hadn't needed Travis to tell him he'd blown it on both accounts. But talking it through with his brother last night had solidified a few things in Oliver's mind.

"I really am sorry for how long it's been," he said. "I wish I'd gotten to see you finish growing up. You're even more beautiful than before."

Bethany wrinkled her nose, doubting him and herself.

"I wish . . ." She studied him through choppy bangs the color of grape soda, as if he were a detail for one of her paintings. "I wish it hadn't been so long, too."

"Yeah . . ." And he had no idea how long he could stay this time. Or how many more chances he'd have to make things right. "I've screwed up a lot, Bethie. But I wanted to become something more than another statistic—another kid who washed out of foster care and then trashed his life. I owed Marsha and Joe better than that."

"You were never trouble to me, even after you stayed gone for so long. I . . . I always hoped you'd come back."

"I never forgot you. Any of the family. I was just . . ." How did Oliver say it without saying too much? His beautiful, talented sister deserved her own second chance, as many chances as he could give her, without thinking she owed him anything because of whatever part of it he'd bankrolled. "I was needed . . . elsewhere."

He stalled out at the sadness on her face.

Bethany glanced down at her paint-splattered boots. "Dru seemed a little freaked this morning. It isn't just about Dad, is it?"

"No."

"She won't tell me what's was going on."

"I can't either yet." He'd give anything to not be keeping even more secrets from her.

Bethany eased away, freshly wounded. "I'm pretty much finished out there. I guess I better get."

And before he could stop her, she raced out the Dream Whip's front door.

"Damn it." He headed behind the front counter, pushing through the swinging doors to the industrial kitchen beyond.

Dru was prepping what looked like a batch of the chicken salad that had been a Whip crowd-pleaser as far back as when she and Oliver were kids. He stopped several feet away from her stainless steel work station, expecting her to be pissed after Bethany's warning.

Dru smiled instead, pointing her chopping knife at him. She pinned Oliver with one of her *tell me everything* stares.

"Spill," she demanded.

"You just left Selena there with her mom?" Dru asked after Oliver had recapped yesterday's misadventure at the Rosenthal house.

"What was I supposed to do once Belinda showed up?"

"What happened to all that fancy talking you do with your clients, to get them to throw money at you when they need something fixed? You need to *fix* this, Oliver."

"I tried."

"Who cares if Belinda was there?"

He'd cared. He'd damn near trampled the woman racing out of her house.

"She's scary," he fessed up.

"She's a pushover these days where Selena and Camille are concerned, everyone can see that."

His sister looked exhausted. But she was calm. She was definitely a little freaked—it was there in her eyes and the rapid-fire chop-chop-chop of her knife. But she was studying Oliver with a cool confidence that he could no longer feel about any of this.

"Mom's been obsessed with Selena and Camille, too," she said. "Does that mean you're going to run from Marsha, too, the next time she walks into a room?"

"Of course not. I just thought everyone could use a little space yesterday afternoon."

"Everyone?"

"Okay, *I* needed space." Selena didn't know who her daughter's father was. And worse, she didn't want to know.

"A man who needs space doesn't march into a woman's house and demand she tell him whether or not he's her sperm donor."

"I didn't want to . . ." What? Start making out with Selena again, right in front of her mother? "I wasn't going to make more trouble between Selena and Belinda than I'm sure I already have."

"Trouble?"

His sister lifted her hand, chopping blade pointed up. She wiped her bangs out of her face with the back of her wrist.

"Let me get this straight," she said. "You stared at Selena across the hedge like a ghost the other morning and intimidated her until she couldn't speak to you. Then you botched things at the hospital when she came to visit Dad. But you thought cornering her in her mother's home yesterday about Camille's paternity, while the poor kid's sick down the hall, might avoid trouble? Haven't you learned anything about women?"

"Apparently not."

"Then when Belinda showed up, you bounced, like you and Selena are still teenagers, and you'd been caught canoodling or something."

He spun an onion on the counter instead of responding.

"Oliver?"

Damn it. He needed to talk to someone about it. Someone *not* his mother. Or Travis, who'd gotten an earful about everything else. But he'd never have let Oliver live it down, how Oliver had practically had his hands up Selena's skirt the first chance he'd gotten her alone.

"I left," he said, "mostly because just before Belinda showed up, Selena and I were kissing. And even after her mother got there, I wanted to . . ."

"Get you some more of that?"

Oliver shook his head at his sister. "It wasn't like that."

But if Selena had been there in the kitchen—Dru or no Dru—he'd have wanted to touch and taste and feel her melt all over him again. She'd been liquid fire in his arms.

His sister set her knife down. "You kissed her?"

"It just happened." He sounded ridiculous.

"While you grilled her about Camille?"

"I wasn't grilling her."

"So she was willing to talk about her daughter's paternity?"

"No. But—"

"Then you were grilling her."

"I was asking her to work with me on this, with our family, with you and Brad."

"And she was angry about it."

"You don't know that."

"I know women. She was angry and probably scared and feeling off balance and defensive. And instead of giving her some space before her mother showed up, you—"

"Kissed her and scared her even more." Except for the few moments when she'd been open and giving and loving and wanting. She'd been his Selena again. "I don't know what the hell I was thinking."

"Of course you do." Dru rounded the counter and gave him a hug. And it felt good. Solid. Like old times. Except that now his sister was looking a little too closely at him for comfort.

She let the silence stretch between them and got back to working on the celery that would join the baked chicken she'd diced. She was waiting him out, like their mother did.

"You warned me seven years ago," he finally said, "to be careful with Selena. Even then you thought I was scaring her—or something was. I wish I'd had you nattering that in my ear yesterday."

"I don't natter. I talk reasonably about things. And I don't care how many times my fiancé accuses me of going on and on. I'm an adult now, and adults don't natter."

"You're a downright gorgeous adult," Oliver corrected.

She grinned her approval at his remembering her reprimand when they'd talked at home. "You're not imagining it."

She scooped chopped celery into the metal mixing bowl that held the chicken. Scraps were discarded into the waste bin at the end of the stainless steel counter, into a different container from the one that had received the unwanted poultry parts.

When he'd walked into the kitchen, the bowl had already contained mayonnaise, boiled eggs, and red onion. He watched her add spices next and stir everything together with an enormous metal spoon, its handle half the length of her arm. Then came the plastic wrap, rolled from what looked like a ten-pound box. She covered the mixture with brisk, controlled movements, storing it on a shelf in the industrial cooler. Then she collected everything that needed cleaning and dumped it in one sink. She washed and dried her hands in another, untied her apron and draped it over the sink's edge.

When he still hadn't said anything, she gave him her full, frustrated attention. "Look, let's just cut to the chase. I love you. I love Brad. I'll love Camille, just like Marsha and Joe will, if she's ours. All that leaves for us to discuss is whether in the last seven years *you've* learned how to really let yourself love someone, the way Selena and Camille will need you to."

"Wow." Brad must not have known what hit him. "Did you know before I told you? About Camille?"

"No. I still don't, and neither do you. And now you've made us getting to the bottom of that harder than ever." Dru pressed her palms to the counter. "Mom's pretty worried about Dad."

Oliver blinked. The zigzag shift in topics made it impossible for him not to pull his sister into his arms again.

"We're all worried," he said.

"Are you talking to Selena just because of Mom and Dad?"

. . . whether in the last seven years you've learned how to really let yourself love someone . . .

"Marsha and Joe were a lot of it at first."

"But not all of it?"

Not even close.

Not after holding—kissing—Selena again. Not after speaking to Camille. Not after seeing Bethany and talking with Travis and Dru and Brad. After accepting that coming back home had never been simply just checking on his dad. Oliver had needed all of this, all of them, for months. For years, whether he'd seen it or not. So much that at the moment what he *seriously* needed was a drink, something cold and biting and mind-numbing, to help him forget the rest of what he was feeling: panic and the absolute certainty that he was going to let everyone down again.

"I need to know . . ." he admitted. "I need to know that you're going to be okay. You and Brad, and Mom and Dad. But if Camille's mine, I need her in my life . . . somehow." No matter how hard her mother fought to push him away. "If she's not, I don't want Brad to lose having her in his. Or yours. If she's family, then—"

"She's ours." Dru stepped back. "My advice? Don't make what you do next about anyone but you and Selena. Dad's rallying. He'll get through this. Mom'll hold herself and everyone else together like she always does. Brad and I are going to be fine.

There's a part of me that's still a little pissed at Selena and what she did. But what I think about her or any of the rest isn't important. You need to do what's right for *you* this time, Oliver."

"I don't want anyone getting hurt again."

"That's a pretty unrealistic goal, wouldn't you say?"

"I'll get things under control."

Dru snorted. "Good luck with that."

Oliver ran a hand through his hair. "I'll figure something out."

She checked her watch and winced. "I have a staff meeting in a half hour."

"You have a staff? I've been running my own business for five years, and I've never had a staff."

"Stick with me, kid. I'll get you to the bigs." She placed a palm over his heart, her engagement ring flickering like living fire. "Wanting Selena and Camille for yourself is a good thing, Oliver. Don't worry about me."

"I'm sorry about all of this," he said.

"I'm sorry you've missed so much time with everyone." His sister's gaze was steady. Her forgiveness, solid. "And from what I hear, you might not have much time to set things right with Selena before you miss even more."

"And you've heard . . . ?"

Dru backtracked to the sink to deal with the dishes. "Gossip mostly. The Whip is an epicenter for the stuff. I'm never sure what to believe. Talk to Selena again. Get the real story from her."

"Selena's not speaking to me."

"You had her talking yesterday. Get back on that horse, Oliver, and stay on this time."

"You stretching the musketeer metaphor a bit."

Dru ignored his sarcasm. "No Belinda."

"I can work with that."

"*No* kissing."

He avoided her gaze.

"You know I'm right," she pressed.

He did. He also knew his chances were slim to none of *not* being all over Selena the next time he saw her.

"You've got to smooth things over," Dru said.

"Smoothing things over is my day job."

"Then saddle up and get to work."

His cell phone rang before Oliver could respond. He pulled it from his pocket and saw Marsha's name on the display.

"This has to be about Dad." He hugged his sister to his side and answered the call. "Hey, Mom. I'm at the Whip. What's up?"

"My name is Oliver," he announced to the room that evening. "And I'm an alcoholic and an addict."

After talking with his mom over the phone, taking care of Teddy all day, then visiting his dad at the hospital while his sister spelled Oliver again at home instead of getting her afternoon off, he'd officially hit the wall.

Joe's spirits were still high, though the angio had sapped even more of his energy. And now he was due back in surgery—later that night if Kask could line up a surgical team and an OR. There hadn't been enough improvement in Joe's latest tests. Bypass was his best shot at recovery now. And Travis had taken one look at Oliver leaving their dad's CICU room and agreed to be at the house tonight—because Oliver had needed to be here.

"Hello, Oliver," replied the AA group gathered in a strip mall just outside the Chandlerville city limits.

Everyone met his gaze, patiently waiting for him to continue. Everyone, except for Selena.

She'd zipped through the doors at the last minute, after he'd caught sight of her barreling into the parking lot practically on two wheels. She'd parked her excuse for a car as far away from the meeting space as possible. He'd considered slipping out the back door and sparing her knowing he'd been there at all.

Except he'd been waiting to speak first, once the opening business of the meeting concluded. He was there to work his program. To cling to his commitment to stay clean. Selena, presumably, was dealing with her own sobriety in an equally responsible way. And she didn't need him to look out for her anymore. She'd made that clear enough. Now she had her coffee and was sitting at the back of the room, making eye contact with no one. Not since she'd heard his voice and realized he was there.

"I'm only in town for a visit," he continued. "My father's having health problems that got a lot worse today. My family needs my help more than ever. Plus there's a lot more going on than my dad possibly . . . dying." Oliver clenched his fists. "I'm not coping with things nearly as well as I should be. And the last time I felt this way and didn't take care of it by working my program, I found myself at the bottom of a bottle of pills, wondering if I'd screwed up everything that was important to me for the second time in my life."

Selena looked up, the honesty he might never have been able to give her one-on-one connecting them across a roomful of strangers.

"Alcohol," Oliver continued, "was how I destroyed my best shot at a normal childhood. I haven't had a drink since I was nineteen. I've made something of myself. I had everything in my life exactly the way I wanted it. Then two years ago I chose taking prescription drugs over dealing with things that most days I still don't want to deal with. I relapsed. Hard. I thought I'd fully recovered from that. The last few days . . . it's clear I haven't."

He took a breath, felt the light-headedness of too little sleep and escalating stress. He saw again the downright frightened look on Travis's face a few hours ago, when Oliver had nearly lost it in the CICU hallway.

"The meds were legally prescribed. I saw them as necessary, to keep me working harder and faster at an impossible job I do better than most anyone. My career is who I've become. It's how I take care of people. Modifying my workload was out of the question. Time off meant letting people down. Stimulants kept me going, on my feet and functioning. They very nearly trashed my life. I almost blew a contract for a client who could have shot my reputation in the industry. I nearly destroyed my chance to make up for my hell-raising youth to my family. But . . ."

He thought about what Travis had said. And Dru. And Selena. Oliver looked her way again. Made sure he still had her attention.

"I'm starting to wonder if that's not what I wanted from the start. If my relapse was somehow my excuse to come home. At least close enough to home to feel a little more of it, to want a little more of it, until I got my chance to dive all the way back in. My dad's health crisis means I'm needed here, not just at work. I get this town back. People care about me here. And maybe I'm letting myself really take that in for the first time."

He saw tears in Selena's eyes. That's when he realized his gaze was wet, too.

"At least," he said to her, "that's what I've been figuring out the last few days. I've made amends with people I didn't think I'd ever see again. My rehab counselors tried to talk me into doing that from the start. My family's wanted me back for years. But I knew . . . somehow I knew how hard it would be to come home, and then return to the work I do. And my family will be needing the money my business generates even more now. Especially when it's looking like . . ."

He kept his attention focused on Selena, which kept him going.

"I don't know when my dad will be able to work again. If he'll be able to. So I'll work my ass off instead. No problem. That's who I am. Except that will mean leaving him again. All of them . . ." Oliver cleared his throat. "So an hour or so ago, while I was talking with my dad, and I was scared out of my mind by how old and fragile he looked, I found myself thinking how easy it would be to stop by the pharmacy on the way out of the hospital and have a backup prescription for stimulants refilled. So I'd have a pill, maybe two or three—no more than a half dozen or so—to get me through this. Just while I'm home. Just while I'm starting back to work."

Selena wiped her eyes with the back of her hand. So did he. And then she did the most remarkable thing. She smiled, and she nodded, supporting him the way he'd once tried to be there for her.

He smiled back, to let her know how grateful he was. He took a deep breath, the knot lodged in the center of his chest loosening a little.

"And that's when I knew I had to be here. Because I can't help the people I care about if I don't take care of my sobriety first. I'm no good to my dad or anyone if I'm high."

Heads all over the room nodded, strangers, brothers and sisters he'd never met. And Selena, even though she still looked as if she might sprint back out to her car.

"I have things in my life that are more important," he said directly to her, "than a few hours of escape, or convincing myself that feeling nothing is the only way for me to get through this. So I'll stay clean today. Tonight, when my dad's back in surgery. Tomorrow. Whatever happens, I'll figure out where I need to be for my family and the people I care about—and I'll make sure I'm there for them." Remembering what his brother and sister and his rehab counselors had said, he added, "I'll make sure I'm there for myself."

With the audience clapping their support, he stepped away from the folding table that the meeting coordinator, a local businessman named Walter Davis, had set up with fliers and other paperwork. It also served as a makeshift lectern. He shook Walter's hand and took a seat on the front row of olive-green plastic chairs that looked to be seventies-era castoffs. A man Walter had introduced as Law Beaumont occupied the seat beside him.

A decade or so younger than Walter, a few years older than Oliver, Law's handshake earlier had been firm, his energy intense but steady. He'd said he was recently married to the Chandler Elementary principal, which meant he likely knew Oliver's family the same as almost everyone else in the room. The anonymity of AA only went so far in a small town.

Law glanced over his shoulder toward the back. "Friend of yours?" he asked softly.

"Not exactly, no." Oliver fixed his attention on the next person from the crowd of twenty or so who'd walked to the front of the room.

Law leaned in. "She's here pretty regular, but no more than once a week. If that's going to be a problem, check with Walter. He'll have a line on other meetings for however long you're in town."

Oliver nodded his thanks and crossed his arms, tuning in to the new speaker's sobriety story. Except a part of him knew that Selena never got up, never moved. And that he couldn't let her slip away again, not without trying to fix at least part of what he'd bungled yesterday.

The meeting wound down. Walter invited people to stick around as long as they wanted, to grab something to drink or eat from another folding table sporting a coffee maker, bottled water, and a couple of bakery boxes from Dan's filled with assorted pastries. If anyone needed a sponsor, there was a designated place across the room to deal with that, too. The smoking area was the alley out back.

A blur at the edge of Oliver's vision told him that Selena was on the move. He pushed his way through the crowd—ignoring several people offering a handshake or a welcome—and out the front door into the balmy night. He caught up to Selena as she reached her car.

"I didn't know you'd be here," he said, winded from sprinting across the parking lot.

"I believe you." But she kept her back to him.

Inserting her key, she unlocked the sedan that appeared to be someone's Frankenstein approach to melding three, maybe four, different makes into one. The faded green paint on the trunk screamed at the different tints of blue that covered the rest. The two tires he could see didn't match. Neither did the chrome on the front bumper and the faded metal on the fenders. From the way it sat, tilted slightly on its axles, someone had wrecked the poor thing more than once.

"Talk to me." Oliver stopped her from opening the driver's door, his hand catching it near the top of the window. "Damn it. Just stand here with me for a minute. Help me figure some of this out."

She dropped her head and rolled her shoulders, supple muscles flexing beneath the deep red T-shirt she'd thrown on over tight jeans. Travis had said she was a runner, too. Every morning on the weekends. Damn, Oliver would give anything to see that. A sophisticated city girl turned and stared straight into him, wearing black, square-heeled boots. She planted her palm in the center of his chest and shoved him out of her personal space.

"Figure what out?" she asked.

"Hell if I know." He kept his hands to himself by burying them in the back pockets of his jeans.

"I don't want to do this in public, Oliver."

"You don't want to do it at all. You're never going to want to, and this is the most privacy we're likely to get for a while. I don't know when I'll have another break at the house, now that Dad . . ."

"What's happened with Joe?" She brushed his arm, her touch loving, her expression concerned.

Oliver closed his eyes. "He needs a bypass, as soon as possible. I came here straight from the hospital."

"I'm so sorry. Your family . . ."

"We'll be fine."

That Oliver had no doubt about, with or without his help. Look at how they'd all been pulling together to support him the last few days. Nothing kept the Dixons down, or stopped them from taking care of their own.

"But it's going to be a rough go of it for a while," he admitted. "And I don't know what I'm going to do if Joe doesn't . . ."

He simply couldn't say it.

"I'm glad you had a meeting to come to." Selena's touch dropped away.

"Travis's friend Walter was pretty stand-up about it, meeting me at the door and smoothing the way. I had no idea that you . . . How long have you been in AA?"

"Pretty much since I left town." She scanned the quiet parking lot and then the star-shot sky overhead. "So far, my sobriety is one of the few things I don't think the general public around here is keeping tabs on. I'm betting that's going to change if you don't let me get in my car and drive out of here."

Oliver's fingers closed around her toned forearm instead. "It wasn't my intention to ambush you tonight. Or at Belinda's yesterday. I only wanted to get things out in the open and talk. But when I saw Camille up close, and she . . ." He forced himself to focus. "Can we give this another shot? I'm usually a lot better at dealing with people's difficult issues."

"That's what your website says. No computer problem's too big or too broken for you to fix. You find a way to deal with one client's difficulties, then you move on to someone else's."

His website? "You've been googling me."

"No." Embarrassment pinkened her cheeks. "A little. Not much. Marsha said something to my mom about how proud she and Joe were of you. I may have . . ."

"Internet stalked me?

"Once or twice." Selena shoved soft, sleek hair behind her ear. "Besides, you positively reek of it now."

"What?"

"Success. Control. Business. Everything about you—except your deplorable wardrobe—says you're at the top of your game. A player to be reckoned with, running your own company. Not that I'm surprised as much as some people will be when word spreads. When I saw you the other morning I would have guessed you'd landed on your feet even if I hadn't already known part of your story. I've been around enough of you."

"Enough of who?"

"Corporate types. Movers and shakers. I can recognize one from a hundred paces, long before he throws a Hello Kitty Frisbee over my head. You're eaten up with it, even if you look like you've slept in your clothes for three days. I bet you dominate whatever business environment a problem draws you into. And now your difficult issue is my daughter and dealing with her."

"For my family's sake."

"I was inside just now. I heard how hard all of this is for you. Being home and leaving again soon. I'm assuming learning about Camille—maybe being a dad and not knowing what to do about it—is part of what's thrown you for enough of a loop to need a meeting tonight."

"Okay. It's personal for me. But I have my family to think about, too. And I know you're worried about them, or you wouldn't have avoided my folks for two months, or have looked so guilty at the hospital when you finally visited them."

Selena gazed over his shoulder to where the meeting was still going on. "The fact that Camille exists doesn't mean our worlds have to be karmically linked forever. I never meant to hide her from your family. It wasn't a conscious decision. I never thought I'd come back. Everyone was living their lives . . ."

"But you did come back."

"Shit happens, Oliver. We were supposed to have been long gone by now."

"Yet you stayed." And that reality seemed to be messing with her as much as him. "It scares me, too, Selena. I still don't know how to wrap my head around what family means. Or what it doesn't. But . . . I don't want to just run again, not until I've figured some of this out."

Selena squinted up at him. "I'm happy you want to give Chandlerville and your family a second chance to be in your life. But you don't know if you can actually go through with that, do you? And I'm terrified of what that might mean for my daughter."

"I'm just asking for a chance," he pressed. "Hear me and my family out—the way you listened to me inside. You've always been able to see me, understand me, like no one else could. Do that again, Selena. I'm not a bad guy. I'm not out to hurt you or Camille, and neither is my family."

She seared him with her disbelief. "Are you telling me you could rock your world and be a hands-on father if Camille is yours? Because unless you can, I'm trying—I've been trying since Tuesday—to understand how there's anything but heartache ahead for my daughter if we take her down this path."

"Having Marsha and Joe as grandparents would be a good thing for Camille," he hedged. "Look how happy she is with Belinda."

"She needs consistency."

"Then give her that in Chandlerville."

"Because surrounding ourselves with this town and our families worked out so well for the both of us when we were kids? My mother just announced that she kicked my father out twenty years ago, instead of him leaving on his own. Clearly my childhood was going to be messed up from the get-go."

"That doesn't mean Camille will have the same experience."

"No. But being a part of either of our families doesn't necessarily mean she'll be happy."

"She deserves as much family as we can give her, even if—"

"*We?* You and me? Or me and your family, once you're out of the picture again? Once we tell Camille she has a father and let her know you that way, and then you disappear from her life. She's already known one man who couldn't be bothered to be a real parent to her. She doesn't need another."

"What if Brad's her father?" Oliver felt the possibility twist in his gut.

"Do you want him to be?"

Selena's heart was in her eyes, every lost thing about her that Oliver had once thought he could save.

"See what I mean?" she said when he couldn't find his voice. "See how complicated this gets? You don't know what you're feeling yet. You don't know if you really want my daughter in your life. Or if you just want to not hurt anybody. And all *I* can think about is that you should be furious. All of you should be. And then I worry what that kind of messed-up dynamic could do to my daughter."

"A part of me was pissed at first," he admitted. "Stunned. And then angry again, for like a second, when I met you two out front of your mother's. And then I saw Camille's eyes . . ."

Selena collapsed against the side of the car. "A lot of people have green eyes."

He conceded her point, trying not to let the panic show—how thinking of Camille being Brad's felt like losing something infinitely precious, before it had even been his to begin with.

"I'm sorry about your dad," he said, wishing he could hold her and make her see that the last thing he'd ever want was for her daughter to feel anything but happy and secure. Things Selena had deserved to feel her entire life.

"Yeah," she said. "Me too." She fumbled with her tote bag's strap. "I'm sorry I didn't find a way to tell your family about Camille on my own."

"We need to talk. Brad and Dru and you and me, we need—"

She turned away and got her driver's door open with a screech. She tossed her bag inside. And then she slapped her palms on the roof of the car. Collecting herself, she faced Oliver again, a tough, confident woman.

"We what?" she asked.

"My father might be dying . . ." It wanted to explode inside Oliver—how close his family was to the incomprehensible. "He might have already missed meeting his first grandchild. If he recovers, we have to make sure he'll have that chance."

Oliver watched Selena swallow. Hard.

"Brad and Dru are getting married in a few months," he pressed. "My mother's got a houseful of kids and me—*me*—as her best fallback plan to keep Family Services satisfied until we know how things are going to shake out for the toddler my parents just signed on to foster. I have no experience with kids, a full-time job demanding my attention all over the globe—*if* I don't lose every potential client I have lined up because I can't schedule a damn thing with every minute of my day up in the air the way it is right now. And on top of it all, I'm dealing with maybe having a child of my own to be responsible for. I can't let any of it drop. I won't. I'll find a way to work through it all. And *we* can find a way to deal with Camille responsibly, if you'll let us try."

"My daughter is the best thing that ever happened to my life. She's not something to be dealt with. She's no one else's responsibility. I'm not going down that road again, Oliver, to feeling . . ."

"To feeling what?"

There was some big ugly still playing out between Selena and her estranged husband. Oliver was certain of it.

"Trapped." She choked out the word. "That's what you're telling me. Where my child is concerned, I'm trapped into doing what you want. Or I'll be depriving your parents of their grandchild."

"I'm telling you that you and your daughter already belong with my family, if you'll just find some way to trust that we have your best interest at heart. Are there some hurt feelings still? Sure. But we all made mistakes when we were kids."

He thought about Travis and Dru, his siblings' forgiveness, and how his parents had welcomed him back with open arms. Now there was one other person he needed to make amends to.

"When we were eighteen," he continued, "I pushed too hard for you to get better—for *me*—before you were ready to deal with your drinking for yourself. I made you feel abandoned. And I knew how messed up you still were about your dad leaving. I made you think that if you didn't do what I wanted, you'd have no one. And then I left you behind when it all imploded, just the way you were afraid I would. *I'm* sorry for that, Selena. I hope you can forgive me."

"I slept with your best friend, who may have gotten me pregnant." Self-loathing dripped from each word. "I didn't stick around long enough to even know I was expecting. And by the time I found out, the last thing I'd have considered was begging anyone in Chandlerville for help."

"You wouldn't have had to beg. You're among friends here. Family. A part of you must have believed that, or you wouldn't have come home again."

"I didn't have a choice."

"You wouldn't still be in town, you wouldn't be talking to me now, if you were really . . ."

"Scared? I'm terrified. Of all of you."

"Including your ex?"

Oliver wanted a few minutes alone with this Parker character, to explore exactly what had happened in New York. And no matter his intentions to just talk and nothing else, he wanted Selena in his arms again—to comfort and reassure both of them. To kiss and excite. To need and feel her craving him again.

But her gaze had grown haunted.

"The way I see it, you're fighting to get things right with Belinda so Camille will have a grandmother. So she'll feel safe and secure. Let her have my family to help with that, too. Let them be a good thing for her."

"Just them?" Selena asked, nailing him, demanding an honest response when he didn't have one. "What about you?"

What about him?

Was he a father or an uncle? It shouldn't matter which. But it did. It scared the spit out of Oliver, how much it did.

"I'll make this work" was all he could promise. "Whatever's best for everyone."

Selena looked . . . disappointed, and like she wanted to press the issue. But people were spilling into the parking lot. His and Selena's talk was about to become fresh fodder for the local gossips.

"I won't bother you at another meeting," he promised.

"But what about your program while you're home?"

"I'll find another place."

"You relapsed two years ago. It's been seven for me. I don't come all that often."

"You felt like you needed to be here tonight."

Selena laughed. "And whose fault was that?"

"This is your meeting. Don't worry about me."

"After what I just heard, I *do* worry about you."

Oliver stilled at her admission. The noise and bustle around them faded. A warm breeze blew a tendril of brown hair forward, over her shoulder. He longed to brush it away.

"I can skip for now," he insisted, "if—"

"No. You can't." Genuine concern. Soft eyes. With no effort at all, she blew through all his best intentions.

Oliver allowed himself to touch.

Her hair. The skin on her long, smooth neck above the scooped collar of her T-shirt. Just the tips of his fingers, sliding down to the pulse beating madly at Selena's throat, while he absorbed the wonder of her caring enough to berate him about his sobriety.

"Don't risk your own recovery for me," she pleaded, their mouths inches apart.

"I won't be responsible for you risking yours. You have no idea how proud I am of what you've accomplished." He hadn't meant to let this get personal. But the words kept coming. "You're healthy. You need to stay healthy for Camille. That's what's important."

"That will never change."

Tears glistened at his praise, making her eyes sparkle. She stood a little taller. Her attention dropped to his mouth, slid back up to his eyes.

"From the moment I realized I was pregnant," she said, "I stopped drinking. I found my first meeting. No matter what happens . . . I'll never go back."

"No, you won't. Neither will I. This is hard, I know. But we're both going to get through it sober."

She bit her bottom lip. Then, tentatively, she nodded, trusting him at least that much.

Oliver was proud of Selena's sobriety . . .

And he was touching her. Until his fingertips slid away, so gently she could have imagined them being there at all. Her body betrayed her, wanting to be closer, no matter the people trickling out of the meeting or the cars pulling out of the parking lot. She was flat-out desperate to lose herself in Oliver's commitment to make sure they kept each other healthy and on track.

She forced herself to step back, pressing against Fred's solid presence.

"Be proud of yourself," she insisted. "You're doing this for your family, remember? And we both know what happened the last time we tried to help each other."

He put even more distance between them. "I didn't mean that my family is all I care about. It's just . . . you're important to me, too, Selena. You always will be. And Camille. I'm trying to do what's right for everyone."

His halting admission melted away the last of her anger.

She should leave, before she said or did something more she'd regret.

The world had felt like it was closing in on her all day, while she stayed home with her daughter. The situation with the Dixons. Belinda's revelation. Camille's latest attack. The memory, every time she'd walked past the living room, of how right it had felt to be in Oliver's arms again. His oh-so-logical arguments about getting to the bottom of Camille's paternity. Parker's daily call, pressuring her again to come "home" to him. Her mother had been right. Selena had needed her meeting.

And still, she'd circled the shopping center twice before going inside. *After* she'd talked herself out of driving Fred until she had to fill up his tank. At a station miles away. Run by people she didn't know and would never see again. Strangers somewhere beyond Chandlerville who wouldn't think twice about a woman buying a six-pack and loitering in their parking lot while she drank it. Instead, she'd gotten herself together and made it here. Only to be standing with Oliver again, basking in how good it felt.

It was a slippery slope . . . One with razor-sharp edges that would slice her heart to ribbons if she kept remembering his kiss. Kept seeing him every time her daughter smiled. Kept fantasizing about making the Dixons and their perfect family a part of Camille's life.

"I'm afraid," she said. "Please don't ask me to make what my daughter's going through any harder than it is."

He stepped closer, him and all that tempting heat. "No one wants either of you to be afraid. Trust me not to let that happen. Meet with Brad and Dru and me. We'll figure out a next step that works for everyone." At Selena's disbelieving snort, he dug in. "Just think about it."

He sounded so reasonable, so grounded and responsible and genuinely concerned.

"I'm sorry for all of this," she heard herself say. She thought of what he'd shared inside. "You've been through so much already, and I—"

"I'm not sorry." He grinned at her disbelieving stare. "Okay, once or twice a day I'm desperate to fall off the face of the earth again, because all of this is so surreal."

"Oh, thank God!" She slapped her hand over her mouth to keep herself from giggling. "Thank *God* I'm not the only one who just wants this all to go away. Joe's heart attack, too. I hope he's going to be okay now that he's having a bypass. I really do."

"Yeah. I think worrying about him is part of why I handled yesterday so badly."

She eased a little closer, knowing she shouldn't. "And the other part?"

"I wasn't expecting it," he said. "How much I might want Camille to be mine . . . A daughter? That's a lot to process."

"You *might* want her?" Selena's heart sank. "You have to be sure, Oliver. For the right reasons. I know it's a lot to think about, being an instant dad. But you'll hurt her if you're not sure. No matter how much your family might love her, she'll want her dad, too."

"And Parker wasn't sure?"

"My marriage was a train wreck for a lot of reasons." Not the least of which was that from the start Selena had still been in love with someone else. "It didn't help that Parker saw being a father and a husband as a business asset more than a blessing. Camille was never really a factor in his life, neither one of us was, except for window dressing."

"So you got out?"

"Damn straight. And I'm not setting my child up for more disappointment."

Oliver's touch slid down her arm until they were holding hands.

"Give me a chance," he said, "to prove to you that I can handle this."

"You're good at it now, you know?"

He seemed surprised.

"Handling people." She remembered anew the boy he'd been and the mess they'd made of loving each other. Because her problems had been unfixable then, and he'd refused to accept it. "Negotiating. Maneuvering people, until you figure out how to solve their problems. You've gotten really good at it."

Oliver dug his hands into the back pockets of his jeans, cocking his hip in a bad-boy-done-good stance. "All I'm trying to maneuver you into is talking with my sister and her fiancé and me. Nothing more."

"Good. Because it's more that got us into trouble the last time."

She stretched onto her toes and kissed him softly. Because *more* of him was exactly what she needed before she headed home. He'd grabbed her yesterday while he was angry and frustrated. She couldn't bear that being her last memory of them together. And then she couldn't bear the thought of stopping . . .

He kept his hands in his pockets while she kissed him. But

his lips followed her lead. Then his tongue feathered across hers in a tentative way that had her shivering, seduced.

She eased back, remembering where they were and how many people might be witnessing her appalling lapse in judgment. And . . . she suddenly didn't care about any of it, not while she watched the wonder, the need, spreading across Oliver's face.

"We have to take one day at a time, right?" she warned. "That's what we come to meetings to remember."

"Focus on what we can control," he agreed. "Let go of what we can't." He cupped her cheek the way he had her daughter's. "Tell me you trust me, Selena."

Except she didn't. Or maybe she didn't trust herself with him. But she did absolutely believe he cared about what happened next to Camille. And her daughter deserved to know the Dixons were her family, somehow.

Her hands shaking, wishing she was already home reading her daughter a bedtime story and shutting out everything but Camille's love of fairy tales, Selena pulled her cell from her tote.

"I'll meet," she agreed. "Just to talk. Just the four of us. What day do you think would work?"

"Why don't you shoot me a text"—Oliver snatched her phone away—"once you check your schedule? I'll give you my number."

He typed in his contact information and handed back her cell.

"Text me your number and some dates," he prompted as she gaped at him. "I'll see when Brad and Dru can meet and let you know. Beyond that, I'd only use your number for emergencies. Scout's honor."

He'd never been a Scout.

But she remembered him saying his mother had wanted him to be one as a little boy. Always prepared, always considerate, and putting others first, never backing away from a challenge. Someone anyone could depend on. Exactly what he'd gone off and made himself into—at least for his clients.

She caught Oliver smirking at her sparkly Hello Kitty smartphone cover—the one Camille had picked out at a discount store. Selena texted him a vulgar suggestion, telling him what he could do with his opinion of her accessories. He read it out loud and laughed. Then he saved her in his contact list.

And it was done.

Just like that.

They were officially back in each other's lives.

"It's going to be okay this time," he promised.

She tried with all her heart to believe that she wasn't making an even bigger mistake with him than before.

Behind the wheel, she secured her seat belt as Oliver headed for his truck, tall and strong and in no hurry. Fred took his own sweet time getting with the program. She could feel Oliver waiting, watching while she turned the ignition three times before it caught. Oliver's headlights were already on, his truck's engine no doubt purring like a champ.

She pulled out of the lot, knowing he'd be behind her the whole way to Belinda's. He'd always gotten her home safely when they'd been kids, even that last year on the nights they'd been so reckless. Especially on those nights, Oliver had always made sure she was okay.

I'll love you forever, Selena, no matter what. I'm not like your dad. I'll never leave you . . .

Chapter Fourteen

Marsha stood apart from her family at just past ten that night.

Dru and Travis were on the other side of the waiting room that was designated for immediate families of surgical patients. Marsha had asked for a few minutes to herself. She couldn't remember the last time being in the company of her children didn't bring her comfort. But tonight, feeling them close while their father was being wheeled into surgery made it impossible for her to focus on anything but what could be lost to all of them if Joe's heart took another turn for the worse.

Somewhere in the bowels of Chandler Memorial, in some sterile operating room, a surgical team was preparing to crack her husband's chest open. They'd stop his heart. A machine would circulate blood and oxygen through his body, circumventing his lungs. The damage threatening Joe's life would be repaired—a procedure that would last for hours, perhaps until morning. And then he would be taken off bypass, and they'd wait, Dr. Kask had explained, to see *if* Joe's heart would start beating again on its own.

There was every reason to believe all would go well. Patients successfully recovered from open-heart surgery all the time.

Except that there had been a lot of blockage. And Joe's system was weak already. *And* there were no guarantees with any procedure, Kask had been careful to explain again in pre-op.

And that's when Joe had taken Marsha's hand, when a nurse had been administering the early anesthesia into his IV, to help him relax.

"It's going to be fine," he'd said. *"You'll see. Make sure you help the kids see."*

She would, she'd promised. And she'd been so glad to hug on Dru and Travis when she'd walked into the waiting room and seen them there. She'd been grateful Joe had seen Oliver earlier today, too. But what if . . . The *what if*s were driving her out of her mind.

She couldn't get warm. She couldn't think about anything but the feel of her husband's fingers curled around hers, his brave smile as he'd drifted to sleep, and then her absolute terror when he'd been wheeled away, that she might never have him in her life again. She wouldn't, she absolutely couldn't, let her kids see her this way.

Despite the late hour, people from the community were downstairs in the main lobby, or sitting with their coffee or tea in the cafeteria. Folks had been calling since word spread about the bypass. Friends and neighbors she and Joe had known for decades. And it should have been a blessing.

But Marsha couldn't face them either, wondering if by morning she might be greeting everyone for the first time without her husband, her life forever changed.

She stared out the waiting room windows, three stories up from the streetlights and trees below. She rubbed her hands up and down her arms, trying to ward off the chill. Movement out of the corner of her eye startled her, before a reflection in the windows showed her who had come to stand beside her.

"Oh."

Marsha wiped at her eyes. She turned to Belinda Rosenthal.

"How . . ." she stuttered. "How did you get up here?"

Belinda smiled. "I told the nurses I was family, and that I wasn't leaving until they let me see you."

"Oh." Marsha tried to find the energy to be shocked.

But nothing was penetrating the images and descriptions of open-heart surgery she'd searched for online, on the tablet Dru had brought over days ago so Marsha had digital books to read while Joe slept.

Belinda inched closer. "I made sure no one else could hear when I talked with the nurses. Plenty of rumors are already flying around about our kids. People have seen them together enough to wonder what's going on. I wouldn't want to add to that. But I know a little more than my daughter's thought about her and Oliver . . . and Camille. And I wanted you to know, especially tonight, that I'd be proud to have Oliver be Camille's father, if that's where we find ourselves. I've had my misgivings. I guess a part of me still does. Selena is in such an unsettled place right now. And I worry about Camille . . . but your son seems to have become a fine man."

"Yes, he has." Gratitude flooded Marsha for the effort Belinda was making. Their families had lived next to each other for decades. Belinda was as active in the community as her job allowed. Well respected. Considerate. But reaching out one-on-one had never been her strength.

"What's it like?" Marsha asked.

"What?"

"Being a grandmother. This will be my first time."

Belinda smiled again. "It's the most wonderful thing in the world. And the hardest. Thinking about Selena and Camille leaving as soon as my daughter can manage it, them being somewhere else where I can't help them with their troubles anymore . . . that's hard. My daughter's just starting to get comfortable with us being in each other's lives again. We're getting past all the misunderstandings and mistakes—mostly mistakes I made. I'll never be able to thank her enough for giving me this chance to know Camille. To love my granddaughter all the ways Selena never thought I could love her when she was little."

"You've always loved your daughter with your whole heart. The best way you knew how." Marsha turned back to the windows, both of them looking out now. "Healthy kids want their independence, even when their troubles are piling up. Some leave. Some stay. You'll always miss them, and you can't let them know how much. But if you love them unconditionally, they'll find their way home again."

"I missed her every day she was gone. When she finally called, I couldn't let her see how much. Maybe I should have, but I didn't want her feeling guilty for going off on her own."

"It's hard not to think you've done something wrong. All the time Oliver was out of our lives . . ."

"You and your husband give your kids the chance to be themselves, find themselves. And because of you, look at what Oliver's become."

"He's done that with his own hard work."

"Because you encouraged him," Belinda insisted. "And you've never given up on him. He's still figuring things out. I guess we all are. But you gave Oliver a solid start, even if it took some tough love."

"And you've done the same for Selena."

Belinda stared out at the night, as if she didn't know what to believe.

"We love our kids," Marsha said. "Even when they make it hard to. Even when they don't know how to—"

"Trust us?" Belinda was rubbing her own arms. "I've given Selena so many reasons not to."

"And a world of proof that she can. Especially these last few months. She's stayed, Belinda. She and Camille are still here."

"I've wondered for a long time about Camille's father," Belinda finally said. "I promised myself not to push Selena to take me into her confidence. I've learned at least that much with her. But I wanted you to know . . . especially now. I'd be proud if it turns out that our families are connected in such a wonderful way. And I wanted to say how sorry I am. You've missed precious time with Camille. Maybe I could have helped with that, if things between my daughter and me weren't so strained."

"Joe and I understood. When we began to suspect ourselves, we understood why you needed to keep your distance. Selena has to believe she can count on you first. That Chandlerville and your house are a safe place. I think she's starting to. My husband and I will have our time with Camille."

Marsha could feel it growing again. The certainty. The confidence that she'd get the chance to share this wonderful beginning moment with Joe—like they'd shared so many other new starts.

Belinda was finally opening the lines of communication about Selena and Oliver and Camille. *This* was hope. This was good. This was the sweet promise that came from friends and family caring for one another.

"You have nothing to be sorry for," Marsha told her neighbor. "Joe and I have admired you from the moment you moved in next door and started transforming that yard of yours into a botanical paradise that would put to shame any of those fancy gardens in Atlanta. You've put everything you have into every-thing you do, including loving your daughter and now your granddaughter. We'd be proud to have you as a part of our fam-ily. Not that we don't already know how lucky we are to have you living next door."

Belinda looked positively stricken for a second. And then Marsha was engulfed in a tight, determined, very un-Belinda-like hug.

"Your husband's going to get to know his granddaughter one day very soon," Belinda insisted as Marsha slipped an arm's length away. They clasped each other's hands. "And my garden club is going to throw Joe a fantastic Father of the Year party just as soon as he's up to it. You wait and see."

"How are you feeling?" Selena asked the sleepy angel she'd come home to after AA.

"Better." Camille yawned, stretching in her bed, a flower opening to the sun. She turned her cheek for a kiss.

Selena obliged. "I'm sorry I was late getting home."

"That's okay. I don't mind." Camille scooted over as Selena snuggled in beside her. "'Cept I'm hungry, and Grammy said I had to wait and ask you if I can have a snack."

Selena propped herself against the wall behind the single bed she'd slept in her entire childhood in this house. Her daughter was already drooping back into her pile of pillows.

"You don't exactly sound hungry," Selena said.

"How do I exactly sound?"

Selena smiled. "Like you want an excuse to stay up now that I'm here."

"But dinner was a long time ago." Camille yawned again. "And Grammy only gave me soup and crackers."

"Your stomach's still grumpy from yesterday. And Grammy's homemade soup is yummy."

"But I want one of Mrs. Dixon's cookies. You said I could."

"When you were feeling better. Maybe tomorrow for breakfast."

"Grammy won't mind me having cookies for breakfast?"

"We'll sucker her in," Selena conspired with a wink. "We'll bribe her with a cookie of her own."

"Grammy never eats cookies. I don't like being sick," Camille groused. "I hate it."

Selena watched her daughter rub sleepy eyes with tiny fists.

"Me too, Cricket." Yet saying Camille's nickname made Selena smile, same as always.

Her daughter had loved being outdoors practically from birth, playing in every park Selena took her to in Manhattan. She'd been mesmerized by the grass and the trees and the birds and breeze from the moment she could crawl out of Selena's lap and explore. Before Camille could walk or run or dance as she did everywhere she went now, she'd hop up and down, in her baby carriage, in Selena's arms, clapping her hands whenever they'd left behind the high-rise apartment Parker kept atop one of the oldest residential buildings near Central Park.

It had always made Selena wish that her daughter had more room to run and play, in a place where nature didn't have to battle for its existence between towering buildings and avenues of endless concrete and traffic jams. Somewhere like Chandlerville.

"One cookie?" Camille begged. "Please, Mommy?"

Selena held on a little tighter, relieved that her child felt well enough to wheedle. Camille's doctors had warned that each minor reaction to something increased the possibility of a more severe outcome.

"One cookie," Selena caved. A special treat. For a very special little girl. "*If* you can keep your eyes open long enough to eat it."

Camille beamed. Then her forehead crinkled in confusion. "Did Oliver have one before he went home yesterday?"

Selena shook her head, slowly finding her voice. "He left before he could. But I'm sure Mrs. Dixon has lots of cookies at her house."

Oliver's truck had pulled into the Dixon driveway as Selena let herself inside to face Belinda—who as it turned out had been dressed to go out. She'd left a few minutes ago.

"Whose father is Oliver looking for?"

"What?" Selena stared into her daughter's innocent eyes. Camille had felt too miserable to talk much since Oliver's visit.

"He wanted to know who someone's father was." Camille played with Bear's long bunny ears. "He was asking if you knew. If he's trying to help someone find their daddy, you should help, too. Everyone wants a daddy." She looked up at Selena. "Even if they have the best mommy and grammy in the world, and not every daddy is a good daddy, everybody wants one."

Selena hurt for the loneliness Camille hid so well most of the time.

The last year or two, Camille had zeroed in on any and every conversation about fathers she was around. She'd begun to pull away from Parker, on the rare nights he'd made time for her and Selena. She'd sensed on her own, no matter how much Selena had tried to cover for her husband, that being a father was a convenience for Parker, often a chore.

"I'm glad Parker's not my daddy." Camille cuddled with Bear and frowned, her attention zipping away from Oliver.

"I am, too, Cricket." Parker's chronic neglect of his personal life unless the timing suited his business interests would have continued to hurt Selena's little girl—regardless of whether Camille one day caught on to the host of other problems in Selena's marriage. "You deserve the best daddy there is."

Camille nodded enthusiastically. "I'm glad we're here, instead of New York still. Even Fred loves it here. He hasn't broken down once, the way you thought he would when we bought him. And Grammy's here. And I like my new school, and I like Mr. and Mrs. Dixon and their kids being next door, and now Oliver. New York wasn't nearly as much fun."

"I like being home, too," Selena admitted, even though she was terrified that her decision might end up hurting her daughter as much as marrying Parker had. "But we talked about Grammy's not being where we'll stay forever, right?"

The whole world was waiting for them, she'd told Camille when they'd headed to the Deep South. Life was theirs to conquer. They would find a home neither of them would ever want to leave again. Selena had just never contemplated Chandlerville being that place.

You're important to me, too, Selena. You always will be.

She looked around at the pink walls and pink shelves and pink little-girl desk that had been hers back in the day. At the Hello Kitty decorations all over the place—Selena's obsession when she'd been younger. Now it was her daughter's, too. Several of Belinda's hand-sewn quilts were draped over a chair and the foot of the bed. Camille had become fascinated with them. She'd fallen in love with all of it.

"We'll make you an even better room," Selena promised, "wherever we end up next."

"I want one like this one, pink everywhere, in a house, not an apartment, where there's lots of flowers outside my window and a backyard I can play in anytime and lots of nice people living next door and maybe even a puppy. Can we have a puppy, Mommy?"

Camille's ability to rebound, to zoom from the bad on to the next happy moment had become a lifeline for Selena. She pecked the tip of her daughter's nose with a kiss and smiled into pleading green eyes.

Every other time the topic of a pet had come up, Selena had wormed out of committing, not wanting to get Camille's hopes up. Not knowing if a pet would be possible wherever they moved next. But Camille being happy was the point of every change, every struggle, every week and then month Selena had worked herself into exhaustion since leaving Parker. So why was she holding back on something as simple as agreeing to a pet? She could make it work, just like she had whatever else her child had needed.

"Once you and me and Fred are settled, once we know we're not going to have to move ever again"—Selena brushed her fingers down Bear's bunny ears—"then we'll go out and find the cutest, floppiest-eared puppy we can."

"Really?" At Selena's nod, Camille pumped both fists in the air. "That's so cool. Yay!"

"Yay!" Selena cheered. "What will you call him?"

Camille's eyes rounded. "I get to decide?"

"He'll be yours."

"All mine?"

"You're a big girl now. You'll be a great mommy."

"Just like you." Camille threw herself into the happy, easy hug Selena had needed.

"Being a good mom's a cinch, when you're working with the right kid material."

"We'll find the right puppy, too. And I'll train her and"—just that quickly, their future pet was a girl—"she'll sleep with me on your old bed, and she'll play in Grammy's backyard. And . . ."

Selena felt her daughter catch herself. Camille slipped out of her arms.

"Or whatever backyard we have when we move," Camille said.

Selena wanted her happy hug back. She longed for the luxury of knowing for certain that the job next year at Chandler, and Kristen's offer to help Selena make night school work, would be the right decision for her daughter—for them. She wanted to trust Oliver's logic that they could all be one happy family once Camille's father had been identified.

And she actually wanted to talk through it all with Belinda. About whether Selena and Camille should stay in town for good. How to approach the rest of the Dixons after talking with Brad and Dru. How to end the secrets and limit the collateral damage and make things simple and calm and settled for everyone.

"We'll bring your puppy to meet Grammy as often as we can," she heard herself promise, the words slipping out and feeling right. "We'll make sure you get to sleep with your new puppy in my old bed, and play with her in Grammy's garden,"

Give me a chance to prove to you that I can handle this, Oliver had asked.

How on earth were they going to handle any of it?

Joe's bypass was happening tonight. Belinda had said as she headed to the hospital it was time she supported her neighbors in person. Oliver was next door with the Dixon kids, alone. Selena had heard Travis's cruiser pull away, presumably so he could be at the hospital with Marsha. While Selena found herself grappling with the absurd impulse to pop across the hedge once Camille was asleep.

"We'll do more puppy planning tomorrow," she said instead of indulging in the fantasy of kissing Oliver again. "Once—"

"Blossom!" her daughter exclaimed with another enthusiastic fist pump. "That's what I'll name my puppy."

Selena couldn't help laughing. "And what if the right puppy for us turns out to be a boy?"

Camille's forehead wrinkled.

Another kid might have shrugged the question off. But ever since Selena had explained her reasons for calling their heap of a car Fred and talked about the magic of names—including how Camille's had come from Selena's very favorite flowers in the world—her daughter had been fascinated with what each name she heard meant. Her expression suddenly brightened in triumph.

"And the winner is?" Selena knew she was in for a treat.

"Bud?"

Selena scooped her daughter close. "You're too good to be true, kiddo. 'Bud' it is. Now, let's get you that cookie and tuck you in for the night."

Selena stroked her daughter's soft hair and carried her to the kitchen, Camille's head resting on her shoulder.

It was a perfect moment. Since leaving New York, Selena had been determined to give her daughter as many of them as she could. Now Camille loved living with Belinda. And she was dreaming of a house and a puppy and a big backyard to play in.

Except every little girl wanted a daddy, she'd said. One who'd play with her and come home to her every night and make her feel like she was the center of his world. How did Selena explain to her daughter that there'd never be a family like that for her with her biological father? The way it never would have worked out for Camille with Parker.

Brad was marrying Dru soon. God willing, they'd have kids of their own. Oliver traveled the globe and worked 24-7 for his job. What about any of that wouldn't mean even more disappointment and heartache for Selena's little girl?

She settled Camille into a kitchen chair and kissed the top of her head. "Cookies and then bed. I want my favorite flower in fighting spirits tomorrow."

"Because no one waters Grammy's begonias better than I do?"

"You're the very best, Cricket." And Selena was making that house and yard and puppy and happy family of her daughter's dreams come true. "I don't know what I'd do without you."

Chapter Fifteen

Late Friday night, Oliver paced his mother's dimly lit kitchen with a sniffling Teddy in his arms.

He'd diapered the kid—he was a pro at it now, since the toddler seemed to take a dump every two hours. He'd given Teddy a late-night bottle, even though caving to it sat squarely in the Do Not Do column of Dru's two pages of instructions, pinned to the kitchen bulletin board. He'd read the boy a book and played a favorite nursery song on the battered kid-proof tape player that Teddy was supposedly addicted to. Nothing had worked.

Night four of Oliver's return to Chandlerville wasn't going to yield any more sleep than the other three. He suspected Teddy wasn't settling down completely until Marsha walked back through the front door for good.

"I know." He jostled a cranky Teddy up and down, thinking about whimpering himself. "You're getting a bum deal, man. I'd be kicking up a fuss, too."

It'll be another day at least before they'll move Dad to stepdown, Dru said when she'd called earlier. Oliver had seen Joe only once since the bypass, and his father had been asleep the whole time. *They're trying to regulate his heartbeat and pressure. He's having trouble breathing still. They're watching him for pneumonia. Mom said Kask's team is talking about possibly moving him to a rehab facility first, before he comes home . . .*

Oliver stroked Teddy's back. The boy's cries were softer. He rubbed his head against Oliver's shoulder. Teething was a bitch on little guys, from what Oliver had read online. Dru's advice for how to handle it? Oliver should make a night's worth of strong coffee. They hadn't spent enough time together yet for her to realize he'd sworn off the stuff. It wasn't as if he were sleeping, regardless.

A few hours ago, he'd sent the e-mail to kill Monday's client pitch with Canada.

"It's going to be okay, buddy," he said to the restless, drooling, inconsolable child in his arms. "We'll make everything okay."

"And here I figured you'd be long gone by now," a voice responded.

Oliver stared. Teddy lifted his head from Oliver's soaking wet shoulder and looked behind them both.

"Over here, dumb ass," the voice said again.

"What are you doing up?" Oliver asked Fin, a fourth-grader who according to Marsha had come to the family street-smart and world-weary and with some of the same attachment issues Oliver still struggled with.

She'd also said Fin was the one who'd first found Joe in the front yard having chest pains.

The boy grabbed milk from the fridge and a glass from the cabinet beside the sink. He poured, dropped into one of the high-backed stools at the kitchen's center island. When Oliver put down another glass, the kid filled his, too. Oliver downed half the milk before spilling most of the rest, when Teddy reached for the rim and tipped it almost completely over.

"Damn it!" Oliver thunked the glass to the counter and fumbled for a kitchen towel. He dabbed at Teddy first and, juggling the toddler, crouched to sop up the floor.

"Give him to me." Fin got off his stool. "It's not like I was sleeping anyway."

He grabbed a pacifier off the counter next to the toaster and plugged the baby's mouth. Teddy rewarded them with silence. He snuggled his head against Fin's neck, snuffling and suckling.

Oliver snapped his fingers. "Forgot about the pacifier."

"Don't you know anything about kids?"

Oliver tossed the soiled towel toward the laundry room, ignoring how it landed short, in the middle of the doorway. He leaned against the island and drained the rest of his milk in a single long gulp, the way he once would have a beer.

"Did you know how to take care of babies before Teddy came along?" he asked.

Fin sneered. When Teddy raised his head, Fin gave him a goofy grin. Teddy giggled, drool oozing out from around the pacifier.

Oliver patted the toddler's back. "You seem to be pretty good at it now. How long have you been here, anyway?"

"Like a year or something."

"I've had four days." Not even that, if you counted the distraction with Selena and Camille, and him visiting the hospital whenever someone could spell him at the house. "Wanna cut me some slack?"

"Why? It's not like you're staying. What do you know about anything around here?"

"I know that not sleeping sucks. And it usually helps me feel better to have someone else to chew on until the sun comes up. Me, I find subcontractors to argue with, because their coding's not working or they're not working fast enough or I want them working on something else. There's always someone to rant at when I need to sleep but can't. You"—he pointed at Fin with his empty glass—"evidently decided to come downstairs to gripe at me and hold the baby."

"Because you couldn't get Teddy to shut up."

"Or holding him calms you down." Oliver had been watching Fin's eyes grow drowsier the longer he had the toddler in his arms.

Fin promptly handed the baby back.

"I used to hang out with Dru sometimes," Oliver said before the kid could make it to the kitchen stairs. "We were both up a lot in the middle of the night. Or maybe I was up first, and she somehow knew it and didn't want me to feel alone."

"So?" Fin glared at him, his hand on the stair's railing.

"So, I haven't talked to Marsha about it, but if hanging with Teddy at night helps you sleep, it's okay by me. No one else has to know if that's what you're worried about."

The boy had come searching for his nighttime pal. Oliver was sure of it. While Oliver had done bed check the last two evenings, he kept finding toddler toys on the floor beside the bunk beds Fin shared with Gabe.

"I don't care if I'm alone at night," Fin scoffed. "I was alone for a long time before I came here. In a lot of places a whole lot worse than this dump. I don't need anyone else to be okay."

"But you're not alone now." Oliver deposited their glasses in the sink and filled them with water. "And neither is Teddy."

Fin eyed him with the instincts of a survivor who wasn't sure yet if he'd met a friend or an adversary.

"Does Teddy sleep better with you at night," Oliver asked, "when he's not feeling well?"

"Maybe. So?"

Oliver headed for the stairs. Walking the floors with Teddy for another night wouldn't be a hardship. He had too much on his mind to do more than think. But if he'd learned anything from the last four days of chaos, it was to follow his instincts with these kids the way he did with his computers.

"So." He handed over the toddler again. "Marsha and Dru both said to tuck Teddy in with me if he got cranky. But as you've so wisely pointed out, I don't know jack about kids. And you're an old pro, right? You and the rest of the house could use some peace and quiet. Tomorrow you can give me a crash course on—"

"Not being a total loser at babysitting?" Fin said snidely. He cuddled Teddy against him. The baby actually sighed.

"You bet." Oliver headed up the stairs, Fin following. "I'll learn from the master."

And after that, maybe someone could teach him the secret to getting through to Selena.

No one in his family was thinking about anything right now but Joe's recovery from surgery. But Dru and Brad had said they were ready to meet with Selena once things settled down. Oliver had called Selena's cell that morning. He'd texted her that afternoon and again a couple of hours ago. She'd ignored every attempt he'd made to get in touch. So much for taking one day at a time and making this as easy as possible for everyone.

After Fin and Teddy were settled, Oliver headed for his parents' bedroom and walked to the window that overlooked the Rosenthal property. As the shadows deepened each night, Selena, not work, consumed his thoughts. Her new strength and confidence. The wonder of her kiss, her touch, her compassion for him even when she'd been spitting mad—and more than a little scared of him still.

He'd left the ball in her court. He'd done all he could this time, calmly explaining his family's side of things. Where he and Selena went from here was up to her, unless he wanted to make things ugly. But he had to see her again, talk to her, hold her. Because of Camille and his parents and Brad and Dru, yes. And because *he* needed Selena close.

She'd kissed him last night, after he'd promised Dru he'd keep his hands to himself. Why the hell had Selena gone and done that if she was going to ignore him all day today? Meanwhile he'd been out of his mind remembering the fire that had streaked through him as her sweet lips innocently brushed his. He stared out the window at Belinda's hedge of camellias.

Don't make what you do next about anyone but you and Selena . . . Dru had said. *Do what's right for* you *this time . . .*

Problem was, Oliver had no idea what was right anymore. Seattle was gone. Toronto was gone. Work had been a black hole of nothing for him since he'd come home to Chandlerville. And he . . . he couldn't get his head around caring, not enough to focus on landing his next client. Not until his dad was better. And Joe *was* going to get stronger. Before long he'd be back at the house, and he and Marsha could take over the family again.

Then Oliver would be free to refocus on the high-pressure job and fast-paced life that suited him. He would find a way to get back to work, exactly as he'd planned. Only when Selena had flat-out asked him what he'd do if he turned out to be Camille's father—whether he'd be leaving Chandlerville—he'd had no answer to give her.

He still didn't.

It's not like you're staying, Fin had said.

It had never been as if Oliver was staying. Then he'd seen Camille and talked to her, he'd seen Selena again, kissed her, and let himself want everything they'd once had back so desperately he'd barely stopped himself from walking next door about a dozen times today—he couldn't think about anything else.

I have things in my life that are more important . . . he'd told the AA group last night, looking straight at Selena when he'd said it.

All of it was important. His responsibility to his career and his family. His relationships with his parents and brother and sister and even the younger kids. His responsibility to his daughter, if Camille really was his. His feelings for her mother that had never gone away.

Oliver stared out at the night and the Rosenthal house—a cutthroat problem solver who didn't have a clue what his next move was. Or how the hell to make it, without hurting any of the people he cared about.

"Couldn't sleep?" Belinda stepped onto the shadowy porch and took a seat on the swing cushion beside Selena's.

Then her mother seemed satisfied not to say anything at all, while they both stared into the night.

Selena remembered it vividly, Belinda finding her on this same swing, crying, their first night on Bellevue Lane. Because they'd finally moved away from their bigger house way across town, where they'd lived with Selena's dad. And Selena had accepted that her father was never coming back.

She'd only heard from him a few times since. On her birthday when she was younger, a card would arrive in the mail with his signature alone beneath some sappy saying. He'd have tucked a five-dollar bill inside, as if that were all she'd needed from him anymore. The last birthday card before Selena lost contact with him had come when she was eighteen. A few months before she'd broken things off with Oliver.

"Couldn't sleep," she finally answered.

"Seems to be an epidemic tonight." Belinda motioned toward the lights still on downstairs in the Dixon house.

"Why are you still up?" Selena asked.

She'd stayed home another day with Camille. Her mom had gotten up early and gone to work, the same as always. They'd shared a simple dinner—another pot of Belinda's soup, in deference to Camille's still-queasy tummy. Otherwise, Selena and her mom had kept to themselves. The same as last night, when Belinda had returned from the hospital, and Camille had already been asleep, and Selena had been in her room . . . needing time and space to think.

"I fell asleep earlier for a few hours," her mom said. "It didn't stick. I heard you come out here awhile ago."

Belinda stared straight ahead while Selena pushed them both in the swing.

"How are the Dixons?" Selena asked, knowing her mom had called Marsha to check on things.

"Joe's still in CICU. Marsha's a wreck while they wait for him to stabilize. But she's staying strong for her kids. You know how she is."

"Just like you stayed strong for me, after Daddy left?"

Belinda hesitated, then nodded. "After I told him to hit the road. Because we were better off without him."

"Why . . ."

Selena inhaled, fighting the long-ago anger, the outrage at being abandoned, the unfair blame that she'd heaped on her mother. For hours, she'd been picturing herself twenty years from now, having a similar talk with her own daughter about the father who may or may not have decided to be a part of Camille's life.

"Why," she tried again, "did you let me think all this time that Daddy just up and left us for no reason?"

"Because that's exactly what he did, the day he decided to carry on an affair, and to keep seeing the woman for over a year."

Everything inside Selena froze. "What?"

"Then when I confronted him about it, he expected me to accept it as part of our marriage. It was a minor matter I should overlook, because he was so good at putting food on the table and keeping the lights on. Besides, if I left him and his money, what the hell was I going to do without the pretty life I'd grown accustomed to?"

Selena planted her feet on the ground. The swing jerked to a stop.

"What?" she croaked. "Why didn't you tell me?"

Belinda kicked off and relaxed into the brightly covered cushions as they swung. "Have you told Camille about Parker's other women?"

Selena shook her head. She'd barely been able to admit it to her mother, when Selena had called to say her marriage was over, and she wasn't sure she could pick up the pieces of her and Camille's life on her own.

"Would you have stayed with him?" her mother asked. "For your daughter's sake, would you ever go back to him, no matter how he treats you, now that you know how difficult it is to make ends meet on your own?"

Selena shook her head again, understanding more, and less, about her mother by the second. "Is that why you took Camille and me in? Because of what Daddy did to you? And now Parker—"

"I took you in"—Belinda inhaled the summer spice of the night air—"because I love you, and I wish I'd never let you go in the first place. I know it's hard for you to believe that, or to want to come back for good. And I'm grateful to have you and my granddaughter here before you move on. But before you leave again, Selena, I want you to know . . . I've always wished you'd come back. I've always wanted you to be happy here, make a life here, raise your daughter here. No matter what's happened."

Selena curled her feet beneath her.

"You let me miss Daddy." She needed to know it all. "All these years, you let me be mad at both of you and miss *him*, when you'd done what you had to, because he—"

"He was your father. You were already brokenhearted. I didn't want to take more of him away from you than I already had."

Selena thought of the hazy photograph that was all of her dad she had left. A picture of them that she'd once kept in the last book he'd ever read to her—*Alice in Wonderland*. After he'd disappeared, she'd dreamed of falling down a rabbit hole and finding him on the other side. Her entire childhood, she'd craved the magical future they should have had together. When all along, that magic had already been hers—here in this tiny house with her mother, who'd done the best she could to protect and raise Selena. The way Selena was now loving and protecting Camille.

She'd taken *Alice in Wonderland* with her when she'd left for New York. But she realized she had no idea where her dad's photo was anymore. She'd put it somewhere when Camille had fallen in love with Alice, too. Selena had always meant to look through her things for it. She'd thought maybe one day she'd even go searching for him. But now she knew—her father hadn't deserved to be found. He didn't deserve another second of Selena missing him.

"You protected me," she said to Belinda, gently stroking her arm.

"Your father loved you, I think, in his own way. Just not enough to keep his fly zipped up when he wasn't home."

"And not enough to want to stay a part of my life once you tossed his cheating ass out."

Belinda chuckled. She took a cleansing breath, then exhaled. "He was a bastard. There's no getting around it. I know it's been hard on you, honey. *I've* been hard on you. But all I ever wanted was for you to make the right decisions, the ones that'll finally give you some happiness. And I want you to do the same thing for Camille."

"You mean about Oliver?" Selena wished there was enough light to clearly see her mother's expression.

"Oliver and Parker."

"Oliver's nothing like my husband, or Daddy." Selena was certain of that, if nothing else. "He's not the one who . . . he'd never cheat on me the way I hurt him with Brad."

Belinda swung some more. "You can't seem to stay away from the man he's become, any more than you could when he was a boy."

"I went to the hospital his first day back to apologize. I'd hoped that would be enough for both of us."

"You were wrong."

And maybe Selena had *wanted* to be wrong. Maybe she still did, about so many things.

Belinda looked at her. "The choice you make next for you and Camille will affect a lot of people."

"I don't think the choice is mine alone to make alone any longer." By now, Belinda must have heard about Selena and Oliver talking outside their AA meeting.

"Do you love him?" her mother asked.

"Since when has my loving Oliver ever been enough?"

The swing creaked on its hinges.

The night drew a little closer.

"I wanted Camille to have a fresh start," Selena said. "No more disappointments. No more fear and confusion and worrying what's wrong or what's going to happen next."

"And she can't have that if you still care about Oliver?"

Selena let them swing for a while, knowing the moment had come, knowing her mother probably already knew, but, Lord help her . . .

"When Oliver was here the other day when you interrupted us," she said, "it wasn't just to see me. And now I have to deal with . . ."

"*We* have to deal with it," Belinda reminded her.

Loving her mother for the *we*, Selena pressed on. "He wanted—he still wants—to discuss something Marsha somehow guessed. Something I should have been straight with you about before now. With everyone. You see . . ."

Selena's stomach bounced into her throat, choking her.

"I do see, honey." Belinda said. "Marsha Dixon's not the only one with eyes and intuition where her child is concerned. Or her grandchild."

"You knew."

"Do you?" Belinda took Selena's hand, where Selena was clutching one of the swing's cushions. "Do you know who your daughter's father is?"

Selena shook her head, feeling it all. The past and the regret. "It wasn't a conscious choice at first. I was on my own when I found out."

"You wouldn't have been, if you'd told me." Her mother sounded sad, not disappointed the way Selena had thought she'd be. "And it's my fault you didn't know back then that I'd have helped you, no matter what. I can be a critical person, Selena. After your father . . . I became too focused on getting through life. Surviving and making things work when I had only myself to lean on. I couldn't fail. I wouldn't let that happen to you, too. So I worked hard at everything, and tried to do the very best for you I could every day. But I left you feeling lonely. Until you turned to someone else for the love you thought you didn't have at home. It took me too long to realize that I was losing you."

"You haven't lost me," Selena insisted. "I'm so sorry. For everything. I made myself believe nothing would ever be right for me here after Daddy left, and then Oliver left. I made my own problems, not you. And I thought I could run from them, even after I had Camille. I wanted her to have more than I had. I convinced myself Parker could give us that. When all this time . . . she had a grandmother who would have doted on her. None of this is your fault."

Belinda patted Selena's hand. "It's never wrong to want more for your child. But, honey, there's nothing you can do for your daughter—nothing you can do because you love her and you want the best for her—that I'll think is wrong. I'll support whatever decision you make."

Selena caught the glimmer of tears in her mother's eyes.

"You have supported us, Mom. You've saved us more than I had a right to expect."

"You're saving yourself. I'd like to still help with that, as much as you'll let me." Belinda dashed at her eyes. "I spoke with Marsha a little last night . . . about Camille."

"Mom . . ."

Belinda raised her hand. "Whoever the girl's father is, Marsha and Joe Dixon want only the best for you and your daughter. I'm convinced of that. In your heart, I think you know it, too."

"Do I?"

"Thinking about having them on your side scares you is all."

"That's not true . . ."

"If we all get behind whatever you think is best for Camille," Belinda said, "you have one less reason to convince yourself that you need to run again."

Selena left her mother and the swing behind, moving to the other side of the porch.

"Camille wants the fairy tale," she said. "And she deserves that. White picket fences and perfect yards and bubble wands and happily ever after."

"Why can't she have that and have the Dixons, too?"

"While her father is marrying someone else and making a new family for himself? Or if Oliver's her father, while he's so caught up in his crazy busy career that it keeps him from being with his family except when there's an emergency?"

"Camille will have you to help her through all that. And me. And her other two grandparents. Brothers and sisters. It won't be easy, but . . . is the fact that it'll be hard a good enough reason for you to run again and keep your daughter away from all of us?"

Selena looked out into the sleeping yard she and her daughter had helped Belinda coddle. Every beautiful thing out there was waiting for the morning sun—for another chance to thrive.

"What do I do, Mom? I could bring her back for visits. I've already told her I will. But she loves it here. If she knows she has even more family in Chandlerville, that she belongs with the Dixons, too . . . if I explain about Oliver or Brad . . ." Selena paced across the porch. "What if one of them hurts her somehow, even if they won't mean to? Or if I still decide to leave, and knowing about the Dixons hurts her? What if just telling Camille at all screws everything up again for her, after what she's been through

198

already with Parker? I can't stop thinking I should just leave it alone, no matter how much I want . . ."

No matter how much Selena wanted Oliver and the Dixons for herself, too.

"Maybe I should settle Camille somewhere else first," she reasoned.

All day, Selena had been trying to rationalize moving at the end of the school year—somehow getting the money from Parker and piling herself and her daughter and everything they owned back into Fred and leaving Chandlerville behind.

"Maybe then I could explain to Camille about her father, once we have some distance from all of this."

Selena knew she sounded ridiculous. But Belinda had sat through it all. No judgment. No advice. Just waiting and supporting.

"What do I do, Mom?"

"You stick." Belinda stepped to her side, the swing creaking softly as it rocked without them. "You stick it out this time, until you're sure you know the right answer."

Selena hugged her mother, desperate for the soft, loving feel of it.

"I've learned a lot from my own mistakes." Belinda held on. "From living with them for as long as I have. We are what we are, inside—wherever we go in the world. My moving us to this house didn't change the damage that came from losing your father—for me or for you. Any more than you leaving New York has erased what happened with Parker. But growing up in this house brought you closer to the Dixons and Oliver. And coming home has brought you and your daughter closer again. Don't run this time, until you're sure letting go is what you want."

"So I should stick?" The very opposite of what Selena's instincts were screaming for her to do.

"As long as it takes to figure things out. Not for Camille or me or Oliver or Parker or Brad or the Dixons. This is your life, Selena. Your choice to make, for you and your daughter. For your family. There's no right or wrong decision. There's just what you think is best."

"Like you did when you told Daddy to go?"

"Yes." Belinda eased away. "As hard as it's been, I love my life in Chandlerville. The way I never would have if I hadn't told your father to leave. I've figured out how to be happy, Selena. Now it's your turn."

"I . . . I don't know how to do that." For so long, damage control had been all Selena could think about.

"You will." Her mother wrapped an arm around Selena. Together, they stared at the landscaped view they couldn't quite see. "And once you do, I'll be right here, fighting for whatever you decide."

Chapter Sixteen

"Whoever the girl's father is . . ." Camille's grammy had said. *"Marsha and Joe Dixon want only the best for you and your daughter."*

Camille hugged her tulip quilt that Grammy had said *her* grammy had made when Camille's mommy was born. It was so early in the morning, there was hardly any sunlight at all outside to keep Camille company. Grammy and Mommy had stayed up late talking on the porch. Their voices had gotten Camille up when the Hello Kitty clock on her wall had said two o'clock.

The sound of their voices had made her feel weird, even when she hadn't been able to make out the words. They'd sounded mad or scared or something. Things Grammy and Mommy didn't like for Camille to hear them being. She'd snuck down the hallway anyway, to get closer. Now she kinda wished she hadn't.

Why hadn't Mommy told her?

Why hadn't Grammy?

Camille snuggled deeper into the window seat she loved—her room at Grammy's had the coolest window. Big enough to sleep in, so sometimes she did at night after everyone else had gone to bed. Because it made her feel like she was sleeping in Grammy's garden, just outside. Last night, she'd stayed in the window all night with her flower quilt, looking at the Dixon house next door, even though Grammy's hedge hid most of it from where Camille was sitting.

Next door was her family, too?

Is that what her mommy and grammy had been saying? Her grandparents, her brothers and sisters, and . . . her daddy might be over there? Then why had everyone pretended they were just neighbors, and Oliver was just a friend from when Mommy was little? Even Mrs. Dixon had pretended. And why did Mommy want to move on again if they had another family in Chandlerville, plus Grammy?

Or if Oliver's her father, while he's so caught up in his crazy busy career . . .

Is the fact that it'll be hard a good enough reason for you to run again and keep your daughter away from all of us?

Camille didn't want to leave, now more than ever. Even if she didn't understand how Oliver could maybe be her daddy. And she wasn't sure she wanted him to be. And who was Brad? And why wasn't anyone telling her about any of it?

Mommy had sounded so sad and scared, like she had right before they'd left Parker. Camille wanted the Dixons to be her family. That would be the coolest thing ever, besides coming to live with Grammy and maybe getting a puppy. But she didn't want her Mommy to be scared again.

And Camille wanted a real daddy. She wanted to be part of the Dixons' fun family. But if she couldn't know about them and stay in Chandlerville, too, then she just wouldn't tell Mommy or Grammy she that she knew. She'd pretend, the way she used to pretend she didn't know that her mommy and Parker were fight-ing, and that Mommy was getting sad about staying in New York.

She snuggled with her quilt and looked out at the Dixon house.

How long, she wondered, 'til people were up next door? And how long 'til Mommy and Grammy wouldn't notice if Camille snuck over there? She could stay outside all morning if she had to, and take her quilt and her bubbles and Bear and play in the shade by the back hedge no matter how hot it got.

Then when everyone was too busy to notice, she'd sneak over. Just to play. Just to see Mrs. Dixon and everyone and everything that might be hers, too. And maybe she could ask someone over there what was going on. Maybe that way, without making Mommy sad at all, Camille could find out for sure if the Dixons were her family, too.

Chapter Seventeen

"Shoot me." Oliver slapped the lid of his laptop closed and stared at Marsha's infernal stove. He was beginning to believe the thing was possessed.

It was late Saturday morning. He'd been up since five with Teddy. Fin had brought him to Marsha and Joe's room at the crack of dawn, the toddler fussing again. Turned out the kid had been running a slight temperature. When Oliver called Dru, she'd said not to worry unless the fever got any higher. Oliver should push fluids—yay! more diapers—and give Teddy baby Tylenol at careful intervals.

Which had been a relief to hear and Oliver had almost gotten the kid back to sleep, when the rest of the tribe had woken up to their last Saturday before summer break, ready to rumble. Waiting for updates on Joe was wearing on all of them.

The kids had taken turns all morning giving each other and Oliver a hard time. And now his plan for a crowd-pleasing lunch that didn't come in a pizza box was officially a bust.

"Just shoot me," he said.

The pot of boiling macaroni heckled him by continuing to bubble over. Smoke seeped through the oven vent. His rep as a man who could fix any problem he set his mind to had just hit a record low. If only Xan Coulter could see him now. He snatched up the pot by its handle and dumped the half-cooked macaroni into a steaming pile in the sink.

"Is the oven s'posed to be doing that?" Lisa asked. She'd followed him from one room of the house to the other all morning, *helping*. "It never smells like that when Mom cooks. I don't think there's s'posed to be smoke."

Fin sauntered in and laughed. "Told ya. He can't even make crap macaroni and cheese and frozen fries. Let's see if he can ruin PB&J."

"Look, kid . . ." Oliver caught himself before he lost his cool.

If some loser with zero domestic skills had barged into Oliver's life when he'd been the same age—needing the kids' help most of the time to get through the simplest tasks—Oliver would have been a smartass, too. His eye tracked to the fire extinguisher on the wall by the sink. Did he even know how to use one? Cracking the tight muscles in his neck, he dragged on purple oven mitts and opened the stove he'd just turned off.

"Shut the door to the living room," he said, "in case"—the fire alarm bleated its eardrum-shattering warning—"the detector goes off."

He dumped the charred fries into the sink. The edge of the sheet pan brushed his wrist and singed him.

"Damn it!"

"I'll get Teddy," Lisa said over the blare of the alarm, racing into the living room where the toddler had finally gone down for a nap.

Oliver grabbed the broom and with the end of the handle stabbed at the squealing demon in the ceiling until it shut up.

"I'll get the peanut butter." Fin trudged to the pantry, lugging out a hernia-inducing-sized tub of extra-chunky. The kids had made a serious dent in it since Oliver arrived on the scene.

"Maybe Dru can bring something over from the Whip," Oliver reasoned.

"Who's as old as you," Fin griped, "and can't cook?"

Sandy-brown hair, athletic and growing into lanky, he wore a ripped soccer jersey this morning and almost-too-short jeans. He dumped his burden onto the island and flung the refrigerator door wide to root for the grape jelly Oliver had seen lurking behind the pitcher of orange juice he'd mixed up from concentrate for breakfast. A meal Oliver had finished cleaning up less than an hour ago.

Followed immediately by starting laundry, figuring out from the chore chart on the laundry room wall who was on vacuum duty on Saturdays and who got stuck with the bathrooms, *and* dragging half the kids back to their bedrooms to make the beds Marsha insisted be straightened at the start of every day. Lunch should have been a cinch after all of that.

"I cook just fine." Armed with a pot holder, his wrist still stinging, Oliver scraped the burned remains of what used to be crinkle-cut fries on top of the failed mac and cheese.

Fin fake gagged.

Oliver pulled two loaves of bread from the cabinet under the island. "PB&J isn't so bad."

"Boris's jelly only." Fin flicked a thumb over his shoulder at the reminder list tacked to the white board that took up half of the refrigerator door. "Allergies."

"Right." Rule number one in Dru's mind-numbing list of helpful reminders: Don't send anyone to the hospital. "Thanks."

"You're no good at any of this."

Oliver hadn't failed at something this badly since high school math. Marsha had actually laughed at some of his horror stories when they'd talked over the phone an hour or so ago. "Good thing being a domestic goddess isn't why I'm here."

"Why are you here?"

"Because I've already done everything all of you might think you can get away with, just because Marsha and Joe aren't around—long before you figured out that rebelling is a natural high. So spread the word. Don't waste your time." He brandished the spatula for emphasis. "Not only will your chores double each time you test me, but I'll be waiting for you at the starting gate, ruining your fun from the get-go."

Fin rolled his eyes. "So if you're so tough and badass, why come back now just to push us around? Dad might be dead soon . . ." The kid was suddenly furious. Except he sounded like he was going to cry. "And then we all gotta go somewhere else, right? Who cares if you ride our asses about making our beds?"

Lisa returned, the baby squirming in her arms, almost too big for her to hold. She'd heard Fin's tirade, and she was looking scared—the way Oliver suspected all the kids were feeling, no matter how they acted like nothing had changed in their ever-changing worlds.

"I'm here because I'm your big brother. Like Travis is. Like Dru's your big sister. And brothers and sisters stick together. That's why I'm back. And Joe is *not* going to die. Mom says he's doing better and about as cranky as you guys this morning. He wants to be back home, sleeping in his own bed. Sounds like the doctors might okay him moving to another room as early as this afternoon."

"And that's good, right?" Lisa fed Teddy snack crackers from a box she'd snagged from the pantry.

"It's huge."

Oliver looked between Lisa and Fin, feeling for them. Feeling too much like them some days. Even now after all he'd accomplished with his life, it was easy to expect whatever good he had not to stay that way for very long.

"I know I'm a disaster around here," he said, "messing up all the things Dru and Travis do better than me. But that doesn't mean I'm not good at listening, if you need to talk about Joe, or if—"

"Who wants to talk about him?" Fin stomped to one of the cabinets for enough plates to feed everyone. He yanked open the utensil drawer, grabbed knives and spoons. The sound of everything clattering onto the counter started Teddy crying again.

Oliver pressed his thumbs into his eye sockets, close to screaming himself.

"Can I help?"

Everyone pivoted. Camille stood in the doorway to the backyard looking fully recovered from being ill, wearing pink shorts and a yellow top. There were dirt smudges all over her, like she'd been rolling around on the ground outside. She headed straight for the baby, smiling as if they were best buds. Teddy's arms opened wide. Lisa handed him over.

"Does your mom know you're here?" Oliver watched Camille cuddle the toddler. She reached into the box of crackers Lisa had left on the island and started feeding him.

"She comes over sometimes." Lisa picked up a spoon. Fin had already dragged bread out of the bags and divided out two slices for each plate. He was smearing peanut butter on half of them. Lisa started covering the rest with jelly.

"She does?" Oliver crouched in front of Camille, who was looking guilty but determined not to let it show. "How often?"

She didn't answer.

"Saturdays mostly." Lisa looked up from the sandwiches. "It's no big deal. She helps Mom sometimes is all."

"Do you come for the cookies, too?" Oliver asked.

Camille nodded. "I helped make them last weekend. Your mommy made them with stuff I can eat, which makes cookies taste gross. But hers don't. She says it's 'cause I'm good help."

She's sneaked over to the house a few times . . .

We've had some lovely chats.

Oliver's mother had been *baking* with the girl. While Selena wanted Camille protected from his family, until Selena was ready to explain things to her daughter her own way. He tweaked Camille's nose with his thumb and forefinger. He took Teddy before she collapsed under the toddler's considerable weight.

"Those were the best cookies I've had in years." He patted Teddy's back. The baby fussed, reaching for Camille again. "Now I know why."

Camille smiled.

"Where's your mom?" he asked.

"Jogging. Every Saturday morning. Grammy doesn't have to work on Saturdays. I help her in the yard. Mommy runs. Even when it's raining. Running makes her happy. She says it helps her think. Sometimes at night, too, after I go to bed. But always on Saturday."

"And your Grammy knows you're here?" He found that hard to believe.

Camille bit her lip and shook her head. "She thinks I'm—"

Teddy barfed all over the only clean T-shirt Oliver had left. Oliver barked out something not suitable for children of any age to hear. Likely not for most of the adults in Chandlerville, either.

"Eeeeeew." Fin stabbed his knife into the peanut butter jar and backed away. "I'm not cleaning that up."

"He does that when he cries too much," Lisa said with authority, while Oliver held Teddy at arm's length.

Footsteps clambered from where the other kids had either been upstairs cleaning stuff or in the living room doing the homework they hadn't finished yesterday. Suddenly Oliver had four more spectators surveying his latest disaster.

"Lunch!" Gabe and Shandra said at the same time.

The high schoolers grabbed their plates. Gabe snagged a bag of chips from the pantry while Shandra took orange soda from the fridge. They sprinted for the dining room as if they hadn't nearly polished off a box of cereal between them just a few hours ago. Shandra giggled as she passed Oliver.

"Man," she said, "you smell like baby puke."

"That's because I'm covered in baby puke."

"I'll take him again." Camille held up her arms. "He likes me."

Fin and Lisa deserted Oliver, too, with their plates and drinks. Boris grabbed his food and left without saying a word. Oliver was intimately familiar with the maneuver. In a big family, you kept your head down, you kept moving, and good things happened. The slow and careless were given *projects*, as Marsha and Joe liked to call them. There was always something to do. Especially when there were babies around.

Oliver shook his head, alone now with Selena's smiling, helpful, not-supposed-to-be-there child. He got another whiff of himself and, resigned, handed Teddy over.

"Just for a second." He shoved a kitchen towel at Camille in case there was another eruption and edged toward the laundry room. "Then we're getting you home. My shirt from last night's run is filthy, but anything's better than this. I'll be right back."

He pulled the thing from the laundry room floor and shucked his soiled T-shirt off. At the sound of the doorbell, he hung his head and stared at his tattered tennis shoes. They were sporting even more character now, compliments of Teddy.

"Perfect."

Still holding his running shirt, he used the puked-on one to wipe down his sneakers. Leaving it with the rest of the laundry, he turned back into the kitchen and rushed past Camille.

"I'll be just a few more seconds," he promised.

She had Teddy on the floor. The kid was giggling and playing with her ponytails and the pink polka-dotted ribbons tied around them. Oliver slowed, his heart beating frantically at the perfect picture they made—his maybe daughter and his youngest foster brother, sharing a happy, careless moment. Then the door-bell pealed again.

He headed down the hall. He tripped over a backpack half-tossed into a corner. It spilled onto the faded runner that had looked a hundred years old when he'd last lived there. The bell rang twice in a row this time, impatient, demanding. He yanked the door open, pulling his shirt over his head and one shoulder.

"Yeah?" he asked the young woman in a suit standing on the top step. She stared at his half-exposed chest. He shoved his other arm into his T-shirt and pulled down the tail. "Can I help you?"

"Um . . ." She seemed to mentally shake her thoughts back on track. "I'm Ms. Walker. Donna Walker, with Family Services. I'm Teddy Rutherford's caseworker. Actually, several of the kids are mine. Well, not mine. But you know what I mean." She took a deep breath. "I apologize for the inconvenience on a Saturday.

Our office was informed by Mrs. Dixon about Mr. Dixon's heart attack. We already had this unannounced site evaluation on the schedule, and my supervisor wanted me to keep it considering the strain Marsha and Joe are going to be under for the next while. We need to be certain Teddy's placement isn't too much for the home. If other arrangements are needed, it'll be important to make them as quickly as possible. Waiting too long might contribute to any attachment issues Teddy could experience after making another change so soon. That is . . ."

She paused and really looked Oliver over for the first time since staring at his pecs.

"Excuse me," she said. "But who are you, exactly? And where are the Dixon children?"

"I'm Oliver Bowman."

He pulled his cell from his pocket. Though what he'd accomplish with it at this point by calling Marsha, or Travis or Dru, he wasn't sure. His mother was entrenched with Joe, and his brother and sister were both elbow-deep in their demanding Saturdays, working full-day shifts.

"I aged out of Marsha and Joe's home seven years ago. I'm back to help the family. My mother was supposed to have let someone in your office know."

Ms. Walker consulted her notepad. "I have a record of her call. But I see nothing about you supervising the kids in Mrs. and Mr. Dixon's absence. We'd assumed your local siblings would be taking care of that."

"I'm giving them a break. The kids are eating lunch in the dining room," he said. "They're being well supervised, and—"

A toddler wail unleashed, loud enough to be heard all the way from the kitchen. Though it could have been laughter—with Teddy it was always a toss-up.

"Is that the baby?" the caseworker asked, a second shriek echoing down the hallway. "Is he hurt?"

"No, he's . . ."

Oliver glanced over his shoulder. Ms. Walker brushed past him.

"Damn it." He followed in her wake, bringing up his contacts on his phone.

He had his brother's and sister's numbers on speed dial. Marsha's, too. But none of them needed the distraction of knowing he couldn't handle the one thing his family had asked him to deal with while he was in town. He stopped scrolling at another number and hesitated.

Teddy kept fussing, crying for sure. Ms. Walker was in the kitchen now—with a toddler Oliver didn't know how to soothe and a little girl who might or might not be Oliver's daughter. The Family Services caseworker would wonder about Camille being there without her mother. And Oliver would have to come up with some explanation that wouldn't send Ms. Walker next door for a chat with Belinda Rosenthal. Lord knew what Selena's mother would have to say about him.

He selected the number and texted, *911. My parents' place. Hurry.*

Emergencies only, he'd promised Selena. He rushed into the kitchen.

"Hello," Ms. Walker was saying to Camille over Teddy's sobs. "And who do we have here?"

This most *definitely* qualified as an emergency.

"What?" Selena panted on the Dixon front porch, sweaty from her run and freaked after Oliver's text. "What's wrong?"

Nothing had looked at odds when she'd sprinted by Belinda's house: no fire, nothing exploding, no cops at the curb. The same with the Dixon place. She'd rung the bell and stopped short of pounding on the door to get in. Oliver had yanked the thing open before she could change her mind.

"I need your help." He grabbed her hand and pulled her through the cluttered but empty living room, then down the hall.

God. She hadn't been in this house in ages. But it still felt the same. Like a large family, like a lot of love, like a home you could be yourself in. Like heaven, she'd always thought.

"My help with what?" She staggered over a backpack that had been left on the floor, then gasped. Oliver's arm had curled around her waist to keep her moving toward the kitchen. "You said it was an emergency."

"It is. Just follow my lead. Please."

"Oliver . . ."

"Please."

His second *please* was partially drowned out by another woman's voice. They rounded the corner and Selena stared for the split second it took her to recover from finding whoever else was in the Dixon kitchen—a woman she didn't know, wearing work clothes in the middle of a Saturday—kneeling and talking with a happy-as-you-please Camille.

Selena rushed forward, alarm bells ringing again.

"Is everything okay?" she asked over her shoulder. "What's my daughter doing here?" She drew Camille to her side and confronted the other woman, who was standing now. "I'm sorry. Who are you?"

"Camille's fine," Oliver explained. "She's been keeping Teddy company. And this is—"

"Teddy?" Selena asked.

"Marsha and Joe's youngest," he explained over the low-level racket of what must be the rest of the Dixon brood doing something in the dining room—presumably eating lunch. "He was sleeping while Fin and Lisa made—while I was making sandwiches for the kids. He spit up on me, and Camille was playing with him on the floor while I changed and the kids took their food to the dining room. That's when Ms. Walker—this is Donna Walker from Family Services—rang the bell. So I called you. I thought it would be a good time for Camille to head home, before things got any more offtrack for Marsha and Joe's site evaluation. You remember how important those can be for a new foster child's placement."

He sounded so certain he was making sense.

"What are you talking about?" Selena sputtered as Camille lifted the cute, red-headed little boy into her arms. "How did my daughter get here?" Selena cast Camille a disbelieving look. "You're *supposed* to be next door playing while your grandmother works in the yard."

"I'm Ms. Walker." The other woman reached out her hand, all business. "Family Services. How exactly do you and your daughter know the Dixons?"

The rest of what Oliver had said, his stoically in-control expression with just a hint of desperation around the edges, sank in.

This was the Dixons' caseworker.

"Teddy likes me," Camille insisted. "He likes it when I come over to play, and Mrs. Dixon doesn't mind." She grinned at Ms. Walker. "I've known him for weeks now. So it's okay. Mrs. Dixon said it was okay if I play with him sometimes."

Which most definitely *wasn't* okay with Selena.

But neither was Oliver making any worse an impression on Ms. Walker than he already had, thanks in part to Selena's wandering spawn. Camille seemed fine, Selena consoled herself. And

Teddy certainly was content in her daughter's arms, whatever had happened before Selena got there. The enthralled baby reached a slobbery hand for Camille's hair and tugged. Camille laughed. He let go of her ponytail and clapped.

Selena snagged the opening and knelt in front of her daughter.

"Sweetie, why don't you let Oliver tend to Teddy now and head back next door to Grammy's? Does she know you're here?"

Camille shook her head as Oliver took the baby. She looked down at her favorite flip-flops. They had fabric daisies glued to the top of them.

"I heard noise from the kitchen," she said. "The windows were open. The kids were talking and laughing, and there was a loud sound, and Teddy started crying. And I knew I could help. You weren't back yet, and . . ."

"And I told you I would be only half an hour. You're not supposed to leave the yard without an adult with you."

"But I thought Mrs. Dixon was here, and I could help her bake for just a few minutes like before, and—"

"Like before?" Selena looked to Oliver. "How long has she been coming over here?

He shook his head, shrugged. His attention flicked toward the social worker.

"Am I to understand," Ms. Walker said to Selena, "that you had no idea your daughter was here alone with Mr. Bowman?"

"She was never alone with me." The tightness around Oliver's eyes was the only hint to the degree of panic he was controlling.

"The baby doesn't count," Ms. Walker corrected.

"Lisa and Fin were just here," Camille said, as if two more of Marsha and Joe's foster kids were her good buddies. "They were helping make lunch."

"And I knew she was here the entire time," a voice said from the door to the Dixons' backyard.

Belinda stood there. She'd been listening for who knew how long. She walked the rest of the way into the kitchen.

"Mom?" Selena asked.

"I stepped into my house to take a phone call and was watching through the window while Camille played," Belinda explained to the social worker. "I saw my granddaughter scamper through the bushes and head over. Marsha's never minded her coming for a visit before. I figured Oliver wouldn't, either, until I had a chance to fetch Camille home."

Selena skewered her mother with a *we'll talk* glare.

"Mrs. . . . ?" the social worker asked.

"Belinda Rosenthal."

"How well do you know the Dixons?"

"They've been my neighbors since I moved to Bellevue Lane, long before Oliver joined them." Belinda matched Ms. Walker's no-nonsense stare. "If Marsha trusts him with her kids, I've got no reason to worry about Camille being here for a few minutes while he's taking care of the house for his parents. No one's more careful with their children than the Dixons. And Oliver was just visiting our house the other day. Wasn't he, Selena?"

Selena nodded. She clamped down on the rest of what she intended to say once Ms. Walker was gone.

"And I helped with Teddy." Camille's wide, innocent eyes, begged Selena to understand. "I'm really good with him. Right, Oliver?"

"Better than me," he said.

"High praise," Selena muttered.

"I planned on sending her home as soon as I realized she was here," he explained. "But things got a little out of hand. Teddy woke from his nap early." He turned to Ms. Walker. "Why don't you take him in and talk with the kids while I finish up with my neighbors?"

Ms. Walker took the toddler.

"I have another appointment this afternoon." She looked less than thrilled at being dismissed but turned on the heels of her conservative, stylish pumps and struck off for the dining room. "I'd hate for your parents not to get the most benefit from my time here."

"Thank you," Oliver said when she was gone—to Belinda and Selena. "I can't screw up Teddy's placement for my parents."

"It's the least we could do." Belinda looked down at Camille. "You promised me you'd stay in the backyard, young lady. I was scared out of my wits just now when I couldn't find you."

"So you didn't see her come over?" Selena asked.

Belinda shook her head.

"You had no idea she's been over here before?"

"No. But I didn't want to make trouble for Marsha and Joe with their social worker."

Oliver sighed. "Thank you, both of you, for covering my ass."

"I'm sorry, Grammy." Camille hung her head. "But—"

"She really was a big help with Teddy," Oliver offered.

"Evidently, they're fast friends," Selena added.

"But—" Camille started to say again.

"Mom, would you mind taking her home?"

Belinda scolded Camille with an admonishing look. "It sounds as if someone's not going to get any more outside playtime unless she stays with me or her mother."

"But—"

"We'll talk about this at home." Belinda tried to lead Camille toward the back door.

"No." Camille refused to budge. "I don't wanna go. I won't. I won't go!"

"Camille?" Stunned, Selena knelt in front of her.

Her daughter's face was bright red, her breath rushing in and out. She was trembling and close to tears.

"You shouldn't have snuck over uninvited," Selena insisted, "even if Mrs. Dixon's let you before. You shouldn't have wandered over without your Grammy knowing. But we can talk about it at our house."

"But this *is* my house." Her daughter stomped her foot. "I belong here, too. You said so, and I wanna stay. I wanna play with Teddy and the other kids before we move. Why do we have to move? Why do I have to go now, when—"

"This is not your house." The words choked Selena. Or maybe it was the panic of watching her worst nightmare come true—her child hurt and scared because of something else Selena had screwed up.

She hadn't stopped worrying over what to do about the Dixons since talking with Belinda last night. She'd stayed gone longer on her run than she'd intended, going over and over things in her mind while she'd rationalized continuing to avoid Oliver. How did she tell Camille? What did she say to Brad and Dru? What if Oliver wasn't her daughter's father like Selena had always hoped? What if he *was* and there was no chance for them to be a real family?

And now Selena was gazing into her daughter's confused expression, wishing there was some way to make the next few minutes less scary than they were always going to have been, no matter what Selena said.

She felt Oliver's hand on her shoulder. He knelt, too. She saw Belinda's concern lock onto the three of them.

"When did I say this was your house, Cricket?"

"You told Grammy the Dixons were my family, too." Two tears spilled from Camille's eyes. Oliver gently thumbed them away. "Last night, on the porch. I couldn't sleep. And I snuck up to listen. And you said you didn't know how to tell me. Or 'splain about Oliver and . . . someone else. You said . . ."

Camille stared at Oliver, her tiny chest rising and falling while Selena's heart imploded.

"Could you really be my daddy?"

Oliver stared into eyes that looked exactly like his. Or did he just want, badly as it turned out, for Camille to belong to him?

He'd lain awake the last two nights wanting another chance to talk with her, get to know her, make her smile and maybe look for himself a little in how she acted and talked. But now she was hurting, the way Selena had said she would. More tears trickled down her cheeks.

"Yes, Cricket." Selena turned her daughter to face her. "Oliver might be your father. But we're not sure."

Camille looked back to him. "That's what you were asking, when you were looking for someone's daddy."

Oliver nodded, his voice a no-show. His heart was a puddle of mush as Selena stroked her daughter's arm and Camille flinched away.

"Oliver had just found out, sweetie," Selena explained. "And . . ."

Camille backed into Belinda, and her grandmother's arms closed around her.

"We wanted to be sure before telling you," Oliver finally got out. "That's why we've waited to tell you."

We.

He caught Selena's surprised glance at him making her decision to delay dealing with Camille's paternity a *we* thing. Because he didn't like how Camille was looking at her mom, as if Selena were suddenly the enemy. He took Selena's hand and ignored the way she tensed at his touch.

"You're not sure you want me?" Camille looked down at her flip-flops, gutting Oliver when her bottom lip quivered.

"Of course I want you," he said. "And my parents for sure want you as their granddaughter, whether you're mine or not. Everyone in this family will be thrilled to have you—look how much Teddy lights up when he sees you. But we're worried about confusing you. We wanted everything to be okay for you when you found out."

Camille stared at him. Hope, doubt, fear . . . it was all there.

"I always wanted . . . to be part of your family." She snuck a peek at Selena and then up to Belinda. "It's why I came over today, even if I wasn't supposed to and I shouldn't have listened last night, and I wasn't going to tell what I'd heard. But I still wanted to be . . . to have a family like yours," she said to Oliver. "But you knew and you didn't tell me. You didn't want me to know and . . ."

Her attention flickered to Selena before she turned in Belinda's arms and buried her head against her grandmother's tummy, crying so hard now she could barely catch her breath.

Belinda lifted Camille into her arms. "I'll take her home and calm her down while you two talk." She gave Oliver her full attention. "I really am sorry I lost track of her and set all of this into motion."

Selena stood once her mother and daughter were gone, her hand covering her mouth. "How did this happen?"

"Fast." Oliver winced at the memory of the frantic beginning to Ms. Walker's visit. "It was all happening too fast. That's why I sent you the 911. Camille walked into the middle of a complete meltdown. And then I didn't know what to tell the social worker about her. Family Services might crucify my parents because of how I've handled things. But I couldn't tell Ms. Walker that on top of everything else that I had an unsupervised minor over who'd been told *not* to visit the scary people next door. And I didn't want to upset Camille. The last thing I wanted was to make her cry."

Selena dropped her arm. Her hand slapped against the thigh of her jogging pants. "I guess that plan's moot."

"Hey, I'm not the one who let the paternity cat out of the bag to your daughter." He rubbed his temple. "Damn it, I'm trying to do the best I can for everyone. And *not* ruin my parents' chances to keep Teddy. There was no one else to help me this morning, no one close enough. So, I—"

"Knew I'd come running?"

"I knew you'd do the right thing once you got here. Just like you'll do the right thing now that Camille's asking questions about me and my family."

"The *right thing* being telling her everything?"

He had no idea anymore. "I want to protect her, too, Selena. I want to protect you both. But I'm worried about my parents, and I know you care about them."

"And?" Selena looked as flabbergasted as he felt.

"And *you* kissed *me* the other night. You agreed to talk things through. Then I don't hear from you for over twenty-four hours. I'm turning myself inside out, destroying potential business opportunities to stay in Chandlerville for my family—and for you and Camille now." Staying for himself, too, because leaving felt more impossible by the hour. "Hell, Camille's already figured out most of it for herself. But I bet you're still trying to think of a way to deal with who her father is without *dealing* with whatever this is between us. Meanwhile, we can barely keep our hands off each other when we're alone."

Selena smoothed both palms down her thighs, drawing his attention to her toned, trim body. She looked like she could run for days. But she couldn't run from them now. He found himself closer. He reached for her shoulders. He held fast when she went to pull away.

"You don't distrust me nearly as much as you want to." It had been a stunning conclusion he'd come to somewhere in the middle of last night. "And you don't like it one damn bit."

"No," she admitted. "I don't."

"You've wanted me far away from *you* from the start," he said, "not just from your daughter. This has never been entirely about Camille, has it?"

"Of course not."

"Because you still feel guilty about things you did seven years ago?"

Selena shook her head, looking like she despised the both of them for her weakness.

He aligned their bodies until her heart beat next to his. She was warm from her run. She was looking up at him, seeing and feeling him. She was soft against him, like she'd been a lifetime ago, like in his dreams of her ever since.

"Because you wouldn't have been able to stay away from me," he said, "whether Camille was involved or not. And it terrifies you, what that could mean. There's something in you for me, Selena Rosenthal. There's something between us still."

She nodded in silent agreement.

"And you don't want to trust me again," he repeated. "Even if this—you and me—could help Camille feel safe and happy?"

Selena tensed against him. "Parker started out saying he wanted to make me and my baby happy. Almost as soon as I limped into New York and met him in some club I'd heard I could get a job doing whatever clubs paid girls my age to do. I'd screwed up any chance I had to have you in my life. I couldn't face my mother, not knowing whose baby it was. I was desperate. And there Parker was, acting smitten, ready to take over."

The way Oliver had tried to their last few months of high school. The way he was pushing her now to deal with Camille's paternity.

"Take over what?" he asked.

"Me. My *education*, Parker called it, while I learned to be something besides eighteen and pregnant, though college was always out of the question, because no one could know a wife of his had no degree. He was ready to be responsible for my child, though. He'd raise her as his own. A man of a certain age should settle down, he said, and make his life look more stable. And I was so grateful at first. He was going to slay all my dragons. Camille and I were going to be safe, forever, the way I'd once dreamed you'd make life better. All I had to do was better myself and keep Parker happy."

She looked ready to run again. She settled deeper into Oliver instead.

"Except I was never going to be able to make Parker want the kind of family Camille and I deserved," she continued. "Not when there was a big city of other women out there panting to make him happy without the added baggage of being a husband and father. So, good riddance. Now my daughter will be happy because of me. Not because we need someone else to decide whether he loves us enough to walk through the door at the end of the day."

"You think I could still hurt you."

Oliver couldn't keep his hands to himself, sliding them up and down her curves and feeling her body warm for him. He desperately wanted to meet Parker and wring the man's cheating neck. He still wanted to slay every dragon Selena was determined to face on her own. He wanted that chance with Camille, too. But . . .

"No matter how much we might still feel for each other," he said, "you think I could still hurt you. So you're determined not to give this a chance."

"You could destroy me," Selena whispered.

Then she pressed her lips to his.

He took the kiss he'd wanted since she'd driven away from him two nights ago. Once again she'd initiated it, when he'd half expected her to shove him away. To tell him to go to hell. He wouldn't have been surprised if she'd bitten him, given her current state of mind. Instead, she was all over him.

She still expected the worst of him. But she was rising onto her toes to give him more, take more, want more with him. Just like when they'd been kids, only better now. She was still afraid. But not in this moment, while she arched, stretched, luxuriated in his hands sliding from her waist up her ribs, his thumbs caressing the sides of her breasts. Her hands slipped under his T-shirt, her nails scraping across his belly and then around and up, down, smoothing over his butt, the backs of his thighs, as if she'd never stop.

God, he hoped she never stopped.

He deepened the kiss, shutting out the sound of Ms. Walker talking with the kids in the next room. Selena angled her head so their mouths could feast. She still had doubts, but he could feel her need blowing through the compulsion to be careful. There was honesty inside her, too, for him and what they could have.

And trust. Somewhere deep where she couldn't stop it, she still wanted to trust him. He'd never been more certain of it.

Her complete openness while she explored his body again was sexier than her gasp, her touch, her tongue seeking his. This was his Selena, giving everything, taking more. And he wanted every taste, every sip, until he was drowning in it, in *her*.

There'd never been half measures between them. All-consuming had been the only way they'd known how to love as teenagers. The same all-or-nothing would be the path they'd travel as adults. And it had Oliver spooked, the same as Selena. Because this time around if they failed, it wouldn't be because they hadn't known better.

He ached to lift her to the kitchen's island and settle in. She was all but wrapping her body around him, smooth skin and sleek muscles and slippery running gear that hid next to nothing of her. She kissed his neck. He reciprocated and tasted salt and Selena, nibbling beneath her ear, licking at the goose flesh rushing over her.

"Oliver," she whispered. "Please."

"Selena . . ."

They were begging. Their bodies were demanding. And they couldn't do this. Not yet. This needed to be slow and sure and in it for the long haul, before they sank any deeper into the flood of it. He curled his hands around her shoulders. Hers cupped his face.

She broke the carnal rhythm of their kiss and pressed her lips to his, over and over. Healing, gentle touches that had him promising himself to protect her, Camille, and everything that was important to them.

The raging, relentless tide of desire finally began to ease. Leaving her smiling gently, her eyelids closed as if she were having the best dream. He let his fingers trail through her hair, where it had escaped the ponytail she'd caught the mass of curls into for her run. Her smile widened. Her eyes fluttered open.

"Hello," she said.

He lifted her hand and looked down at her palm, nestled trustingly in his. "Hello."

He drew the backs of her fingers to his lips. And then he let go, so she wouldn't have to.

Her features lost some of their softness. Worry crept back. Doubt, as she swallowed and bit her lower lip.

"What are we going to do?" she asked. "We can't just . . ."

"No," he agreed, "we can't. But we *can* work through all of this together, especially things with Camille. I'll deal with Ms. Walker, and then get Travis over here on his lunch break. You and I can walk Camille through her questions. And then we'll—"

Selena's cell phone played *Mission: Impossible.*

He chuckled. She smiled and rolled her eyes. She pressed the call through.

"Mom?" she said. "I have you on speaker. I'm still with Oliver. I'll be home in just a—"

"It's Camille," Belinda said in a rush. "Her EpiPen's not working. She's really having trouble breathing. I've already called her pediatrician. The nurse said to bring her straight to the ER. We have to get her to the hospital, Selena. We have to go right now."

Chapter Eighteen

"The doctors know what they're doing," Belinda insisted, her arm circling Selena's waist. They were waiting outside the ER cubicle Camille has been whisked into, shooed aside by the nurses so the critical care team could work on Selena's daughter without distraction.

"Of course they do," Marsha reassured them both, hugging Selena from the other side. "You got Camille here quickly. That makes all the difference—"

"In severe anaphylaxis cases," Selena finished for her, whispering the doctor's description of Camille's condition.

Selena was shaking so badly, if the other women hadn't been supporting her, she'd have collapsed.

Severe.

It was a word she'd never heard used about her daughter's allergies. But she knew the horror stories. Worst-case scenarios. This had been her nightmare since Camille had been a baby and first diagnosed with food sensitivities. And all she could do was wait now, while specialists tried to stabilize her baby.

"They have her on oxygen." By the time Selena had rushed her daughter into the ER, Camille had been lethargic, almost unconscious. A team of nurses and the doctor had been waiting. So had Marsha, who'd hurried down from the cardiac floor. Oliver had called ahead and energized everyone into motion. Within seconds, Camille had been taken from Selena's arms and into a treatment area.

Now Selena couldn't tear her gaze from the image of her daughter lying immobile on a treatment table. Her play clothes had been cut away from her chest so monitors and heaven knew what else could be hooked up. One of her flower flip-flops lay on the floor beneath the exam table. The other was still on her left foot. There were two IVs, one in each arm. The frantic activity around her had settled down in the last few minutes. That had to be a good sign. Right?

"They're just taking precautions," Marsha assured her. "The paramedics did the same with Joe when they came to the house. They're stabilizing her. Making sure whatever's happening doesn't get any worse."

Selena nodded. Then her breath caught as she remembered everything Marsha had been through earlier that week.

"You should be upstairs with your husband," Selena insisted.

"Dru's with him. Joe's spirits are up. We just received the approval to move him to the step-down unit. Travis headed over to the house so Oliver can be here—Oliver feels so bad, thinking it was something Camille ate when she was with him. Everyone's exactly where they should be, Selena. Including me. Camille is important to us. You both are. We'll get through this. Don't you worry."

We can work through all of this together, especially things with Camille . . .

Selena fought back tears.

Belinda's hold on her tightened.

"Thank you for being here," Selena said to both women.

"Ms. Rosenthal?" The very young trauma doctor who'd been working on Camille stepped around the half-closed green curtain that had been pulled around Camille's ER bed.

"Yes." Selena rushed toward him. "How is my daughter?"

"We have her breathing and heart rate better controlled. She's still pretty out of it. We're treating her with a high dose of steroids for the asthma symptoms, other meds for the primary allergy. We'll be admitting her and observing her closely for the next twenty-four hours. Depending on her response to treatment we may need to keep her longer than that. But for now . . ." He smiled. "I'm cautiously optimistic that we're out of the woods with this attack. She's a very lucky girl that you got her here so quickly. Her airway was almost completely obstructed, and her blood pressure was dangerously low, compromising her heart's ability to beat properly."

"What . . ." Selena couldn't finish. She felt Camille's grand-mothers join her.

"What caused this?" Belinda asked. "She's never had a reaction this bad before, has she?"

Selena shook her head. "But her pediatricians warned me this might happen. They said to let her lead a normal life but to be careful that the adults around her knew what to do in case of an emergency."

And that had been the beginning of the end for Selena and Parker—long after she should have left him for other reasons, but had stayed thinking she owed her daughter to try to make their family work. Parker's carelessness where Camille's allergies were concerned, his refusal to take precautions or learn anything about how to help her if she became reactive, had been the final straw.

"There was no way to foresee this." The doctor shoved his clipboard under his arm. "Your daughter could have outgrown her allergies without an extreme anaphylaxis episode ever happening. Most kids do. It sounds like you've done everything just right. My team will take it from here and get her back on her feet and playing again in no time."

"But can you tell us what caused it?" Marsha asked.

"One of the nurses will take a history of what you think she might have been exposed to immediately prior to the onset of symptoms, but unfortunately that might not tell us anything for certain."

"I wasn't with her the whole time—" Selena started to say.

"I was." Oliver appeared at her side.

Marsha and Belinda faded away as he took Selena's hand, his grip firm, reassuring, his eyes concerned but calm. His attention strayed to where Camille was lying so still on the table beyond the green curtain. He quite simply melted.

"I'm so sorry," he said to Selena.

"It's not your fault," she assured him. "You couldn't have—"

"She was with me this morning when she—"

"And me," Belinda interrupted, behind them. "We don't know what she came into contact with or when."

"And even when we are sure," Selena said, "the doctor was just saying no one could have predicted this. And she surprised you this morning on top of it. Don't blame yourself."

"She's so sick," Oliver said. "And she could be my . . ."

Selena pushed onto her toes and kissed him, loving him for being so concerned.

"Yes," she said. "She could be. So pull yourself together, like any parent would have to. She's going to be okay." Selena was more able to believe that now, with Oliver beside her.

Oliver kissed her back, then inched away, steadier now. His focus returned to Camille.

The ER doctor cleared his throat. "As I was saying. Someone will be by with a survey for you to fill out, so we can try to identify the cause. I've already gotten my staff started on admitting Camille to pediatrics."

"Thank you," Marsha replied.

The doctor left as one of the ER admissions nurses rushed over. "Mrs. Gryphon?"

Oliver's attention shifted to the nurse, then to Selena. Given his startled expression, it was the first time he'd heard her married name.

"Your husband's on the phone at the desk," the nurse said.

"What?" Selena and Oliver both asked.

"We had some admit questions regarding her insurance," the nurse answered while she eyed the man Selena had just been kissing. "The insurance company must have contacted your husband. He insists on speaking with you before he'll deal with us."

"You can't be serious." Belinda sounded ready to explode.

Selena was right there with her. From the rising fury on his face, so was Oliver.

"He was asking for details about his daughter's condition," the nurse said, "but you told us you were her primary guardian. We weren't sure what to say to him so . . ."

"She's not his daughter," Selena corrected. "He wanted to adopt Camille," she said to Oliver, "but . . ." She looked to Belinda. "He wasn't the father I wanted for her."

The nurse, eyes rounded at the personal details, pointed a thumb over her shoulder to the admissions desk. "Whoever he is, he's on the phone. Your daughter's listed as a dependent on his policy, and at the moment he's refusing to provide the insurance rep confirmation about her status."

"I'll take care of the bill," Oliver said.

"What?" Selena shook her head. "That's not necessary. It could be thousands of dollars if they keep her here for a couple of days. And we're still covered by Parker's insurance. He's just—"

"Trying to control you. He's harassing you while your daughter needs urgent medical care." Oliver pulled a credit card from his wallet. "Use this to cover her account, then hang up the damn phone and cut him out of the loop."

"Oliver, don't . . ."

He had to stop. It was a wonderful if overly generous gesture. The rational part of Selena could see his point. Eliminating Parker from the situation was the most efficient way to handle things. But she couldn't take it—Oliver throwing money at *her* problems the way he'd bankrolled his family from a distance.

He had to stop. *They* had to stop. Everyone, everything, had to just stop for a minute, until Selena could think straight and didn't have the urge to shove the man's gold card down his throat.

"I don't want this," she told him. "You don't have to do this. You don't know anything about Parker and me and Camille. Please, don't put yourself in the middle of our problems."

"It's done." He handed his card to the nurse. Once she was gone, he said, "What happened between you and the bastard you married is none of my business, if you don't want to talk about it. But Camille's family, whether I'm her biological father or not. She's going to get what she needs—without you having to do your husband's bidding while he bullies his way back into your life. That's not going to happen as long as I have a dime in my bank account."

"How long has she been here?" Marsha asked Dru.

They were staring through the windows of Joe's CICU room. He was scheduled to move to step-down tomorrow. He was doing as well as a man could expect less than two days after having open-heart surgery. Which meant he was swollen and puffy and paler than Marsha had ever seen him. And he was in a lot more pain than he wanted anyone to know. But as she had every time she'd set eyes on Joseph Dixon since her first day at college, she gazed at him and smiled.

They were going to get through this stronger than before.

He had so much to live for. Just look at the surprise that had been awaiting her when she'd returned from the ER. Bethany was curled up beside her dad, half on his hospital bed, one leg hanging over the side, her head nestled on Joe's shoulder while he slept.

"Bethie was here when I came back from the bathroom," Dru said, "about half an hour ago. The nurses said she'd just slipped in. And she's already stayed too long. I've run them off twice so she could have as much time with Dad as she wants. Do you think she'll stay once we get her out of his room?"

"I think she should know how much we want her to stay." Like Marsha was hoping Selena and Camille were learning how much they were wanted. Like Oliver hopefully was. "Our family has to pull together now, and not just for Joe."

Dru hugged Marsha to her side. "Bethie's doing a good job at the Whip. Whatever we need her to do. She's even letting me hang some of her work on the walls. Unsigned. Of course it's too good. Everyone knows whose it is. There's so much of her in each painting. But no one bothers her about them. You should see people, Mom. They stop and stare and smile."

Bethany had a gift for bringing her imagination to life so others could experience how she saw the world. It was in handling day-to-day reality that she still struggled.

"She must have heard by now," Marsha said, "that Oliver's back."

"She's talked to him a little. People in town are trying to get her to spill what she knows about Oliver and Selena. But she's not gossiping about the family."

"Of course she's not." No matter how angry Bethany might be at her brother for being gone so long, she'd still protect him.

"Is Camille okay?" Dru asked.

"They're keeping her for a day from the sound of it. But she's going to be fine. Oliver and Selena, though . . . he wants to love those two so much. Selena's terrified to let him try."

Dru watched Joe and her sister for a while before responding. "Selena's afraid he's going to run again."

"We all are."

Dru raised an eyebrow. "Except she's a runner, too. All those years ago from Belinda. From her problems with her husband. From Chandlerville again, from the sound of it. And now Oliver's crowding her too much, too soon. Maybe so he can do what he thinks he needs to for the family—for me and Brad and you and Dad—and then leave again himself."

Marsha took in the peaceful picture of Bethany curled next to the foster father who'd forever claimed her as his own. Tears rushed. Blinking her eyes, she kept them at bay.

"We can't let them go," she said. "Oliver or Selena. We can't lose Camille."

"We won't." Dru leaned her head on Marsha's shoulder. "Not without a fight. Not forever. Not even if they do leave. We'll make sure they know we'll always be here for them. The way you've let Bethany know. And look, she's back. She's with Dad when it matters. Camille will have her chance to know us, too."

"Family stands up for family." The way Oliver had pushed back against Selena's husband's asinine demands downstairs. Marsha kissed Dru's temple.

Her daughter's eyes watered, too. She smoothed her hand over her belly. "Camille belongs with us."

Marsha dug into the pockets of the light cardigan she wore to counter the artificial cold of the CICU. She passed over a bundle of unused tissues. "The way your baby will belong?"

"It would break my heart"—Dru sniffed—"for my baby not to grow up knowing . . ." She stepped back. Stared at Marsha, her secret out. "You knew?"

Marsha pulled her into a hug. "That you and Brad don't want to wait until fall to get married, for more reasons than your dad's health? You've been pushing your food around on your plate when you come for Sunday dinner. You usually have more energy than the rest of us combined, but Brad's been obsessed with you getting your rest since Joe's heart attack."

She eased Dru away.

"Plus," she added, "you're blooming, honey. You're more beautiful than I've ever seen you, and that's saying something. Your fiancé obviously thinks so, too, the way he watches you when he thinks no one will notice. I'm so happy for you both."

Dru laughed, her tears spilling over. "I'm a watering pot. He doesn't know what to do with me. He likes it better when we fight, and then we make up. Now he just sits there when I get like this and holds my hand and waits for me to turn back into my old, cranky self."

"Oh, the cranky will come as the hormones surge and your feet swell and you both are freaking out about how the rest is going to work, now that you're adding a new life into the mix of your jobs and your marriage and everything else you both love to do around town."

"We'd already do anything for this baby," Dru gushed. "Anything. We stay up at night, dreaming of how it will be, everything we'll have once we have our own family to raise. I don't know how you and Dad do it, so many kids from so many different places, and somehow you made us all feel like we were your priority."

"Each of you was." Each of them still was. Every child Marsha and Joe had fostered still belonged to them. Would always belong with them. "Just like this baby, and Camille, if she's Brad's, will be your priority from now on. That's how love works. No matter how full your heart feels, there's room for more when someone you love needs you."

"Like Camille and Selena need Oliver, regardless of what some paternity test says. They're meant to be together, Mom. We can't let them screw this up again."

Chapter Nineteen

Selena gathered her purse from the small table in her daughter's hospital room. She was still wearing her jogging gear from that morning. She smelled like her run and like a mother who'd been scared out of her mind for the last four hours. She needed to clean up before she tackled more drama.

"You'll make the right decision." Belinda had settled into the chair beside Camille's bed as soon as Selena stood.

Once Camille had been moved to the pediatric unit and fallen asleep, Selena's mother had split her time between pacing back and forth across Camille's tiny room grumbling about Parker, and silently pacing in the hallway outside. She'd stepped back in a moment ago, saying Oliver was waiting to give Selena a ride home. Where, Selena had no doubt, she and Oliver would be dealing with Camille's questions, Parker's latest asshole move, and Oliver's determination to intervene on Selena and Camille's behalf. All before Selena could get herself cleaned up and back to the hospital in her own car.

"Is there a right decision?" she asked.

"You're worried about the money Oliver wants to shell out?" her mother asked. "And what it means?"

"I don't know what *any* of this means. Or how I'm going to explain what happens next to Camille."

Belinda pulled her newspaper from the canvas bag she'd had the presence of mind to grab when they'd raced out of the house with Camille. Selena's mother had brought her bag, Camille's flower quilt from her window seat, and Bear. Meanwhile, Selena didn't even have her purse. Her mother had said she'd sit with Camille while Selena took whatever time she needed to pull herself together.

"One of these days," Belinda said, "you're going to have to completely trust someone."

"I trust you now." It was still a little shocking, how easy and right that felt.

"Did you ever really trust Parker?"

"Did you ever trust Daddy?"

"Gabriel . . ." Belinda slipped on the sliders she used to read, then pushed them up to rest on the top of her head. "Your father wasn't cut out for family. I knew that when I married him. But you were on the way, and we loved each other, and I thought he'd grow into the rest. Just because he couldn't, just because Parker thought success meant money and things and a family everyone in his corporate world could admire . . . doesn't mean every man, even one who's had trouble settling down, won't come through if you give him a chance."

Selena shook her head. "After all these years. After how much you disapproved when Oliver and I were dating . . . now you're practically shoving me at him."

Belinda laid her paper on the table by the bed. "It's okay to want him, Selena. It's always been okay, even in high school when I was terrified of how reckless you two were being. I didn't want to believe how much you loved Oliver. How much you needed him. And I didn't want him to make you even more unhappy than you already were. But I believe that he loved you back then, no matter how badly the two of you ended things. I think he could be good for you still, if that's what you want."

"But what . . ." Selena thought of all the dreams she'd fought about building a life for her and Oliver and Camille. "What if Camille turns out to be Brad's?"

"And you've given your heart to a man who isn't her father?"

Selena nodded.

"A man," her mother added, "you think won't want you or your daughter once he doesn't have to feel responsible for you?"

"He's trying to be responsible. But . . ."

"You want to be loved."

And Selena so wanted for that love to be Oliver's. Look at the way he'd held her and kissed her at the Dixon house. The way he'd talked so carefully with Camille when she was upset, and tried to help her understand. Even how he'd overstepped and pushed back against Parker downstairs when it had technically been none of his business. It all sounded so good.

But was it love?

"If it's not going to last," she said, "I have to put a stop to it, for Camille's sake." For both their sakes.

You could destroy me . . .

"How?" her mother asked. "Camille's asking her own questions. She'll be looking for her own answers. You can try to stop what you're feeling for Oliver. But you can't decide for your daughter who and what she's going to care about. Trust me. I've done the legwork."

"But what if she's hurt all over again?"

"What if she loves the Dixons and Oliver, or Brad, or all of them, and everything turns out fine?"

You wouldn't have been able to stay away from me whether Camille was involved or not. And it terrifies you, what that could mean.

"What if *I* mess it up again?" Selena said, voicing her deepest fear. "What if I can't love Oliver enough to stop . . ."

To stop being terrified.

"You can, Selena. Take my word for it. I've seen you with your daughter. Kristen Beaumont can't stop talking to people about how the kids at school adore having you sub for them. You've given me a second chance, and I know I haven't made that easy. You don't know how *not* to love, honey. You're just going to have to trust the rest of us—including Oliver—to love you back."

"Thanks, man," Oliver said to his brother. He punched the call closed and tossed his phone onto his truck's dash. "Travis says to take as long as we need."

Selena didn't move in the seat beside him. She hadn't said a word since they'd left the hospital, driven down Main, grabbed the takeout Dru had called in for them at the Whip, and finally pulled into Belinda's driveway behind Selena's junker.

"How the hell," Oliver said, needing a target for the frustration he'd been suppressing for hours, "did you manage to make it all the way south in that heap?"

She swiveled toward him. "Fred's good as gold. He's never let us down."

"Fred?"

"Flintstone." She waited for Oliver to work it out.

He smiled when he did. "Does that make your daughter Pebbles?"

"Cricket." Selena tucked her hair behind her ears. "I call her Cricket. The way she's always loved to play outside. She hops all over the place, dances, rolls in the grass, like a—"

"Adorable little bug. I get it. You never used to be able to sit still, either. Like mother, like daughter."

He watched some of the wariness ease from Selena's expression. Hopeless, bottomless love took its place.

"Camille likes to spread out one of Belinda's quilts," she said, "and lie in the sun and read. Over by—"

"The camellia bushes? I saw her out there the other afternoon. It made me think of us, when we'd hang out back or in some field somewhere, like the one in Bethany's painting in the Dream Whip."

"Yeah. I saw it. The first time I did, it made me think of Camille."

"Why?"

"You." Selena looked down at the fingers she'd clasped in her lap. "And me. It was my birthday, and we made love by the tree Bethany painted, just before we . . . the week before I broke up with you. I've always told myself that was the afternoon we made Camille. Even if I didn't know for sure, I've always wanted her to be yours. I see so much of you in her. But wanting doesn't make it so, Oliver. I appreciate what you did this morning. But I don't want you to feel obligated—"

"She's my family, Selena. As much as Dru and Travis and Fin and Teddy and all the other kids."

"Yes. But . . ."

"But what?"

"It's different with her. With you and me and her. I couldn't bear Camille being just an obligation for you. For Brad or for your parents."

"You know my family better than that."

"But do I know you? Really? What do you want, Oliver?"

She was the one who'd given up on them when they were kids. He should have gone and found her in New York. Maybe then she wouldn't have married that slime Parker. Oliver should have kept loving her until she was strong enough to love herself better. But that was seven years ago. And even then she hadn't known if he was what she wanted.

"You first," he said. "Stop making this about a daughter we may or may not have together. Camille will be taken care of and loved, whether I'm in the picture or not. Your secret's out. But you're still pulling away, waiting for some other shoe to drop. Tell me what this is really about. One minute you're kissing me. The next you're telling me to back off because you don't need me in your life unless I meet some list of conditions you seem to add to on an hourly basis. Why—"

"Why are you here with me now?" Selena demanded. "Why aren't you at the hospital with your family, or over at your parents' house looking after their kids? Because you're trying to make everyone happy? Which, by the way, is impossible. Or because being here for me now, or at the hospital for Camille this morning—worried and angry and out-of-your-mind furious at Parker on her behalf—is what makes *you* happy?"

Oliver clamped his hands around the steering wheel. He knew what she needed to hear. Why couldn't he just say it? "I'll give you everything I can, Selena. I always would have if you'd have let me. I didn't come back to town thinking this would happen. I can't honestly tell you I wanted it to. My family needs me to keep doing the work I do. Working to help them is what my life's been about pretty much since I left Chandlerville. But—"

"But what? You'll take one for the team with me and Camille? Be a good guy and pay for whatever it takes to be involved in our lives, too. Love me a little whenever a client doesn't need you—as long as you don't have to commit emotionally for any longer than you want to. Until I wake up one day and realize I've been alone all along. And that you've been finding someone else to console you, because being with me and my daughter has just gotten too damn complicated for you to handle?"

Selena's rant hiccupped to a halt.

She'd inched away, her back pressed against the passenger door.

"Parker?" Oliver asked.

Don't think you can bully me, she'd said when Oliver first confronted her about Camille. And after the ugliness that had gone down in the ER, he had no trouble believing her bastard of a husband had been mistreating her long before she filed for divorce. Oliver was going to meet Parker Gryphon one day. His next excuse to travel north, he was hunting the slime down and working a few things out man-to-man.

"He cheated on you?" he asked.

"If that's what you want to call it."

"Slept around?"

"And around." Selena's laugh had Oliver wanting to use the travel app on his phone to book a red-eye to New York that very night. "But Parker is a good provider. And he was willing to keep providing, as long as I could adjust to our arrangement."

"What arrangement?"

"The one he'd made entirely on his own, where he found a ready-made family that gave him the appearance of stability he needed. And he gave me the security I'd been so desperate for when he saved me from having to run back to Chandlerville at eighteen and beg my mother for help. He provided for Camille what on the outside looked like a family that any little girl would love, in a stylish high-rise apartment in the heart of Manhattan . . . and I just couldn't. I couldn't abandon her to that, Oliver. She deserves to be surrounded by real love, even if it's only mine."

"And what do you deserve?" Oliver asked.

"I . . ." Selena's lips trembled, just like her daughter's did when she lost control.

"Whatever this is between us, I don't want it to stop again. But you *can* stop it if you're determined to. Like when we were teenagers. I was loving you the only way I knew how then, too."

"And now your way is by throwing money at people to keep them from expecting more. Like you do with your family. Like this morning with Camille in the ER. I know I sound paranoid. But I'm not setting myself or my daughter up like that again. Especially with someone I love as much as I've always loved you."

Selena looked at him, into him, shocked by what she'd revealed.

Before he realized what he'd done, Oliver had hauled her closer. Or maybe she'd launched herself at him, stretched across the truck's center console, her hands gripping his arms, her beautiful eyes searching. Like in his dreams, it was just them, and Selena was needing him like she wouldn't survive without him. The way he wouldn't without her.

They took each other's kiss, and he was transported back to where they'd been as kids, where they'd always be—loving each other with everything they were. With Selena in his arms, he'd be home for as long as she'd let him have her. He framed her face with his hands, angling her mouth for more. Her fingers threaded through his hair, gripping and urging him closer, their kiss roughening, desperate.

This was what he wanted.

More. And then more. And always. He'd always wanted it with Selena. No matter how many women, how much time, how much work he'd used to fill the emptiness, or how far away he'd traveled . . . being here, home, with Selena had always been where he'd belonged. Enough to keep moving on forever if he was never going to have her back.

She was still in her workout clothes. He kissed down to her neck, tasting salt and sun.

"I think of you when I run," he whispered into her ear, feeling her tremble. "I was thinking about you the night before I came back, after I was supposed to have let go of the past as part of my recovery . . . but I couldn't stop myself."

He kissed her lips, the tip of her nose. He watched her eyes flutter open.

"Anytime," he said, "I'm free of the work I've filled my life with, whenever I try to sleep, when it's quiet and just me—you're always there, making me want you. All of it, everything I've done since I left has had something to do with you, Selena, and how good we once were for each other. How much I want that back. I'll never be free of you."

The need in her brown eyes deepened until he swore he could see her heart. A tentative smile spread across her face. Her tongue was a flirty temptation, caressing her bottom lip. His body tightened just shy of pain.

"Really?" she whispered. Her chest rose and fell in rhythm with his. "I couldn't forget, either. This. All the rest. The hours we'd just sit and talk, or sit and do nothing, out back by the camellias, in town somewhere, some quiet place where no one would find us. I could never forget you. And when I run now, to clear my head so I can think . . . I never can, completely, because you're always there."

"I thought I'd never see you again," he confessed. "And I couldn't be in Chandlerville without you. I'm starting to understand that. Without you I couldn't face coming . . ."

"Home." She kissed him.

Oliver drew her hands from around his neck and placed her palms against his chest, knowing he was taking a risk. She'd just had a shock. Camille was still in the hospital. And Parker was ramping up the pressure to get Selena and her daughter back. Selena was off balance and still not one hundred percent sure of Oliver, or of them. But what if this was their last chance?

"We're both here now." He searched her expression, seeing her love and fragile strength. Craving both. But did she really see him—the way he was, instead of the mixed-up kid she'd once known? "We've been circling this for days, for years. You can't tell me what you're going to need next—for Camille or yourself. And I can't promise I can be that person for you, not until we sort things out. But we can have this."

He gave her the gentlest kiss he could. Like their very first kiss—when she'd shown him how to love again.

"This can be ours," he said. "No being afraid. No one, nothing between us. Please, Selena. Be with me one more time."

She watched him for what felt like hours. For too long. She smoothed her palm over his heart like she would push him away. But then she was in his arms again, holding him as if she'd never let go.

"God, Selena." He crushed her closer. "I love you. So damn much."

It was his last coherent thought.

Selena surfaced from drowning in Oliver's kisses, her vision as clouded as her mind.

"We can't do this," she gasped.

"We can't?" Oliver gritted his teeth, his jaw tightening in brutally harsh lines.

She drew him into a soft kiss this time, afternoon sunlight slanting through the windshield of his truck, nearby trees caressing them with swaying shadows.

"Not here," she explained. "Where anyone could drive by and see us."

They'd been the talk of the town since the night of the AA meeting, since before that. Now they were making out in his very recognizable truck, in her mother's driveway.

"Right." Oliver fumbled his keys out of the ignition. "Inside."

He was beside her door before she could get it open. Hand in hand, they hurried across Belinda's yard and to the porch and through the front door that was still slightly ajar from Selena and her mother rushing Camille to the hospital. Selena closed it behind them, turned, and Oliver backed her into its wooden surface. He pressed his body to hers. His mouth tortured her again, everywhere, anywhere, not nearly enough places at once.

She stretched into him, wanted to feel every inch of him.

"Too many clothes," she panted, tearing his shirt from his jeans.

"Bed?" he asked.

She shook her head. "I sleep on a couch in my mother's sewing room."

His attention strayed over his shoulder. "Couches can be good."

"Yes, they can," she agreed and was swept off her feet and carried across the room to her mother's love seat.

"This one's closer," he insisted, "even if it's so small I'll be a cripple before we're done."

She giggled as he lowered her to the cushions. She inhaled when his chest pressed against hers, his body pinning her again, right where she wanted to be caught. She wrapped her arms around him and dragged his shirt completely off. He buried his face in her neck, kissing the sensitive skin behind her ear, setting her body raging for more. She caught a flash of color over his heart.

"Let me see," she said.

He pulled back, his expression questioning. When she brushed her fingers reverently over her discovery, he stilled.

"It's beautiful," she said. So delicately done, it could have looked feminine, but not on Oliver. Not even with its crimson-red flower and the soft curves of its petals and leaves. "It's a—"

"Camellia," he said. "So I'd have something to remind me of you."

Like Selena had had Camille, and prayed in her most secret heart that her daughter was Oliver's.

A rush of . . . rightness blinded her. She blinked away the emotion so she could see Oliver clearly. She caressed his tattoo, the strong beat of his heart answering her touch.

"You okay?" he asked. "If this is too much . . ."

"No." She smiled. "It's just been a long time . . . since I've let myself want something as much as you make me want."

He smiled, too, with wicked intent. "Wanting can be good."

She kissed him again and again, while he made fast work of her jog top. "Very, very good."

His breath hissed in at the sight of her. His hands and fingers caressed while hers did, too, relearning his touch and, with her tongue, his taste. His mouth took its own journey, worshiping her breasts and then her belly. While her nails scraped down and back up and around, and then down again to the quivering muscles of his belly, the buckle of his belt.

"Hurry." She needed more. She needed now.

"Yes."

Oliver helped her make quick work of her running pants and socks and shoes. His jeans and the rest of his clothes melted away. She wrapped her arms and legs around him, rocking with him, kissing him and needing him.

"Yes," he chanted. "Selena."

They became one slowly. The world stopped completely. Her body thrilled, shimmering all over, as he held them both still, held them back, keeping her from rushing.

"Oliver. Please . . ."

"Look at me." His thumb tilted her chin up until her eyes opened. His face hovered above her in the deepening shadows of the unlit room. "Stay with me."

He began to move, set the rhythm. She reveled in the perfect feel of it, of them. He took her slowly, as if he wanted to make it last. She didn't want it to end either. Ever. But she couldn't bear it. It wasn't nearly enough. Not when her body knew what was coming, what they'd always found. A place only theirs, where need became love and they'd never be alone again. Wild. Untamed. Desperate. But never alone.

She urged him on and cried out when his next kiss deepened, seduced, dragged a groan from her lips. His hands lifted her higher, held her, encouraged her to want more of him, all of him.

"Now," he breathed, "take me with you, Selena."

She saw stars, she saw him, them. She saw their perfect connection mirrored in the brilliant green of Oliver's eyes. And then they were flying, clutching at each other, loving each other, on fire and soaring and tumbling and knowing nothing but the truth neither of them had outrun. That this, their bodies straining closer, deeper, harder, and then caressing softer, holding, comforting . . .

This was intimacy. Belonging. True love.

And it *would* destroy her again if she had to give it up.

Chapter Twenty

Selena pulled the hand-pieced throw from the back of Belinda's couch, while Oliver stood and slipped his amazing backside into his jeans. The lean muscles of his shoulders and torso disappeared under his T-shirt. Only then did he turn around.

He'd said nothing since they'd finished making love. He'd grown quiet almost immediately, slipping away emotionally even while he'd still been holding her. Now they were back to staring at each other without saying a word, the same as when he'd first pulled into the driveway next door. Her body was shaking. Her heartbeat might never settle. Entirely too weak and wanting him back, she'd felt . . . relieved at his withdrawal. And flash-fire furious.

"I didn't know a man could do the walk of shame," she said, "practically standing in one place. If you need to wash up before you head to your mother's, there's a hose out back. Feel free to drown yourself under it."

Absorbing her uncalled-for outburst, he ran both hands through the dark hair she'd mussed. He sat in Belinda's recliner.

"I don't regret what we just did," he said.

God, Selena.

"Making love?" she asked.

"Yes."

"I can see that, what with half of the room between us and all."

He clasped his hands together, his forearms propped on his thighs. "It meant a lot to me. *You* mean a lot to me."

She'd felt that while he'd been holding her, like she was his everything again, exactly the way she'd needed to feel. But he *was* regretting it now. Or maybe she was just overthinking things, worrying too much, looking for all the ways this could still end badly.

You can't tell me what you're going to need next. . . And I can't promise I can be that person for you . . . But we can have this.

She was freezing without him. The way she'd been frozen inside for the last seven years. And she was tired. Tired of landing on her ass, on the letdown side of yet another dream. And that's what this felt like. She'd always known it would, and she'd let herself wish her way here, regardless.

"This isn't your fault," she conceded. "You're a good man, Oliver." He was the best. The best for her. There was no denying it. Just moments ago, in his arms, all she'd been able to see was forever.

"But?"

"But we're looking for different things, I think."

"Are we?" His voice was clipped, deeper, warning her to be careful. Maybe warning himself.

You don't know how not *to love, honey. . .*

"Do you want me?" she asked. "Camille? A life with us? A *real* life, where you're a part of our every day, and when you're away you can't wait to come home to us? Can you tell me that?"

He looked down at his linked fingers. She looked back at the two other times she'd been at this crossroads. When she'd made a destructive choice and broken up with Oliver the first time around. And when she'd made a healthy decision to walk away from her marriage to Parker.

"You don't know what you want," she said to the man who carried a reminder of her over his heart. "Except that you don't want to let anyone down. You're not sure what any of this means. Except that it means we have to do this—really talk about us."

"And we have to do that now?"

"I won't be careless with Camille's happiness again. Or mine. You care about my daughter, obviously, and I'm grateful for that. And for your family's acceptance. But if she turns out to be Brad's, or even if she's yours, you're not sure what any of this will look like to you tomorrow, or next week, or when Joe's better and it's time for you to get back to your real life."

Oliver stood and slowly returned to the couch, sitting beside her. He stared at where she was clutching her mother's quilt to her chest. He looked down to the tennis shoes they'd both kicked under the coffee table—lying in a jumbled heap like they might every day if he and Selena lived together, ran together, came home together on a free afternoon to sneak a chance to make love while no one would miss them.

"This is a lot for me," he said. "I've turned my life inside out in less than a week. I'm still trying to do the right thing for everyone." He shook his head. "Like any of us knows what that is. Except that I was terrified this morning. From the moment Belinda called until I could get to you and Camille at the hospital, I was terrified of losing my chance to have you and your daughter in my life. Of never knowing what that could be like again—a forever family of my own."

A forever family. That's what foster kids called it, he'd told her a lifetime ago. What they all secretly wanted, even the ones whose behavior and choices made it impossible to find. A place to belong to forever, no matter what. Exactly what Selena had been searching for, too, ever since losing her father.

"Oliver . . ." She curled into his hug. She squeezed her eyes shut.

"You're right about one thing." He kissed the top of her head. "I don't dwell on long-term things. Now is what I'm good at. Making money now. Where I'm going to be making money next, so other people can live their lives and take care of their long-term things. I'm good at doing that for my family. I haven't let myself want more than that for a long time. But I swear, Selena, back in the truck with you . . ." He kissed her again. "When I held you in my arms just now. Since I first caught sight of you Tuesday morning . . . I've realized how much I still need you in my heart."

"Today. But what about tomorrow? When you're gone from here tomorrow or next week, how much of us will still be in your heart then? How long will it be before we see you again?"

She wanted to beg him to reassure her. Except the truth was more important. It was the most important thing they could give each other.

"It's complicated," he admitted. "*We're* complicated."

Yes, they were. "There are other things, other people to consider—besides how good we are when it's just us."

He stared at their bare feet, so different but so right resting beside one another under the coffee table. "I know I want to give you and Camille everything I can."

"Then I guess it's up to us to decide."

"Decide what?"

"If that *everything* is going to be enough. If the complications are worth it. Or . . . we get honest with ourselves about how different our lives are. We leave well enough alone and agree to stop fighting reality. And this time, we at least stay friends."

"You'd really walk away without even trying? Because I need time before we put a label on something that just started up again. We're supposed to give up now? Because it's too hard for you to keep trying? What does that make what we just did—a booty call?"

"It was what it was." The first step toward her having Oliver's heart forever, or him breaking hers for the last time. "It was a moment. A wonderful moment. But now it's back to the real world. No fairy-tale endings. No completely right choices. No instruction manual for what to do next. We have to figure us and our families out. To make that work, it's going to take being together for more than a moment. It could take a lifetime—Camille's lifetime. And you don't even know where you'll be next week."

"You don't trust me, Selena. That's what this is really about." Oliver walked over to stare through the gauzy front curtains, at the waning light beyond. "Not enough to stick things out until they run their course. You never did."

Her phone sounded off, making them both jump as it played "Danger Zone." Oliver's cell rang, too. He retrieved her purse from the entryway table beside the front door. Handing it over, he fished his cell from his jeans and read the display.

"Brad," he said without answering.

"Parker."

Selena was surprised it had taken her husband this long to make his next move.

"Shit," she said on an exhausted sigh.

"Trade with me?"

"What?"

Oliver held out his phone. "You set up a meeting with Dru and Brad, to discuss Camille. I'll deal with Parker."

"But you—"

"I understand his type, too. I can work with you to get him out of your life. You work with Brad and Dru and me to make the right choice about Camille's paternity."

Selena couldn't move. Why couldn't she move?

"Trust me, Selena." Oliver laid his phone on the coffee table. He held out his hand for hers. "Let's start dealing with the complications and the confusion and figure out today and tomorrow and next week—together. This is it for us. This is our chance. Are we in, or are we out?"

Oliver answered Selena's phone. The tight-ass slime on the other end began talking immediately in his slick, Upper East Side accent.

"This is ridiculous, Selena," Parker said. "*You're* being ridiculous. My tactics are unseemly, I know. But *you* know I'm not going to stop. Come back and talk with me like an adult instead of running away. You'll be free of that Podunk place and your mother for good. You don't need anyone else's help for you and Camille but mine. If you'd just—"

"Neither of them are coming back to New York." Oliver kept his tone reasonable. He wanted to reach through the phone and strangle the guy. "Selena doesn't need your money, your two-timing, or your help for her child. She has friends here, real family. And she's the best mother I know. There's no way you're going to convince her to come back. Give it a rest, man. It's over."

Selena nodded—at what Oliver had said, or to whatever she and Brad were discussing on Oliver's phone.

"Tonight?" she asked both him and Brad. "At the hospital, you two will come over after the Whip closes?"

Oliver nodded in agreement.

He'd cover the house and the kids for Travis until then, so his brother could check in on Joe or whatever else he needed to do. Travis wouldn't mind stepping back in for a while tonight, once he heard what it was for.

"I want to speak with my wife," the slimeball insisted.

"Ex-wife."

"Not yet."

"Soon." Oliver bit out. "Very soon."

Selena flinched at his fraying control. He took her hand.

"You can speak with her lawyer from now on," he said more calmly. "You're done manipulating Selena with money and everything you think she should still want with you. Leave her alone."

"Her lawyer?" Parker scoffed. "Clearly you don't know my wife or the position she's put herself in. *Her* lawyer is one of a fleet that I keep on retainer. I talk to the man every day. Now put Selena on the phone."

Oliver gently squeezed her fingers. "Her lawyer is my lawyer now. Let yours know to expect our filing to turn over all records pertaining to the divorce."

"And just who the hell are you?"

"I'm Camille's father." And the satisfaction of saying it out loud, whether it was true or not, felt right.

"Okay," Selena said to Brad. "We'll see you tonight."

She finished her call and slipped to her feet, wrapped in her mother's quilt. She grabbed her clothes and walked silently down the hall, presumably to her room.

"*I'm* the only father that little girl has ever known," Parker growled. "I wanted to adopt her."

"Before or after you decided to bang everything that moves

all over Manhattan, and who the hell knows where else? Selena and Camille are out of your life. Get used to it. And tell your lawyers to strap themselves in. Mine are about to make sure Selena is compensated for the years she spent trying to make a marriage to someone like you work. She won't be asking for child support. She won't need it. But don't think that means you're off the hook for the way you stomped all over her heart. Stop harassing her. End this, man. You're just embarrassing yourself."

Oliver thumbed the call closed, Parker still fuming on the other end.

Selena had returned, fully dressed in jeans and a loose sweatshirt, her face looking freshly washed. She'd heard the last of what he'd said to her husband.

"You won't have to deal with him again," Oliver promised.

"Because you're going to take care of it?" She passed him his phone and held her hand out for hers. "Another project for you to add to your list?"

"Because you're going to take care of it by allowing me to help." He pocketed his phone. "We're not kids any longer, Selena. You're clearly capable of managing your life and your choices. You were when we were teenagers, too. You've always been smart enough to take a friend's offer of support, if it will get an asshole like Parker permanently out of your daughter's life."

"A friend?"

"That's what you said. Friends at least? I'll give you my lawyer's number. What you do with it is up to you. Or you can trust me to contact the firm on your behalf."

"As my daughter's father?" Selena's voice broke. She pressed her fingers to her lips. She swallowed before continuing. "Why did you tell Parker that?"

"Because I want to be." More than Oliver could have believed. "And even if she's Brad's, I still want to be in her life, helping you both any way I can. Trust me on that, if nothing else."

Selena folded the quilt she'd returned with and laid it on the arm of the couch. She was so close. Her beauty, her heart, her capacity to keep loving fiercely, the way she loved Camille unconditionally, no matter how hard life knocked her around.

And Oliver wanted it all.

"I should give Travis a break," he said.

"Yeah. I . . . I need to get back to Camille."

She reached for Oliver first—thank God. It had been killing him, wondering if she ever would again. He held her, her head pressed to his heart.

"Thank you," she said. "For making being done with Parker possible. I can't imagine how much it's going to cost. The hospital and now your lawyer."

Oliver massaged her nape. Her hair curled madly, silky soft through his fingers. "The money isn't important. You'll be free. That's what matters. *You* matter to me."

"You matter to me, too." She pushed away to stand on her own.

But did he matter enough? Would she give him a chance to make sense of all the things he still had to? She reached for the purse she'd set on the coffee table and scooped up her keys.

"We're on with Brad and Dru?" he asked.

"Brad said they'd swing by the hospital after ten or so, meet us at Camille's room if that works for you."

"I'll be there."

Facing the rest of the day without Selena would be excruciating. But he was going to move his truck next door and out of her car's way. This time he wouldn't push her for more than she was ready to handle.

"Thanks again for what you did this morning for Marsha and Joe. You and Belinda standing up for them with Family Services could make all the difference in Teddy's placement."

"Your parents and their kids are lucky to have you back."

He inhaled. "I'm the lucky one."

His family had welcomed him home, no matter how much he'd put them through. And Selena had loved Oliver just now, like she never wanted to let him go. That's what he'd hold on to until tonight.

Things were still in chaos. But there had to be a path to making all of it work—for his family and Selena and Camille and himself. He'd come up with the right solution for everyone. He was certain of it.

As long as Selena found her way to trusting her heart.

And trusting him, one more time.

Chapter Twenty-One

Camille wanted to go home.

She wanted her Mommy.

She wanted to go back to when she'd been at the Dixons' with her mom and Oliver and Grammy. And she wanted not to have asked what she had. And she really, really wanted not to have gotten sick. She'd snuck just one cracker when she'd been helping with Teddy. She'd been hungry after playing outside, and she'd thought it was okay this time. It was Mrs. Dixon's house, and Mrs. Dixon's cookies were okay.

She liked helping with Teddy. She did not like having allergies. Or being in trouble. She shouldn't be in trouble because she'd wanted to know the truth about if she had another family. But she was. She just knew she was. Look at everything she'd made go wrong, because she'd gone over to the Dixons' house. Now she might not ever be able to help with Teddy again before she and Mommy moved.

Grammy walked into Camille's hospital room and smiled, not as if she was mad at all.

"How are we doing in here?" She kissed Camille's cheek. She

smoothed where a needle was still stuck in Camille's hand, attached to a tube that had a bag at the other end, hanging beside her bed. "Does it still sting?"

"A little."

Camille had woken up a few times before. Sometimes her Mommy had been there. Sometimes Grammy. But this was the first time Camille had felt like she was getting better, the way everyone kept saying she was—even though people had kept telling her to rest.

"Can we go home now?" she asked.

"Tomorrow, honey. But once your Mommy and I get you home, I'm going to pamper you with the biggest bubble bath I can make."

Camille liked bubbles. Grammy liked them, too, though Mommy hadn't believed it until Grammy had shown Mommy and Camille the bottles of bubble bath she kept in her bathroom. Bubbles always cheered Grammy up, she'd said, and made her feel special. She'd shared every kind of bubbles she had with Camille, and she'd even bought Camille a special bottle all her own—a Hello Kitty bottle, and the bubbles smelled like flowers.

If Grammy was going to make Camille a special bubble bath when they got home, Camille couldn't be in too much trouble for asking Oliver what she had.

"I didn't water my flowers this morning," she said.

The ones right under her window that needed water every day. Except today, she'd played out back all morning instead, and her flowers had to be really thirsty.

"Please," she begged. "I want to water them. I won't do anything else. I'll stay in bed. But I want to go home."

"I'll take care of your forget-me-nots in a little bit." Grammy smiled. "Once your mommy's back and I can slip out."

"Am I in a lot of trouble?" Camille asked. Then before Grammy could answer, she said, "I didn't mean to eat Teddy's crackers, it just happened. He handed me one, and I was hungry and . . . I won't go over to the Dixons' again, if Mommy's mad and doesn't want me to. But why doesn't she want them to be my family? What's so bad about them? Or about Oliver being my . . ."

Camille didn't say *daddy*.

She tried again, but she couldn't.

Grammy sat on the bed next to her. She pulled up the tulip quilt she'd wrapped Camille in before she and Mommy had brought Camille to the hospital. Camille had taken it outside to play that morning. Grammy had brought it back after they left the Dixons. Camille looked at her favorite quilt now, and it made her sad instead of happy.

"Your mom's got a lot to think about," her grammy said.

Grammy sounded sad, too, no matter how glad she said she was that Camille was okay. Something must be really wrong.

"Your mommy doesn't think the Dixons and Oliver are bad," Grammy insisted. "And you're not in trouble."

"Going next door by myself was wrong." Camille's stomach felt gross again. "And I shouldn't have snuck up front last night and listened to you and Mommy talk. But . . ."

"You wanted to know." Grammy rubbed her arm. "There's so much that you need to know. And you have every right to want to."

"I like the Dixons. They're fun. And they're so big, and they'd want me, Oliver said. And I want Oliver, if he's my . . ."

Daddy.

"Would it be so bad," Camille asked, "for me to belong to Oliver and his family?" Camille sat up in the bed, squeezing Grammy's quilt close. "I like it next door. I like it with you and Mommy at your house. And playing in your yard and staying in Mommy's room . . . But I like the Dixons, too. And they like me. Teddy and Fin and Lisa and everyone. I know they do." She *hoped* they did. "Would it be so bad, to want to be part of them, too?"

Grammy looked at her for a long time, like Grammy looked at Mommy a lot—when Mommy thought Grammy was going to be mad, but Camille thought Grammy was just trying not to say the wrong thing. "I don't think having more family in your life is ever a bad thing."

"Really?"

Grammy nodded. "Even if sometimes family makes us angry or scared."

"Like I was this morning? And Mommy, too?"

Grammy nodded again. "Family, real family, is never a bad thing, no matter how it happens into your life." She smoothed her hand over one of the tulips her mommy's mommy had sewn a long, long time ago. "Do you know why this is my favorite quilt?"

"'Cause it's pretty, and your grammy made it?"

Camille's grammy brushed her hand wider, across the colors and prints that made the different flowers and pieces of the quilt. Everything was white and pink, or something close to white and pink. The pieces were all different shapes, but they were so pretty together.

Her grammy had told her, when she'd let Camille pick the quilt from the stack in her bedroom closet, that some of the pieces had come from worn-out clothes and even the sacks people used to sell stuff in, like corn and beans and things. And Grammy's grammy had cut it all up into different shapes and sizes, when people stopped using their old things. She'd made the quilt out of stuff that would have been thrown away.

Grammy smiled. "Families are like quilts, honey. All kinds of people, coming together, sometimes from all kinds of places. Just look at how different your mommy and me are now. How long we've lived without each other—most of your life. But we're still family, right? You and me and your mom."

Camille nodded.

"All families," Grammy said, "even the ones with different parts that don't look like they'd fit together, can be beautiful—if you put enough work into them. And once you get the work right, like my grammy did with this quilt—because she knew all the different-shaped pieces would make lovely flowers for me—what you create can be the most beautiful thing you've ever seen."

"It's so pretty." Camille brushed her hand over the quilt, just like Grammy.

"Some people think quilts look messy," Grammy said. "But a good quilt, if it's strong enough, will last forever. And more than anything else, that's why this one's *my* favorite. My grandmother made it a long time ago, and it's been used a lot. I used to drag it all over the place, the same as you do. And look how beautiful it still is. It's still strong, even if it's not perfect anymore. And now I get to share it with you. Because our family's turned out to be strong, too, honey. No matter how different your mommy and I are, I get to share my flowers and my bubble bath with you. And your mommy's old room in my house. And the town I love so much. It's all even more special to me now."

"Because you love me so much, too?"

"I love you and your mommy both, sweetie. I'm so glad to have you in Chandlerville with me. That's why I wanted you to have this quilt. I want you to think of me every time you use it. Just like when I see it, I think of my grammy."

"I . . . I can keep it?"

"It's yours now."

Because Camille and her mommy were still going to leave?

"Do you . . ." Camille couldn't stop herself from asking again. "Do you think the Dixons would be glad to have me, too?"

Oliver had said they would.

"Of course we're happy to have you as part of our family," a voice said from the doorway.

Mrs. Dixon was standing there.

And so was Camille's mommy.

"I brought you a visitor," Mommy said. She was smiling like Grammy had—like Camille wasn't really in trouble at all. "Are you feeling up for it?"

Camille stared as Mommy sat next to her, while Mrs. Dixon stood next to Grammy.

"I'm so sorry, Cricket." Mommy kissed Camille on the forehead. "I'm so sorry I didn't tell you the truth, and you had to hear me and Grammy talking about the Dixons and Oliver, instead of me talking to you myself."

"But I shouldn't have snuck next door. I shouldn't have eaten one of Teddy's crackers. I thought it would be okay," she said to Mrs. Dixon. "Because your cookies are okay. But I should have asked first. I shouldn't have come over to your house at all."

"Yes," Mommy said. "You should have. You should have gotten to know them a long time ago, as soon as Mr. and Mrs. Dixon wanted us to visit. You wanted to go, and I said no, because . . ."

Camille picked at the biggest flower on her quilt.

Because her mommy was sad. That's what was wrong. It's what had been wrong for a long time. Camille wanted Oliver to be her daddy, and his family to be her family. But she wanted her mommy to be happy more than anything. More than staying at Grammy's. More than being a Dixon.

"I won't go back next door." She crushed a flower in her hand. "If you don't want me to, I won't want the Dixons to be my family.

I won't visit them anymore or play with Teddy and the other kids or see Oliver. I won't want them to be my family ever again."

"But they *are* your family," her mommy said.

"They . . . they are?"

Mommy smiled. "And I'm very glad they are. I shouldn't have kept them from you. I shouldn't have made you afraid of talking to me about it. You shouldn't be afraid of any of this, Camille."

Camille looked up at Mrs. Dixon, wondering if she was glad, too. She checked with her grammy to see if it was really okay.

"This must be a lot to take in." Mrs. Dixon sat on the edge of the bed. "You must have tons of questions."

Camille couldn't think of any of her questions anymore. The Dixons were really hers. All of them different. All of them together. Like everyone sitting around Camille now.

Mommy had said once that she looked a lot like *her* daddy. The granddaddy Camille had never met. Grammy was smaller, with blonde hair and blue eyes like Camille had sometimes wanted, though Grammy had said Camille's green eyes were prettier. Mrs. Dixon had red hair, and lots of white hair, too, and really white skin. And they were all Camille's, Mommy was saying. Like the tulip quilt—different things, but they were so pretty when you put them together.

"I get to be in your family," she asked Mrs. Dixon, "no matter who my daddy turns out to be?"

Mrs. Dixon looked tired, and maybe like she might be sad a little, too. But it must be a happy kind of sad, 'cause she was smiling.

"Always, Camille. Joe and I have lots of kids who come from lots of different places and mommies and daddies. And that's never stopped us from loving any of them as much as they'd let us. We already think of you as our granddaughter. Joe's in the hospital, too. And he heard you weren't feeling well, and he wants me to hurry back and tell him how you're doing. He'd love to see you, now that he's getting his new room and the doctors will let kids in before long. Do you think you'd like to visit your grandpa one day soon?"

Camille held on to her quilt, the way she had that morning, staring out her bedroom window and wishing she understood everything she'd heard her mommy and grammy saying. And then she'd dragged it outside, so she could be close enough to the Dixon house to sneak over. And now she was hugging it and wanting to hug Mrs. Dixon, too.

And then she was in Mrs. Dixon's arms, and Mrs. Dixon was holding her like Grammy always did. Like she wanted to keep Camille with her always.

"Can I?" Camille asked her mommy, still hugging Mrs. Dixon. "Can I go visit my grandpa soon?"

Chapter Twenty-Two

Selena had stayed with Camille until her daughter fell asleep, Bear in her arms, tucked in beneath her quilt, dreaming happy family dreams.

Belinda and Marsha had slipped away a half hour ago, leaving Selena to read to her daughter about Alice's adventures finding her way home. Selena's baby had finally run out of questions to ask about the Dixons and Joe and Marsha and Oliver. Answers Selena couldn't fully wrap her head around yet. Not all of them. So she'd kept telling Camille that everything was going to be okay. Just like Oliver had promised Selena when they were teenagers, and again just a few days ago.

She shut the door to Camille's room behind her and faced the trio in the hallway. She'd heard Belinda and Marsha talking with Dru and Brad and Oliver as the women left. Dru was at Brad's side, both of them leaning against the wall across from Camille's door. Oliver stood slightly separate, on his own. He stepped toward Selena, then stopped in the middle of the hallway, his hands digging into his jeans pockets, his gaze intense but uncertain. Waiting. But for what?

"Camille wants to see her grandpa, as soon as Joe's up to visitors," Selena told him. "I'm sorry I've put this off. For Marsha and Joe, and for all of you. I let myself worry about . . ." Belonging, leaving, never wanting to leave again. "I shouldn't have let anything get in the way of my daughter knowing your family."

She shifted her attention to Brad.

"I behaved selfishly. Seven years ago. The last two months. I wouldn't blame you for never forgiving me. I really am sorry, for all of it." She looked to Dru. "How much I hurt you, especially when Oliver left and then Brad. When I think of what you and Brad might have had for all these years if it wasn't for me . . ."

No one said anything, and Selena was grateful. This was her moment—the one she knew she finally had to deal with, or she'd always be looking back.

"Brad . . ." She shook her head at him. "I don't know what to say. Except that I never meant to use you. I was just so scared back then. But there's one thing I'm not sorry for."

She sensed Oliver hanging on every word.

"I'm not sorry that my daughter is the result of my mistakes," she said to him, to all of them. "I've been grateful every day that I've had Camille with me. I didn't deserve such an unexpected blessing. Just know that from the start, I was trying to do my best for my daughter. I still am."

"Of course you are." Dru inched closer. "We're all grateful to you for bringing her home."

Selena wished it could be that simple. "That's nice. But after I slept with Brad, you—"

"I was pissed for a while, sure."

"A while?" Brad joined his fiancée.

"Okay." Dru elbowed him in the ribs. "For a few years. But"—she smiled at Selena—"I have a niece to play with now. Or a stepdaughter. And Brad and I are getting married. And you and Oliver are . . ."

Selena and Oliver were what?

She had no idea. And Oliver was just standing there, close but still distant somehow.

"Oliver and I want what's best for Camille," she said.

"We all do," Brad agreed.

"No matter what . . ." Selena had sat listening to her daughter's chatter about the Dixons and her new grandparents and family and all the things she wanted to do with them. And Selena had known she'd made the right choice, asking Marsha to join her in Camille's room. "I want my daughter to have the life she always should have with your family."

"Does that mean you're staying in town?" Dru asked.

It would be so easy to say yes, spur of the moment, and figure out the details later. But Selena looked to Oliver instead. Their crazy roller coaster of a day seemed to be swirling through his mind as much as it was hers.

I don't want this.

It's done.

This is it for us. This is our chance.

Except by Oliver's own admission, he was no good at long-term things. Meanwhile she needed his love every day, every up and down, every moment. Facing it all together, like Oliver's parents had, because there was no other way for them to live.

"I don't yet know if Camille and I are staying," she admitted. And she saw him wince. "There's so much else to deal with first."

"We heard about this morning in the ER." Brad's features hardened with anger. "That husband of yours sounds like a real bastard."

"And I've let him affect me and my daughter's life for too long," Selena said. "I should have gotten out of my marriage years ago, when . . ."

"When what?" Oliver asked.

"When Parker started pushing to formally adopt Camille, and I knew I couldn't let that happen."

"Because he was cheating on you?" Oliver asked, prompting more outrage from Brad. Dru looked as if she might cry.

"That," Selena said, "and the judge would have required that we notify her birth father. And I just couldn't . . . I wasn't ready. I've been a coward all the way around. It's taken me too long to realize what my secret was depriving my daughter and your family from having."

"And you." Dru stepped closer. "We're here for you, too, Selena. Not just your daughter." Her expression grew fierce. "And we're not going to let this Parker asshat bully you into going back to him. Tell her, Oliver. Brad?" Both men inhaled to answer. Not that Dru seemed to notice. "Okay, I'll tell her. No one in our family's going to let Camille or you go back to New York, to that man, if that's not where you want to be. Screw what he has in the bank and how many lawyers are on his payroll. Let him get a look at us. He won't know what's hit him. I have half a mind to fly to New York myself and introduce him to some Southern-fried justice."

Selena had watched Dru's ascension from righteous indignation to avenging angel with fascination and growing amusement. A small laugh trickled out. Followed by a burst of giggling. And then they were all chuckling.

"I'm sorry." She wiped at her eyes, the tears from laughter, yes. But also in gratitude for being included in such an easy, belonging moment. "I appreciate the venom on my behalf. But Parker isn't worth getting yourself worked up over. I'm done letting him play me that way."

Oliver nodded his approval, finally smiling. She resisted the compulsion to beg him to wake up beside her every morning and smile just like he was now.

Dru shrugged and accepted Brad's kiss.

"I've been a little emotional lately," she explained.

"If there is a God"—Brad kissed her again—"it will settle down once you're in your second trimester."

"You're . . ." Oliver spun his sister toward him. He pulled her into his arms. "You're pregnant? Really?"

The joy and excitement on his face pierced Selena's heart with the thought of what Oliver's finding out about Camille a different way, a lifetime ago, might have been like.

Dru disengaged herself and sank back against her fiancé. "No more spinning me around for a while, okay? Not unless you want me to pull a Teddy and hurl all over you."

"And I assure you"—Brad grinned, excited, but a little appalled—"that's a distinct possibility. We have to pull over most of the time just driving around town, so she can puke at the curb in front of some unsuspecting stranger's house. Motion isn't your friend, evidently, when you're—"

"Gestating someone else's progeny?" Dru jabbed him with another elbow.

Then she wrapped him in the sweetest hug. Brad buried his face in her hair and inhaled as if he were holding a miracle. The tender scene had Oliver smiling at Selena again, making the moment more beautiful because they were sharing it.

"Lemon drops," she finally said to his sister.

Dru looked up. "Lemon drops?"

"They'll settle your stomach. And broth, when you think nothing else will stay down. I was sick for nine months with Camille, and . . ."

Selena trailed off, feeling the weight of it fresh and new.

"You'll never get those years back," she said to Brad and Oliver, appalled.

"No." Oliver's strength encircled her, his warmth countering the crazy emotions that refused to settle unless he was near. "But we'll have every new day with Camille you'll let us share. A clean slate. A fresh start. That's all anyone wants."

A clean slate.

It was time to begin again and focus on what came next.

She was standing with Oliver and Brad and Dru, dealing with their problems but joking and cheering about happy news, too. Belinda and Marsha had been with Selena earlier, not judging or blaming her, but helping her explain things to Camille. And Belinda had opened up to Selena last night and over the last few days and months, her support solid in a way Selena hadn't imagined possible.

She had no business being scared of any of these people. *This* could be her and Camille's life, if Selena let it, whatever happened between her and Oliver. And if this was what her mother had meant when Belinda had said for Selena to figure out what she wanted and go for it, whatever the risks, then she finally understood. Her dream come true wasn't the start-over life she and Camille could forge for themselves somewhere else. It was the second-chance family that had been waiting for them in Chandlerville all this time.

She slipped away from Oliver, needing to know that she could say what she had to, do what she had to, even if he wasn't yet ready to take the ride with her.

"We all need a clean start," she said. "We need to move forward without the past hanging over us."

"What are you saying?" Oliver asked.

Selena wasn't exactly sure. But she was smiling up at him, she realized. She was imagining Camille curled up with Joe on his hospital bed, her grandfather reading her a story. And she could see herself and Oliver there, if that's what he wanted, too—standing together, surrounded by family, the beautiful moment even more special because they were sharing it.

"If everyone has some time now . . ." She inhaled, her pulse raging. "I'd like to head down to the clinic," she said, "and see if they're open, so we can start Camille's paternity test tonight."

"How's my granddaughter?" Joe wanted to know the next morning, when Oliver slipped into his father's step-down room on the cardiac floor.

Both of his parents were there.

Two surgeries in a week had taken their toll on Joe. Oliver's dad managed to look both gaunt and swollen. The dark circles under his eyes took up half his face. There was very little of him that wasn't attached to something that was beeping or whirring or taking a reading that one of the nurses could monitor from the desk down the hall—even if Joe's room now had a solid door and walls that weren't windows.

Marsha sat in a chair beside the bed.

"Dru stopped in to see Camille before heading to the house to spell me," Oliver told them. "The doctors are discharging Camille in a little while. Thanks for coming down last night, Mom, and talking with her."

He walked to Marsha, bent and kissed her on the cheek.

She smiled. "You should have come inside yesterday and talked with her yourself."

"Or at least done some *stopping in* of your own this morning," Joe added, "on your way here. Sounds like Selena's warming up to the idea of her girl being part of the family. And we owe a lot of that to you and her mending fences."

Oliver grunted.

"Talking with me upset Camille pretty badly yesterday morning." He laid a hand on Joe's arm, just above the port where whatever was in his dad's IV bag was being shot into his veins. "It's confusing enough to explain to a little girl that she has a father she didn't know about, when you can't actually tell her who that father is yet."

"She was doing much better by the time I left yesterday afternoon," Marsha said.

Oliver shook his head. "Having one of her might-be dads pop in to say hi might set things off again. Especially when I'm on my way out of town."

"You're leaving?" Joe and Marsha responded in unison. They exchanged concerned glances.

"After Selena and Dru and Brad and I went down to the clinic to have blood drawn," Oliver said, "Selena's been locked into watching over Camille. I've been with the kids at the house. Everyone's retreated to their neutral corners to deal with what they have to. It seems like a good time to—"

Travis stepped in from the hallway and shut the door behind him. "How's it hangin', Dad? You ready to blow this joint yet?"

"Your father's still not to get too excited." Marsha eyed Oliver. "So take it easy with the surprises."

"I'm ready to go dancin' as soon as your mother's gotten some rest." Joe held Oliver's gaze. "I was thinking we could double-date in a few weeks. Take our ladies out for a night on the town."

Oliver would love nothing better. "I need to take care of a few things in Atlanta first. But when I get back, I'm game when you are."

"So you are coming back?" his mother asked.

"That's the plan." Oliver finally had a plan he could fight for—after standing with Selena in the pediatric hallway yesterday, watching her battle for a new future for herself and her child. A future he would do anything to be a part of.

"I talked with Chris at the department," Travis said. "I'm cleared for short-term family leave." He slapped Oliver on the back. "I've got things with Teddy while Oliver's gone. If Ms. Walker stops back by, she'll have nada to complain about in her next report. We got along fine yesterday, once Oliver left me to smooth things over. It's all good, right, bro?"

Oliver nodded. He and Travis had texted back and forth, after Oliver had been up most of the night again—thinking about Dru expecting her first baby, and Bethany acting like she wanted to rejoin the family. Joe's long recovery, and the strain it would continue to be for Marsha. Fin and Lisa and Teddy and the other foster kids Oliver was only starting to get to know. And then there was Selena and Camille.

Selena might be wary of what happened next. Hell, so was he. But she was opening her heart to love again. She might have slipped away from the clinic last night without saying good-bye. But before that, Oliver had held her in his arms, and he'd felt how much she'd needed him there. And when she'd committed to discovering who Camille's father was, he'd seen dreams in her eyes instead of fear.

This was his chance, their chance, and he wasn't wasting it.

"I know I promised to stay and help while you got better, Dad." Oliver didn't like the timing of this for his parents. "But—"

Joe stopped him with a raised hand. "There are a few things you might need help with, too?"

Oliver knelt down beside the bed, eye to eye with his dad. His mom's touch settled on his shoulder. Travis was a supportive presence beside them.

"I've needed help for a while," Oliver admitted. "I've been pushing too hard at work. At least I was until a couple of years ago when I landed myself in some trouble again. I've cut back on the deadlines and the stress. A little. Not nearly enough. Not if I want to have any kind of life except my job. Not even enough to sleep, really. And not enough to come home. I thought coming home would ruin everything. So I made sure I couldn't. All I am anymore is balls-to-the-wall getting things done for clients."

He winced, realizing what he'd said in front of his mother. Marsha flashed him another of her unconditional-love smiles.

"Except now," he said, "I'm thinking that . . ."

His dad's hand found Oliver's at the edge of the bed. "That being with your family and the woman you love and her child because *you* need to would be more of a—"

"Life?" Oliver and Travis finished at the same time.

Oliver met his brother's gaze. He propped his chin on the arm he'd braced on the side of the bed. His heart felt like it might burst as he studied the parents who'd given him all the time and support he'd needed to find his way home.

"All this time . . . I figured if I worked hard enough and sent home money, I wouldn't let anyone down again."

"You've never let us down," his mother said.

"All we've ever wanted," his dad insisted, "is for you to be happy and to share as much of your life with us as you can."

"That's what I want now, too, Dad."

"So you decided to leave town?"

"It's a long story." It was Oliver's story, finally circling back to where it had begun.

He'd gotten to the heart of it in the early-morning hours, pacing the floor with a teething Teddy and staring out Joe and Belinda's windows at the flowering hedge between his parents' property and Belinda's. Yes, he was leaving Chandlerville again. This time, so he could make his way home for good.

"I need to close the most important business deal of my life," he told his parents.

Marsha looked dubious. "Business?"

"The kind that will allow me to keep doing what I am for you and the family, and to be with Selena and Camille, too. If they'll have me."

"Hell, boy." Travis thumped Oliver on the back again. "Of course they'll have you. When was the last time you set your mind to anything and didn't manage to get it done?"

Selena pulled into Belinda's driveway just before lunch and parked behind her mother's car. Belinda had headed home from the hospital before them, to make fresh soup.

Selena carried Camille with her as she walked hesitantly next door, through the opening in the front hedge. She stepped to Oliver's side. He'd just placed his duffel bag into the cab of his truck.

Camille gave him a weak wave, her head drooping back to Selena's shoulder, her limp body a sweet, welcome weight in Selena's arms. Her daughter was exhausted—she'd slept in Fred's backseat the whole way home. But Selena knew she'd never have heard the end of it later, once Camille felt better, if Selena had taken her inside first instead of bringing her along.

Oliver had texted just as they'd pulled away from the hospital. And he'd silently watched them approach just now, his expression open, his beautiful eyes soft with what looked like the same jumble of love and confusion and need Selena was feeling. When he opened his arms, she rushed into them, into Oliver, inhaling the just-showered smell of him and curling herself and her daughter as close as they could get.

"I can't believe you're leaving," she said, "now that we've finally . . ."

"No finally." Oliver smiled down at them. "That's why I texted, to be sure we got to talk before I left."

I can't go without holding you again, his message had read. *Both of you.*

He curled her and Camille against his heart. "I won't ever surprise you like that again."

"Surprise me?" Selena sputtered. "The Dixon prodigal son running for the hills now that his Father of the Year is on the mend? One of the neighbors would have made sure to tell me if you hadn't."

"But I wanted to." Oliver's lips brushed Selena's forehead. He kissed Camille's, too, then eased away. "And I'm not running this time. I've already talked with my family about it."

"I know." Selena gave him another quick kiss. A subdued Camille looked sleepily back and forth between them. "Bethany stopped by."

"Really?"

"She'd heard from Dru about you leaving for the city. Dru told her about Camille, too. Bethany found us at the hospital before Camille was discharged. I turned around and she was standing in the doorway, staring at Camille like she was seeing her for the first time."

"I know how she feels."

Selena watched the corner of Oliver's mouth kick up and reveled in how much he wanted Camille to be his. "But it still could be just—"

"Wishful thinking?" Oliver asked. "I don't mind wishing for something that wonderful. Do you?"

Selena shook her head, a little afraid of how close her dreams felt to coming true while she was watching him go. She looked down at the ground and the muddy silk slippers she'd thrown on yesterday along with the change of clothes she'd snatched from her closet after she and Oliver made love.

Oliver's finger tipped her chin up. "The past is just one part of our story, Selena. There's so much more we can be, if we're ready to figure the rest out."

She nodded. "Everyone's lives could have been so much easier if I'd trusted you years ago."

"Maybe." He leaned against the side of his truck—a city man with carefully combed hair for once, wearing jeans and a T-shirt and looking as if he could command any boardroom, anywhere, just the way he was. "Or maybe this is exactly how it was supposed to happen. We've both come home from where we thought our lives were going to be. We've learned a lot about what we don't want. Now we're ready to make the choices we didn't know how to handle when we were kids."

"Except you're going away again."

Camille picked her head up. "Do you really have to go?"

"Not for long, darlin'." He brushed his fingers through her curls. "I'll be back soon. I won't let you down."

Selena wanted to believe him, believe in this moment, she really did. But deep inside, a part of her was screaming for him not to abandon her, the way she'd yelled at him years ago.

"What about all the rest?" she asked. "Everything we don't know yet?"

The paternity test. Whether she and Camille would find a place in Chandlerville or move on. Selena and Oliver's future.

"We wait," he said. "And whatever happens next, we do the right thing."

She angled her head at him. "What's the right thing?"

"Whatever works for *you*." When she blinked in response, he smiled. "Whatever's best for you and Camille. That's what will make me happy, Selena."

"What . . . what are you saying?"

"That I know what I want now. And I have to be somewhere else for a while, so I can make sure I do it right. But I'm coming back to hear your answer."

"To what?" Where was the reckless, greedy man who'd pulled her close in his truck and kissed her until she'd forgotten everything else . . . and then told her he didn't know when he'd be ready to deal with more?

"To whether you want to spend the rest of your life with me."

"You . . . you said you needed time."

"Just a little. Wait for me, Selena. No matter what my next CIO needs or what some paternity test says, I'll be back for you and Camille. Believe that, and keep figuring out what you want— like you did yesterday. Let me love you again, and we'll make the rest work."

"But . . . how long will you be?"

"I don't know yet. I need to set something up that could take a while. Something I should have done for myself. Now I have two more reasons to make it happen." He smiled. "You and Camille."

Selena pushed herself and her daughter into his arms again, needing to feel them around her. Needing Oliver forever. She held on, and so did he, dreaming and wishing and wanting to believe it all . . . together.

"I love you," she whispered.

"I love you, too."

Oliver set them away.

"Save me a cookie?" he asked Camille. "I'll come collecting. Promise."

Camille nodded, a smile on her lips as her eyes closed and she dozed in Selena's arms. Oliver slid behind the wheel of his truck, shutting the door and leaning an arm on the edge of the open window.

"I'll see you soon," he said as he fired the ignition and backed down the Dixons' drive.

Chapter Twenty-Three

"To Chandlerville's Father of the Year." Belinda raised her plastic cup of lemonade in a toast.

Selena joined the rest of the crowded room at the Garner Rehab Center where Joe had been moved, lifting her drink and saying, "To Joe!"

It was a beautiful late-Sunday afternoon, with family and friends and neighbors cheering and celebrating around her. The party Belinda had spent days pulling together had grown until Joe's private room seemed to be bursting at the seams. The crowd had spilled into the center's hallway as more guests and their families joined in the fun.

Adults were drinking and eating—goodies donated by either the Dream Whip or DJ's bakery. Kids of all ages were everywhere. Free from school for the next ten weeks, the younger ones were running wild. The teenagers had grouped off in clumps, playing games on their phones or messaging on social media, basically ignoring the adults. There were balloons, streamers, a Father of the Year banner. It might have seemed corny to some. But to Selena the joy and celebration that filled the room were . . . love.

The love she'd always hoped her daughter would be surrounded by. The home she'd dreamed of for herself.

"I can't believe all of this." Joe's smile was wide, his eyes bright.

He was still too weak to get out of bed without assistance. Marsha didn't like some of the side effects of the array of medications he was taking for his heart and circulation and blood pressure. He was frustrated not to be going home yet. But today Joe's family and community had come to him, to honor him. He was a well-loved neighbor and friend, a doting father admired by everyone in the room and many who'd phoned in their regrets but sent cards and good wishes Belinda and Marsha had taken turns reading out loud—much to the good-natured embarrassment of the man of the hour.

Marsha stood beside her husband now, beaming with pride. Belinda and her garden club—who'd organized the food, the commemorative plaque, the balloons, and the music streaming from Selena's smartphone playlist—were circulating, making sure people were enjoying themselves.

So many locals had gone out of their way to attend.

Ginger and her family and her mother. DJ and Kristen and Walter and Law and their spouses and kids. Several of the deputies from the sheriff's department and their loved ones. Belinda's nosy neighbors, the Ritters, and so many more.

Travis, Dru, and surprisingly Bethany stood with their mother at the head of Joe's bed. Each of them had pitched in, getting the younger Dixons cleaned up and to the center on time. And at Camille's request, she and Selena had strapped a baby seat into Fred and delivered Teddy—who was now happily perched on Dru's hip, being entertained by his uncle Brad. It was a perfect afternoon. Everyone had said so. Only one thing was missing for Selena and the Dixons.

Oliver wasn't there yet.

He would be, Travis had assured Selena. He'd texted with his brother just a few hours ago. Oliver had business to finalize in town that couldn't be put off. But he'd get to Chandlerville as soon as he could.

He and Selena had talked nightly since he'd left. About Camille and how she was feeling. About Joe and his recovery and move, and how Marsha was doing. About Bethany stopping by the Dixon house and then Belinda's the other day, not staying for long, but wanting to meet Teddy and to see Camille again. About Selena's last few days at Chandler Elementary before the school year ended. About everything but her and Oliver and what they were going to do next.

They'd stopped short each night of talking about the future. They had plenty of time to get to that, Oliver had said. Once he was home. Until then, he just wanted to talk, to get to know her again, to hear her voice each night as he stared out at his Midtown Atlanta view. He wanted to know if she'd wait for him, just a little longer. And she had.

Sure, she'd seriously contemplated leaving Camille with Belinda Friday afternoon and charming Fred into an interstate excursion into the heart of the city. But not because she didn't trust Oliver. The as-yet-unopened envelope she'd received in the mail on Thursday had been the culprit. An envelope she'd carefully tucked away instead of opening it or driving to Oliver's condo and insisting they open it together. Instead, she'd saved it for today. Then she'd gotten back to the business of creating the life that she'd dreamed of for her and her daughter. Just as she'd promised Oliver she would.

No details over the phone, they'd agreed. About what either of them were up to. They were trusting each other, no matter what they faced next.

Wait for me, Selena.

I won't let you down.

I'll see you tomorrow, love, he'd said before hanging up last night.

She hadn't heard from him since.

Camille ran up, pigtails flying. She was clutching half of one of Dan's special, Camille-friendly, chocolate doughnuts. At least a third of the other half was smeared all over her face.

"I wanna give Grandpa our card now," she said, hopping up and down.

"Ouch, sweetie." Selena picked her up, to protect her toes.

Her beautiful child was over-the-moon excited about being one of the Dixons. It had made the last week a nonstop celebration. Everyone in the family, adults and kids, had accepted her—and Selena and Belinda—as their own. Yesterday the three of them had attended their first Saturday picnic in the Dixon backyard, having a blast with everyone but Joe and Marsha, who'd been here at the rehab center, finishing getting Joe settled.

Wanting to brighten Joe's transition to the center had been one of Selena's reasons for postponing the surprise now sealed inside Camille's card. Plus wanting Oliver to be there, to hear the news along with his family. The results of the paternity test would formalize Camille's place in the Dixon family, whoever her father was. Selena had secured her daughter's agreement to wait. She'd checked with Marsha to be sure Joe was up for the big reveal, and with Brad and Dru to ask if they were okay with finding out in public.

The family was on pins and needles, but they'd said they'd be thrilled to celebrate one more thing today. Beyond that, to Selena and Camille and Marsha and Joe and the whole tribe, Camille was already a Dixon. Now it was nearly dusk outside and Joe was looking tired. Which meant it was time, whether Oliver made it or not.

"Go on." She put Camille down. It was a wonder her daughter had kept her secret this long. "Be careful with your grandpa. Let Marsha help you up on the bed. But the room is yours."

"Grandpa, Grandma, Grammy!" Camille raced to the other side of the room, where Belinda was chatting with Marsha. "I get to give Grandpa my s'prise now. It's for you, too, Grandma. I drew the pictures for Grandpa, but it's for you, too."

She threw herself into Marsha's laughing hug and practically climbed into her grandmother's arms. Belinda patted Camille on the back. Her smile of pride for Selena was a sweet reward for the hard-fought journey that had brought them all to this happy place.

Selena had turned the divorce over to Oliver's lawyer, who was already engaging Parker's legal team. She'd stopped answering her husband's calls and deleted his texts and voice mails. She'd accepted Kristen's offer to be a full-time sub on staff at the elementary school next year. She was collecting the material and recommendations she'd need to apply for the grants that would pay for at least one night class a semester at the community college. She'd made it to her AA meeting Thursday night. And tomorrow afternoon, she and Camille and hopefully Oliver would be heading to a local no-cage animal shelter to pick out a floppy-eared Blossom or Bud to bring home.

Selena closed her eyes and reminded herself to breathe, to be grateful, to trust, while her daughter chattered away to her grandparents. Oliver would be there. He'd go with them to look for a puppy. He and Selena and Camille would have their new start. And even if for some reason he didn't follow through on his promises, Selena and Camille would be okay. Because look at the beautiful life they were building for themselves in Chandlerville.

"We had it yesterday at the picnic," Camille was saying. "But you weren't there, Grandma and Grandpa."

Selena watched Camille cuddled next to Joe, the large envelope that she'd colored flowers and hearts all over clutched in her hand. Inside was an enthusiastically decorated "Get Well Soon, Grandpa" card from Camille, and inside that, the sealed letter from the hospital's clinic. Camille was smiling up at Marsha. And then she gently, very carefully hugged Joe.

"Open it," she insisted. "Open my surprise, Grandpa!"

Joe took the card, while Belinda steadied Camille, keeping her from bouncing too hard on the bed.

"It's very pretty," Joe praised. "Just like you, Cricket."

Selena blinked away the happy tears that came every time she heard her pet name for her child spoken in the deeper timbre of Joe's voice.

"It's prettier inside," Camille insisted. "But Mommy wouldn't let me color on the letter. Only your card."

"Letter?" Joe asked.

"From the hospital." Selena turned her smile to Dru and Brad, wanting to be certain they were still okay with this. They both smiled as the room quieted around them, the other partygoers catching on that something important was happening. "From the clinic."

"Mommy said we had to wait for all the family to be together," Camille said, "before we could open it."

"Then I'm glad I wrapped up my last meeting in the city, so I could make the party," a deep voice responded from the doorway.

"Oliver." Selena raced through the crowd.

She threw her arms around his neck. She hung onto him the way she'd wanted to the morning he'd left.

"You're back," she gushed.

"I'm back."

He dropped the briefcase he'd been carrying and hauled her closer, delighting everyone into a clapping frenzy when he swooped in for a kiss. His lips were warm and tender and too tantalizing for a public display of affection. But Selena couldn't stop herself from indulging. When he finally set her away, it took her a full sixty seconds to focus on the sexy navy-blue suit he wore, complete with a burgundy tie, a ruthlessly starched white shirt, and gold cuff links.

"Wowza," she said.

"Why thank you, ma'am."

"The party invitation said casual dress."

"I didn't have time to change. And I needed to show off my best stuff at this morning's incorporation meeting. A man can't throw down casual when he's negotiating with his lawyers and new business partner."

"A new what?"

"A peer of mine on the IT contracting circuit, a competitor, really. She nailed my last two prospective clients because I couldn't get my pitches together in time. She's been after me to combine resources for years. I just made her, and myself, very happy by obliging."

"Congratulations, Oliver," Marsha said.

And then everyone was raising their lemonade in a new toast, even if they didn't completely understand what was going on, offering a cheery "Congratulations!"

"But you work alone," Selena said.

Oliver pecked a kiss on the tip of her nose. "Not anymore. Not if I'm going to live in Chandlerville and commute into the city. Not if I can't travel all the time, and can't relocate because a client somewhere needs a tech working at a job site for God knows how long."

"But . . ."

"Not if I want to be here with you and Camille and my family, figuring out how to have a life, instead of making work my whole life. With Xan on board and the plans we've been hashing out for hiring staff and leveraging project loads, I'll be able to do both now."

"Xan?" Selena's head was spinning.

Oliver kissed her again, making her tingle all over. "I'll explain later."

He grinned toward Camille and his parents and Belinda.

"Sounded like I was interrupting something important," he said. "Something about a surprise from the hospital."

"In Grandpa's get-well card," Camille chirped. Her pout made an appearance. "Can he open it now?"

"Grandpa?" Oliver asked Selena.

"I've been working on a few of my own projects." There was so much to tell him.

"I'm intrigued," he teased. "And I'm also going to commandeer the party for just another minute or two, with Camille's permission, of course. I promise to make it up to you," he said to Selena's impatient child.

Camille looked from Oliver to Selena, who nodded her head in encouragement.

"All right," Camille sighed. "What's that?" She stared at Oliver and Selena the same as everyone else in the room.

That's when Selena realized Oliver was holding something out to her. A robin's-egg-blue box, tied with a white satin ribbon.

"Oh my God." She gazed into his smiling green eyes, seeing his love there—and her forever. "Oliver . . ."

"I know it's premature. But my lawyers tell me they've got things moving with Parker, now that he's realized he no longer has financial leverage with you. And from the sound of it, I got here just in time to do this right—the way I've wanted to since I walked into Tiffany's the first of last week and found the perfect ring for you."

"What . . ."

He'd bought her a ring from Tiffany's? Her rebel bad boy from high school who'd spent his entire first week back in Chandlerville wearing wrinkled jeans, T-shirts, ratty tennis shoes, and baby vomit was wearing a designer suit and proposing to her with a ring that must have cost him a fortune.

"What way is the right way?" she asked.

Oliver held out the box and smiled when she took it. "I wanted to ask you to marry me before the paternity test results were back."

He'd dropped his voice, to keep the last of what he'd said between them, not that it was a secret around town any longer. Selena covered her mouth with her hand. Oliver took it and dropped to one knee.

"Marry me, Selena Rosenthal. Marry me and share your daughter with me. Make babies with me. Help me figure out whatever married people have to figure out, so we can make this work the way my parents have. Forever."

It was magical. It was Oliver promising everything that Selena had always dreamed of, for her and Camille. She threw herself into his arms again to the excitement of the wildly clapping partygoers.

Oliver stood and twirled her around, the Tiffany ring box crushed between them. She couldn't wait to open it, to see the beautiful, breathtaking treasure Oliver had picked out just for her. She couldn't wait to tell him everything, most important that *he* was what she'd decided she wanted—him and Camille and her, together—no matter how long it took him to come home. But she had to be sure of just one thing first.

She turned toward Camille and felt Oliver wrap his arms around her from behind. He pulled Selena into the warmth of his body. Camille was still on Joe's bed. Her special card had fallen from her hand, but she was smiling, too.

"What do you think?" Selena asked. She wouldn't make a decision this big without making sure it was okay with her daughter.

"Does this mean we get to stay forever?" Camille asked, her excitement spreading around the room as people murmured their approval and looked back to Selena and Oliver. Brad and Dru, too. They were holding Teddy between them, and they looked thrilled.

"Forever, darlin'," Oliver promised.

To which Camille gave a happy "That's so cool!"

And then she turned back to Joe.

"Can we open your card now, Grandpa, and see your surprise?"

Laughter and cheers and more clapping filled the room. Selena and Oliver pulled the white satin ribbon together and opened the blue box. Her breath caught when she saw the ring. It was magnificent. But its sparkle was nothing compared with the excitement in Oliver's eyes when he slid it onto her finger.

That done, with one more sweet kiss to seal the deal, they turned their attention back to their family and Camille's big moment. Joe carefully read his card, his smile widening. He inspected each and every scribble his granddaughter had painstakingly drawn on both the card and the envelope.

"It's beautiful." He gave Camille a noisy kiss. "I couldn't think of a better way to celebrate being Father of the Year than getting something this special from my very first grandchild."

Camille clapped. And then she held up the sealed envelope that had fallen to the mattress. "But you have to open this, too. Don't you want your surprise?"

Joe ran his hand down Camille's madly curling hair. "How about you help me."

"Yay!" Camille pounced on the envelope.

She nearly tore it in two ripping it open. Her forehead wrinkled at the official-looking form inside, as if she'd expected something far more impressive after the drama of being told at least a hundred times that she'd have to wait to see what it was. She handed Joe the paper.

"What does it say?" she asked.

Marsha leaned over, and she and Joe silently read the report together. They handed it to Belinda, who passed the paternity results to Brad and Dru without glancing at the results.

"What's it say?" Camille demanded. "Grandpa, what's the surprise?"

"Well, Dad?" Oliver asked.

Joe chuckled, looking better than he had since his heart attack. He smiled at Selena and Oliver and pulled Camille into another gentle hug.

"Congratulations, son," he said. "It's a girl."

Acknowledgments

I'd like to thank my friend Jennifer Sewell, mother extraordinaire, for sharing what it's like to raise a child with severe food allergies. We so frequently hear about kids who can't have this or that when we drop our own off at school and play dates. It's easy to lose sight of how quickly these everyday experiences can become dangerous. Or of how challenging getting through them can be for families, when the mere taste of someone else's snack might be life-threatening for a little one. You're an inspiration, Jennifer!

About the Author

Anna DeStefano is the award-winning, nationally bestselling author of more than twenty-five books, including the Mimosa Lane novels and the Atlanta Heroes series. Born in Charleston, South Carolina, she's lived in the South her entire life. Her background as a care provider and adult educator in the world of crisis and grief recovery lends itself to the deeper psychological themes of every story she writes. A wife and mother, she currently writes in a charming northeast suburb of Atlanta, Georgia, not all that different from her characters' beloved Chandlerville. She is also a workshop and keynote speaker, a writing coach, and a freelance editor.

Get to know Anna at annawrites.com and the Anna DeStefano: Author page on Facebook, where she shares her inspirations, her challenges, a healthy dose of honest optimism, and tidbits about upcoming projects.